I felt a chill in the warm morning air. Would Medina have been able to carry that kind of nerve even further— to the point of killing her own son? And assuming she could, why? Because of his criminal past?

Which wasn't all that bad, considering. No, I just didn't see how it could be her.

And her eyes weren't cold like a killer's were supposed to be.

But what about Mose Beadle? His hands were large and calloused from farm work, but he seemed like such a gentle man. And his mother-in-law, Sassy Bentley, had strong hands, but how would she have gotten the body into that ditch, assuming she'd killed her own grandson?

I shook my head, unable to make sense of any of this mess. It had to be the cousin, Jerry. Or even someone else we didn't know. Well, we'd load the car up today and check in with Chief Wilburn. Surely he'd let us go home by now.…

★

Previously published Worldwide Mystery title by
LONNIE CRUSE

FIFTY-SEVEN HEAVEN

Lonnie Cruse

Fifty-Seven Traveling

WORLDWIDE®

TORONTO • NEW YORK • LONDON
AMSTERDAM • PARIS • SYDNEY • HAMBURG
STOCKHOLM • ATHENS • TOKYO • MILAN
MADRID • WARSAW • BUDAPEST • AUCKLAND

For the real Debby Evans Biles,
A friend loves at all times…
—*Proverbs* 17:17

Recycling programs
for this product may
not exist in your area.

FIFTY-SEVEN TRAVELING

A Worldwide Mystery/August 2011

First published by Five Star Publishing

ISBN-13: 978-0-373-26763-7

Copyright © 2010 by Lonnie Cruse

Printed in U.S.A.

Acknowledgments

A special thank-you to all antique automobile owners who lovingly restore and show their ancient cars, thereby keeping an important part of our history alive and working. And to the AACA SIROVC chapter members who have provided support and research information for writing this series. While the setting for this book is the real area of Pigeon Forge, Tennessee, many descriptions of the buildings, such as the police department, library, restaurants, etc., came from my imagination, not from reality.

ONE

"Well, my goodness gracious," said a female voice to my right, expressing those soft words in one of the silkiest Southern accents I'd ever heard. I swiveled my neck toward the speaker.

Out of the corner of my eye I saw my darling hubby snap to attention, whacking his head on the upraised car hood in the process. Any male in the Western Hemisphere worth his salt would've instantly recognized the woman's voice. Ditto for the Eastern Hemisphere. It belonged to the one and only Copper Penny, country singer/songwriter extraordinaire, with more awards than anyone in the business. Not to mention money.

Jack wiped his hands on a rag, patted his hair down over the small bald spot at the back of his head, and approached the mile-long limo now parked alongside our Fifty-Seven Chevy.

"Jack Bloodworth, ma'am. I'm honored to meet you in person. Love your music." Lucky for Jack, he let go of superstar Penny's hand just before I found it necessary to separate him by force.

For the past half hour we'd been trapped on the side of the very busy highway that led into Pigeon Forge, Tennessee. Leaky water hose, a problem that had kept me standing on my bad leg, breathing diesel fumes and swatting away mosquitoes while Jack groused under his breath—until now, of course.

"I don't reckon I've seen a Fifty-Seven Chevy painted

that pretty color of Candy Apple Red since I don't know when," Copper Penny said. Our car was actually Matador Red, but I noticed Jack didn't correct her like he would have anyone else. "Looks like you've got car trouble. Can we help you folks?" she offered.

The early-autumn breeze re-parted my hair. I smoothed it back into place and kept a close eye on Jack while he answered her, afraid he'd crawl through the limo's back passenger window and take off with his idol, leaving me stranded on the side of the highway if I wasn't careful. Any woman who'd been married as long as I had knew real danger when she saw it. The rest of the traffic continued to whiz by us.

"Well, ma'am," Jack dithered, "I'm afraid it's a busted hose. And I don't have a spare one in the trunk." I watched as the red blush slid up his neck, into his face. "I know better than to go off this far from home without extra parts."

"Are ya'll here for the car show?" Penny asked. "Looks like you've got a real winner there to me."

"Yes, ma'am," he said, and I swore if he called her "ma'am" in that reverential tone one more time, I'd give him a swift kick. "Sadie, here, usually brings home a trophy or two." Jack pointed to the Chevy. "I'm hoping she'll win something here, if we can get her on into town."

"I'd be happy to help out," Penny offered. "I love older cars and the memories they bring back."

She appeared to think over our options for several seconds. "We could call a tow truck for you, but it would probably take them a long time to get out here. Traffic's awful heavy with all the antique cars in town. And towing is mighty expensive. How about we give you and your lovely missus a ride to the auto-parts store in Pigeon Forge? It's right on our way, and you can easily pick up the parts you need from them and get a ride back here."

Before I could suggest that someone probably needed to stay with the car, and the someone should be Jack, he reached for my arm and swiftly shoe-horned me into the limo. Sadie was on her own. Jack locked her and climbed in behind me. And we were off to the parts store with the woman Jack Bloodworth had been drooling over for as long as I could remember. I trusted Copper Penny carried extra towels for just such emergencies.

She graciously offered us each a diet soda from the limo bar. I was happy to accept. Standing on the side of the road, handing Jack the correct sockets while he fussed over the car, was thirsty business.

"Don't you all usually travel in a convoy?" Penny said as Jack popped a soda can open and passed it to me.

Jack swallowed a gulp of his own soda before answering. "Yes, we do, generally. But my wife, Kitty—" he gestured toward me, possibly realizing at long last that he hadn't even given her my name, though he had introduced the car "—had a dental appointment this morning, so we got a late start."

"Pleased to meet you," I said, knowing how lame that sounded but unable to come up with anything more spectacular at the moment.

Jack had been extremely miffed at me the entire morning for refusing to cancel the dental appointment I'd had for over two months. But canceling only meant a much longer wait for the next appointment, and I thought I'd chipped a back tooth on the peanut brittle I'd made last week. Thankfully, it turned out to be nothing more than a rough edge needing a bit of polishing. Besides, Jack hadn't decided to accompany the rest of the Metropolis Cruisers to Pigeon Forge for the car show and contest until a couple of days ago.

"This is the first competition we've had a chance to

enter since my wife broke her leg and I broke my arm in a freak accident on my old tractor," Jack said.

I was thankful he neglected to mention the cause of the accident was a cold-blooded killer who'd been determined to do us both in. Some things were better left unsaid before strangers. Both our casts were off, but I was still using my lovely hand-carved wooden cane. Jack, of course, needed no such help to navigate.

I was willing to bet Jack was no longer upset with me for not canceling my appointment, considering my delay and Sadie's breakdown placed him within worshipful distance of his ideal woman. And where was my hero, Yanni, when I needed him?

Copper Penny made what I considered to be a rather large error in judgment at that point and asked Jack where we were from. I leaned back on the butter-soft, cream-colored seat and observed her listening politely while he treated her to practically the entire history of our small town.

"We're the only Metropolis in the U.S. zip-code book, so we were designated the 'Home of Superman' by the Illinois State Legislature several decades ago, and our fifteen-foot-tall statue of him at the courthouse draws tourists from all over. You'll have to come up for the annual Superman Celebration sometime. Second Saturday in June," Jack droned on. Blah, blah, blah.

Up this close and personal, Copper Penny was even more beautiful than she appeared on television or in the movies. And I had to admit, it wasn't just the bright red curls, the smile, or the famous signature piece of clothing, a jacket covered in shiny new pennies. This kind of beauty had to come from within. I was quickly becoming a fan.

To her credit, Penny didn't even blink when Jack launched into a rundown of our private lives—number of children, two, number of grandchildren, two—most certainly giving her more information about us than she could possibly ever want to know. I managed not to grin. Men!

"I confess, I've never heard of Metropolis, Illinois, before," Penny said when Jack finally paused for a breath. "But I do have a concert scheduled in Paducah, come spring. I'll see if I can hitch a ride over to your fair city and see that statue for myself."

We arrived at the auto-parts store, and the limo driver pulled onto the gravel parking lot and stopped.

"I'm due at rehearsal in a few minutes," Penny said, "so I'm afraid I'll have to leave you folks here. But I'm sure Mike or one of the other guys will give you a ride back to your car. If not, call this number and the driver will come back for you. I use this service whenever traffic is bumper to bumper, for safety's sake, and they're very dependable."

She handed Jack a business card with a number jotted on it. Presumably the number of the phone up front with the driver. Jack managed to tuck it into his shirt pocket on the third try and thanked her.

"Sadie and I would be most happy to take you on a tour of Metropolis when you come to Paducah. And Kitty, of course." Lucky for him, Jack remembered to include me in the offer. "Besides the statue, we have a—"

"Jack, Miss Penny is going to be late for her rehearsal if we don't let her go right now." I took a firm hold on his arm. For a minute I was afraid he'd kiss her hand, but he manfully restrained himself—most likely out of fear of me—and we slid out of the car.

"While you're in the area, be sure to stop by Dollywood. I'm doing my one-woman show there all this month. I'd be happy to leave tickets for you at the entrance," Penny said. "I think you'll enjoy it. And be sure to drive through the national park. The leaves are so pretty this time of year."

"Oh, thank you so much!" Now it was me who dithered. "I've been dying to visit Dollywood. I've heard the shows are terrific."

She waved acknowledgment as the limo slid back into traffic. I wrapped my arm through Jack's, partly to help my balance on the gravel parking lot and partly to keep him from dashing back out into traffic on foot to chase down the limo and offer his thanks to Copper Penny again.

"You know I'm not a country-music fan in general, preferring soft piano music or old-time jazz," I said, "but Copper Penny's gracious offer of help when she was obviously in a hurry has certainly won my heart. As soon as we get home, I'm going to swipe a couple of her CDs from your garage and listen to them in my car. When I get a car."

"You'll get your car, just as soon as we find it. I promise," Jack said.

And where had I heard that song before? He'd been promising to restore a vintage Thirties vehicle for me for many years. So far, no luck. Which was part of the reason he'd decided to come to Pigeon Forge at the last minute. Besides the car competition, there would be blocks and blocks of older-model cars, parked facing the highway that cut through town, with For Sale written on the windshields. Most would be priced high, but we might luck onto a bargain. It certainly was worth a shot.

We entered the store, and within seconds Jack and a helpful employee were deep in conversation about busted hoses. So there we were, adrift at the auto-parts store, with a car repair waiting for us back on the highway. What fun.

My cell phone rang. The sound always startled me— even though I'd had the phone for quite a while—because it wished me a Merry Christmas every single time it rang and I still couldn't remember how to change the tune. Well, it would be Christmas again in a few months and I'd be right back in step with the rest of the cellular world. I dug deep into my tote bag and retrieved the phone.

"Mom, where are you guys? Have you found the cabin yet, or is Daddy still lost?" My eldest—not to mention nosiest—daughter demanded to know.

"We're at an auto-parts store. Sadie busted a hose. So we're not lost. At least not yet."

"Tori, give back your brother's toothbrush. And don't you dare try using it to clean the fish bowl again. I don't have any spares left," Maggie ordered her daughter before she turned her attention back to me. "Not a good way to start a weekend at a romantic getaway, is it, Mom? Sitting at an auto-parts store."

Romantic getaway. I snickered. Probably exactly what Jack did have planned to some degree, even though we were sharing our cabin with our best friends. But if I agreed with her, Maggie would be horrified. She'd meant it as a joke.

"I'm not totally certain we'll ever reach the cabin. Traffic is practically at a standstill. Every senior citizen in the United States must have come to this area to view the cars of their youth and dream, if not to buy."

"Sounds like a geriatric nightmare. Just don't let Daddy get involved in a fender bender. You know how he loves to tailgate."

"Your father prefers to call it 'drafting,' and in case you hadn't noticed, you're worse than he is."

"Am not! And you taught me to drive, remember?"

I didn't remember who'd taught her, off hand, but I wasn't about to admit to a brain lapse. "Right now your father doesn't care where he is or how he got here." I told her about Copper Penny riding to our rescue.

"Wow, wait until Sunny hears about that!" Maggie exclaimed. "Assuming I can get her attention. All my baby sister wants to talk about at the moment is her wedding plans. The Pentagon doesn't go into this much detail with their planning. Oops, I gotta run, Mom, the kids are due at soccer practice. Oh, and I hope you weren't planning on wearing chartreuse."

"Chartreuse?"

"To the wedding. Chartreuse is Sunny's current choice for the bridesmaids' dresses. And that includes the matron of honor. Lucky me. Which means you can't wear it to the wedding. Lucky you. She showed me a swatch. Looked like a baby's worst nightmare, strained green peas. I nearly threw up."

Chartreuse. Wonderful. The awful yellow/green color popular in the Fifties that some fool had brought back into fashion again, over fifty years later. What was that famous quote about the importance of learning our mistakes from history in order not to repeat them? And what was Sunny thinking? Chartreuse, for a wedding?

"Mom, you really should check the outlet mall for a dress while you're there. Probably save a lot of money. Billy, stop feeding your cookies to Daisy and go get your jacket. Dogs don't need people food." And with that, she was gone.

I tucked the cell phone back into my tote bag and scrounged for my MP3 player, dusting off a nearby vinyl-and-metal chair and settling in to listen to a Deni Dietz Diet Club mystery on audio. Sadie's breakdown had interrupted me in mid-murder, just as the dead body appeared.

Well, as long as no dead bodies mysteriously appeared

in Sadie's trunk, I'd be happy. Surely no stray murderers would happen by while she was parked out there on the busy highway. Nor would Jack and I be in this area long enough to solve another murder.

TWO

"JUST EXACTLY how lost are we?" I asked, unable to hold my breath any longer.

Mike, the auto-parts salesman, had given us a ride back to Sadie, and Jack quickly made the repairs, washing up at a nearby gas station. I thought it best not to mention that he still smelled a bit of oil or grease. So we were off at long last to find the realty company that rented Jack our cabin. The plan was to check in and get the keys, drop our stuff at the cabin, connect with our best friends—Leo and Debby Evans, who were sharing the cabin with us—maybe grab a nap, and meet up with the rest of the car club at a terrific restaurant in Pigeon Forge. But, like they say, the best-laid plans—

Jack snorted. "How many times do I have to tell you, Kitty? We are not lost. I just don't always know exactly where we are at any given time."

I countered with my own cliché. "And if I had a dollar—" Actually, if I'd settled for a penny for every time he'd said that over the years, I could've created my own penny-covered jacket. And wasn't it a teensy bit illegal to drill small holes in coins of our realm in order to sew them onto garments, like Copper Penny had? Illegal or not, I suspected Uncle Sam wasn't about to challenge a world-famous singer over her trademark clothing. But really, that jacket had to weigh a country ton. How did she manage to strut the stage with it?

I settled back again, admired the beautiful scenery

through the window, and thought of the old joke about Moses wandering in the wilderness for forty years because he wouldn't stop to ask for directions. Too bad they didn't have GPS systems way back then. Too bad Jack didn't have one right now. He always threatened to return it to the store if I so much as mentioned buying him one as a gift. Perhaps it was time to call his bluff?

"If you'd just learn to read a map," Jack said, "it would help."

I didn't bother to dignify that with an answer. All maps looked like gibberish to me, and this late in life I didn't figure they'd gotten any easier to decipher. The few times I'd tried, I'd gotten us lost even worse than Jack's best efforts.

Traffic seemed to be getting heavier by the minute as the work day drew to a close in Sevier County. Visions of us spending the night sleeping in Sadie's back seat, on the side of the highway, weren't terribly comforting. I scrunched down further in the seat, hoping Jack wouldn't try one of his usual short-cuts.

"Hang on." Jack flipped on the blinker, abandoned the safety of the middle lane, and shot between a Nash Rambler and a cattle truck while I held on as ordered, every muscle in my body knotted up tight. The driver of the Nash Rambler signaled his displeasure with what I considered to be a rather original set of horn blasts as Jack waved his apology and took the turn.

About the time my heart rate dropped back below emergency-room level, Jack said, "Can you read that sign?"

"Dollywood is just ahead," I informed him through teeth scissoring against each other. "The rental company is somewhere beyond, on the right."

Jack wheeled Sadie into the cabin-rental company's parking lot just as the last luckless employee locked the front door and rattled the handle for good measure. I was about ready to rattle Jack's back teeth, but he hustled up the porch steps before I had a chance, apologizing to the employee all the way. Not currently capable of hustling anywhere, I stayed put inside the car. Let him deal with it. The smell of wood smoke, probably hickory, in some nearby fireplace, filtered through Sadie's open window.

Apparently Jack dealt well because he returned in moments with door keys and a handful of brochures describing all the local spots of interest for us to visit while we were here.

"The guy said Leo and Debby already picked up their keys a couple of hours ago, so I guess we'll meet them up yonder."

I assumed he meant at the top-most part of the large mountain we were currently parked under, not meet them up in heaven, though either prospect sounded good for a long rest right now. Surviving a downhill drop in a roller coaster is tame compared to riding with Jack Bloodworth when he's in a hurry.

We reached the top of the mountain, and I was afraid I was about to have a nose bleed from the height. I was also afraid Sadie was about to bust another hose from struggling with the altitude. But I had to admit, Jack had done a great job when he chose this cabin to rent. It was perched on the side of the mountain at a rather precarious angle, with a terrific view overlooking Pigeon Forge and the surrounding wooded areas. From up here, the trees looked like a patchwork quilt of green, orange, yellow, red, and all the fall colors in-between.

I hooked my tote bag over my shoulder and hauled myself up the narrow, steep porch steps, holding firmly onto the wooden railing. Jack huffed and puffed behind me, carrying our suitcases. I'd packed as lightly as possible, figuring I wouldn't be much help hauling our stuff to and from the cabin.

I paused at the railing and glanced around while Jack plopped our suitcases on the porch and struggled to open the front door. The smell of the surrounding trees was enough to make me nap worthy.

Once inside the cabin I fell in love with the living room area while Jack checked out the bedrooms. The fireplace was huge, a wood burner, and I was glad Jack had thought to toss enough firewood into Sadie's trunk to keep us warm for a couple of nights.

I placed my tote bag on the large glass coffee table and found a note from Debby waiting there.

Gone to check out the little touristy stores.
See you at dinner. Love, Deb.

"Looks like Deb and Leo gave us the downstairs bedroom, in deference to your bad leg," Jack said. "Their suitcases are in one of the upstairs bedrooms."

"Deb's thoughtful like that. And I do appreciate it. Those stairs look mighty steep to me." I rolled my shoulders to stretch out the kinks. Long car rides left me as limp as the wilted lettuce salad my momma used to make.

"You know, Jack, this might be the ideal honeymoon cabin for Sunny and Craig. And there are several wedding chapels in the area."

Our younger daughter, Sunny, had fallen in love with Craig, the son of my adopted cousin, Will Ann Lloyd, several months back while Jack and I struggled to solve Will Ann's brutal murder and stay out of reach of her killer. Both of the kids had gone back to college after realizing they weren't happy in their jobs, and now, suddenly they were getting married before graduating.

"If only. Young people nowadays can't seem to wait to finish one life-changing experience before beginning another," Jack said, reading my mind as usual.

"True, but I'm not about to complain. We've known and loved Craig Tanner from the day he was born and I've always thought he'd be perfect for Sunny. Naturally, I didn't dare tell Sunny that."

Jack snorted. "Parental approval or disapproval often sets a couple on the opposite path desired." He winked at me. "If your momma hadn't thrown such an almighty fit when she heard we were necking in my car and forbidden us to ever see each other again, we wouldn't have had to elope at such a tender age."

"Well, Sunny's a bit too old for me to forbid her to do much of anything, but I'd give it a shot if I thought she'd opt for a wedding that didn't cost more than the sale of a small third world country."

"Good luck with that."

Jack carried our bags into the bedroom. "Hey, Kitty, there's a king-size bed in here. A fella could get lost in it."

"Not to worry, I brought a flashlight, as usual," I said, peering around the large room.

Jack grinned at me. "Maybe we should check it out right now and make sure the mattress is comfy." He wiggled his eyebrows in that sexy way that still put my tummy in a twist, even after several decades of marriage.

"We don't have time for that right now, Jack Bloodworth. We're supposed to meet the car club for supper. We'll probably be late as it is, even if we leave right this minute."

"You never seem to mind being late whenever we've

got an important appointment somewhere in Metropolis," he reminded me, wiggling his eyebrows again.

So, of course, we were late to dinner. And, of course, I didn't mind.

THREE

THE WAITING LINE at the door of the restaurant snaked down the zigzag, two-story ramp and clean out into the parking lot. Jack and I cut in line behind Debby and Leo. I let Jack tell his Copper Penny story while Leo listened with openmouthed attention. Deb and I exchanged a verbal list of things we wanted to do while we were in the Smoky Mountains, with a visit to the historic Cades Cove area at the top. Maybe see some shows as well, if we could snag the tickets.

"And the outlet mall, of course. I've got to find a dress for Sunny's wedding," I said, "as long as it isn't chartreuse."

"Chartreuse? Of course not. Why would anybody choose chartreuse for a wedding color?"

I explained to her that apparently Sunny had chosen it for her bridesmaids and the unhappy matron-of-honor.

Deb pretended to run her finger down her throat. "I need a dress for Sunny's wedding, too. Maybe we'll both find something at the outlet mall."

"Hope so. But my main mission here is to find the beautiful old car someone is just waiting to sell me," I said, shifting my weight to my good leg. The old wooden stair rail behind me provided a handy place to lean my weary body.

"Judging from all the cars on display we passed on our way to the restaurant," Debby said, "you shouldn't have any problem finding one to buy. I seriously doubt there is a single antique automobile anywhere in this part of the country that isn't parked on the highway with a For Sale sign on the windshield."

"I hope you're right. It's high time Jack got my dream car. He's had his for years." The line moved up several feet all at once, and I nudged Jack, still deep in conversation with Leo.

"And she's just as pretty in person as she is on television," Jack continued his story.

"Wish I'd a been there," Leo said. "I'd a had sense enough to get her autograph on a CD cover. You must have fifty of 'em stuffed in your glove box."

"I know." Jack sighed. "Just didn't think to grab one. I was so upset over the car and excited to be talking to her, and…"

I tuned the guys out as Deb poked me with her elbow. "Listen to that good old country music." She pointed to a trio of musicians nestled between the ramp and the store next door, a woman and two men belting out a country tune for all they were worth, a tune even I recognized.

"How can you not like country music?" Deb demanded of me.

"I never said I didn't like it. I love Alan Jackson, and the Tractors' music always gets my attention. I'm just not rabid about it like the rest of you. Besides, my heart belongs to Yanni. You've known that for years." I was used to defending myself to Debby. We'd had this discussion many times.

I looked the trio over, taking in the worn overalls on all three. Both men had beards, chest length and most certainly hot, judging from the color of the younger man's thick neck. Floppy hats with the required rips and holes topped their heads, and long underwear took the place of shirts. The woman's white T-shirt looked much cooler.

I glanced at the long-nosed, long-eared dog at the older man's feet and was barely able to discern some bloodhound in the obvious mixture. I caught the woman's eye as she strummed on the washtub base fiddle and sang her heart out. She fired up a smile that didn't reach above her nostrils. I wondered if these musicians had other jobs, or if they made a living by singing for their supper.

The young man's banjo case sat open in front of him, ready to receive any donations the waiting diners might be willing to part with. The older man's face burned brighter with each puff into the jug in his right hand. Quaint, but I had to admit the music was surprisingly good. I found myself tapping my good foot in time to the tune.

Behind me, Jack reached in his pocket and threw a handful of change into the banjo case. This time the smile reached the woman's eyes, but the fire inside still burned low. I swallowed hard. The older man's hands were calloused, like a farmer's. Like Jack's hands were from years of putting out crops, and harvesting them into the barn, and working for hours on end to keep his machinery running in-between times.

My job as a school teacher had filled in any income gaps until we'd both been able to retire, him several years ago, me last summer. If this couple and their son farmed and were supplementing their income by entertaining hungry customers outside a restaurant, then times were indeed tough for them. I reached for my own change purse. So did Debby. The woman smiled again, and this time it was genuine. I nodded as the line moved, rounding a corner and taking me out of sight of the musicians.

At last we were seated and ordering. Despite the long line, our club's group of twenty or so had been willing to split up and dine at several smaller tables, so Jack, Leo, Deb, and I were led to a table by the window where we could watch the Little Pigeon River flowing beneath us. The ducks below us darted back and forth, eager to snatch any crumbs thrown by departing diners.

"That lady looked so sad," Deb said.

"And tired," I added. "Must be tough at her age to make a living, singing outside a restaurant."

I'd judged her to be in her late sixties by the lines on her face and her grey hair. I had just recently eased into my sixties, complete with a surprise party and gifts I'd have to keep hidden in the closet until someone else I knew turned the big six-oh, or until I actually needed to depend on a Depend.

Jack and Leo were still going over Copper Penny's attributes, point by point from head to toe. Her ears positively must have been blazing. Like her hair.

"That couple seemed kind of old to have a boy that young," I said. "He didn't look a day over twenty-five, if that."

Deb nodded. "Change-of-life baby, possibly?"

I shuddered at the thought. Raising kids in our thirties had been tough enough. Raising one after forty was not even to be considered.

"Maybe he's a grandchild they took in to raise," Deb said.

I shuddered again. That usually only happened if the parents died or became physically unable to raise their kids, or were simply unwilling.

The waitress arrived and we ordered. I opted for roast beef with all the trimmings. Debby wanted the baked catfish and was horrified that I preferred the beef. We seldom agreed on what constituted a delicious, filling meal. Not to mention healthy.

By the time our meals arrived, Jack and Leo seemed to have at last exhausted the subject of Copper Penny's magnificence, and talk turned to finding a reasonable fixer-upper car to take home for me.

"We'll check out some of the cars parked on this side of the road after dinner," Jack said. "Then we'll go up to our cabin on the hillside and let Kitty rest."

I winked my appreciation, thankful he hadn't said "rest again." Jack wasn't always as discreet about our private lives as I'd have liked. And with or without my cane, I wouldn't be able to walk the over two miles of cars parked in the public parking lots lining the highway that cut through Pigeon Forge. Jack knew what I wanted in a car, and I trusted him to find it at a reasonable price, with or without me. And to fix it up for me to drive.

After dessert, we all lumbered toward the exit, rotating toothpicks and patting tummies. Most of our club members had already eaten and moved back outside for the view. We headed toward the side of the restaurant to join them at the river's edge. I was crumbling the leftover rolls I'd saved to feed the ducks when I heard Deb's outraged shriek behind me.

FOUR

I TURNED BACK just in time to see Deb bounce off the asphalt parking lot as a bulk of black clothing barreled toward me, Deb's purse firmly stuffed under his arm pit. Horrified, I tried to reach out and trip the purse snatcher, but my knees locked in place and my arms buckled across my chest. He blew by me like a freight train passing a bum, face covered with a bandana.

Leo dropped to Deb's side and Jack raced off after the purse snatcher. Both disappeared around the side of the restaurant, leaving me torn between limping after them to help Jack and staying behind to help Deb. I opted for going to her, praying Jack would be safe.

Leo and I gently scooped Deb up off the ground as Jack reappeared around the corner, sweating and panting like a hog at market.

"Couldn't catch the jerk," Jack said, wiping his forehead with his sleeve. "Guess it's been a few years since high-school football."

Actually it'd been a few decades, but now wasn't the best time to point that out. He'd tried to catch Deb's attacker, and that was all that really mattered. Besides, like a dog chasing a car on a dusty country road, what was Jack planning to do if he'd caught up with a determined thief over twice his size, intent on escaping with Deb's purse in hand?

"You okay, honey?" Leo asked, breathing twice as hard as Jack, even though he hadn't moved from Deb's side.

"My arm's probably a bit bruised, which matches my ego, but I'm fine."

I dug for my cell phone. "Your arm could be broken, Deb. I'll call for an ambulance."

"No, Kitty, I'm not hurt. And I'm not going to a strange hospital." Deb dusted off her slacks and gave me her stubborn look.

I dropped the phone back into my tote bag. No use arguing with a brick wall.

Deb's eyes ballooned wide, and she pointed over my shoulder. The guys and I spun around to see the chubby banjo player striding toward us, Deb's purse slung carelessly over his thick shoulder.

"How did you find my wife's purse?" Leo asked.

"I couldn't help overhearing you folks talking on the stairs," he said, grinning up at me.

Did I mention I'm five eight and tower over an awful lot of the school-age male population? A huge advantage during my teaching days.

"About looking for an old car?" he continued.

My head bobbled up and down like one of those ugly fake Chihuahua dogs some drivers kept on their dashboards. What did all this have to do with Deb's stolen purse?

"I was on my way over to talk to you about a car my dad has for sale when that guy knocked this lady down." He handed the purse to Deb. "Not very gentlemanly of him. I cut him off at the front side of the restaurant and yanked your purse back, but he shoved me into the wall and took off running. I'm afraid I lost him."

Deb stared at the rescuer, her jaw swinging in the breeze. Leo stepped forward and shook the young man's hand.

"We do appreciate it. Thanks for chasing him down. I guess we should call the police?"

"Yes, you should," the young man said, "but it will take them a while to get here in all this traffic. Maybe you should take the lady to the first-aid station the car-show hosts set up in the next block and get her checked out, first?"

"I don't need to be checked out," Deb insisted. "I'm fine. I do think we should report the attempted theft. Let me see what's missing."

For the next several minutes Deb scrounged through her purse. "My credit cards are all here, but my cash is gone. Luckily, I didn't bring much cash. Nothing else is missing that I can see."

Good thing her credit cards weren't stolen. That always opened a whole other can of worms. I thanked the young man again, still feeling as if I'd let my best friend down for not beating the thief to death with my own tote bag, which was certainly heavy enough for the job.

"You're most welcome, ma'am. Just glad I was nearby."

"You mentioned you had a car for sale," Jack said, possibly changing the subject because he also felt guilty for not catching the marauder. "We're looking for a car for my wife. Something built in the late Thirties or early Forties. But nothing so expensive that we'd literally have to sell our farm to buy it."

"I've got just the thing," the young man said. "Well, my dad does. It's a nineteen thirty-seven Chrysler, four-door sedan."

"With suicide doors?" I whispered in my most reverent tone.

"Yes, ma'am." He scratched at the long beard and the ugly tattoo on the back of his hand appeared to roll around, an eight ball, slightly lopsided, as if he'd drawn it himself rather than visiting a tattoo parlor.

Then he turned back to Jack. "I'm Charlie Beadle. My

folks own a farm out in Sevier County. I'll give you our address, and you can come out and look at the car. She's in pretty good condition. Dad's had her up on blocks for years."

"So the tires are probably dry rotted?"

I was ready to kick Jack. Tires, shmires, those were easily replaced. How much did the boy's father want for this jewel and what shape was she in? I glared at Jack. He apparently got the message.

He said, "What shape is she in, and how much is your dad asking for her?"

Young Charlie named a figure that made my stomach lurch. "But she's in mint condition, except for a little fix here and there," he added.

Which was exactly what I wanted, but I doubted Jack Bloodworth would cough up that much money, even though we had it put back for a car purchase. He'd want something left over to use for repairs, insurance, and the other little details. I sighed.

"Give me directions," Jack said, surprising me, "and we'll come out tomorrow morning and take a look. I can't promise you anything because that's way more than we'd planned to spend, but I won't have any peace if we don't at least take a look at the car."

I yanked a notebook and pen out of my bag, passed them to Charlie Beadle, and he jotted down the directions. Jack promised we'd call before we came.

"The local police department is sending a unit out," Deb said, closing her cell phone as the young man left us. "While we wait, let's go feed the ducks. They said it would be a while."

We had to pick up her leftover bread off the ground, but I didn't figure the ducks would care. They probably invented the five-second rule.

"Mind if we go along with you tomorrow morning?" Deb said as we each limped toward the river's edge. The ducks immediately abandoned the other tourists and swam straight for us, expecting new treats.

"I'd love to see their farm," Deb continued. "The older couple is so interesting looking, and the boy doesn't match them at all. He looks like a city kid, not someone who's spent much of his young life working on a farm."

"I agree," I said, tossing half a roll at the most demanding duck. He downed it in one quick gulp, leaving only crumbs for the others. "Charlie Beadle's hands don't sport any calluses I could spot. I'm dying to learn more about the family. Something about that boy—"

"Kitty, we are not buying the first car we look at," Jack said, taking a roll out of my stash and breaking it into small pieces.

Probably not even the fourth or fifth, if I knew my husband. But chances were good we would end up buying the first one we looked at, if it was in the shape the young man described. But I'd let Jack do his thing before I began making wifely noises.

A local cop arrived sooner than expected and took Deb's statement, leaving us free to head back to the cabin to tend her scrapes and bruises. And me to wonder what, in particular, had caught my attention about Charlie Beadle. I shook my head, unable to firmly tack the feeling to the little bulletin board that hung inside my head.

FIVE

I WAS UP BY SUNRISE the next morning, staring in awe as the low, smoky clouds slid over the tops of the mountains like a mother's loving hand caressing her baby's shoulders. Our farm was pretty much flat land, all hundred and thirty acres of it, and I wasn't used to heights like this. The vapor clinging to the hillsides didn't completely cover the trees, and the fall colors underneath were spectacular. But I had to wonder what it would be like to travel up the steep, narrow road to reach this rather remote cabin in the dead of winter. My guess was, nobody much did.

Deb stepped out onto the terrace, two coffee mugs in hand, still in her favorite old bathrobe. The newer, prettier versions Leo gave her every Christmas languished in her closet, stashed carefully away for "an emergency." Obviously this vacation didn't qualify, and since she was rarely ill, I feared his gifts were doomed to stay there unless some local charity got lucky.

"The guys are still hogging both bathrooms," she announced, sliding a cup in front of me. "I warned Leo if he complained about how long it takes me to dress just one more time, he'd regret it."

I nodded and sipped my coffee.

"Apple Barn for breakfast?" Deb asked.

"Where else?" I replied.

The homemade apple fritters at the Apple Barn were the best I'd ever tasted, not to mention the apple juice and other apple products they served there. My mouth watered just thinking about it. Maybe with his tummy full, I could talk Jack into buying that car for me, assuming it was in the condition Charlie Beadle described.

"How are your injuries this morning?" I asked.

"I'll live," she said between quick sips of coffee. "I took a couple of aspirin last night, so my arm doesn't feel like it's in the middle of a forest fire this morning. My knee isn't swollen, just sore."

Which was a blessing. Before I could ask anything else, she said, "Think Jack will buy that car for you, assuming it's what you've been looking for?"

"Not today. He'll have to look around at a hundred or so other cars, just to be sure he's getting a bargain. I'll have to be patient."

Deb grinned. She knew I had all the patience of a hungry toddler in a room full of cake and ice cream, but I'd give it my best shot.

"Apparently those people need the money," she said. "How much do you think they make in an evening, singing for tourists?"

"No idea. I've heard tell that the drifters who sit at the off-ramps near I-24, holding those little cardboard signs, announcing they're willing to work for food, do pretty well in a day."

"I suppose they deserve it," Deb said. "Can't be much fun sitting in the hot sun all day. Or worse, in the rain."

"Can't be much fun singing in a parking lot for pocket change, either. The boy looked fat and happy, but the older couple seemed worn down."

"Maybe they—" Deb began as the patio door slid open and Leo's head popped out.

"You girls going with us? Time's a wastin', and it takes you two forever to get dressed."

"Pardon me while I strangle my husband," Debby said.

Despite the injured arm, she declined my offer of help with that task.

One last long look at the wonderful splash of fall colors and I went inside to shower. I wondered if I should take a minute or two to call my younger daughter, first. If at all possible, something had to be done to get Sunny to cancel the chartreuse.

IT TOOK NEARLY an hour's wait in line to get us a spot at the Apple Barn, but I wasn't about to complain when they seated us at a table with wicker porch swings hung from the beams across the ceiling instead of the usual restaurant chairs. The place had enough ambiance to cover all of New York, with some left over. And the omelet I ordered was to die for. Light and fluffy with sharp cheese melted everywhere.

"Think you'll win a trophy this year?" Jack asked Leo, around a mouthful of hot apple fritter.

"Hard to say. I've not entered the truck before, and I don't know how tough the competition is here, or how the judges do their thing."

Jack and Leo each trained as judges for our local car competitions. Whereupon, they discovered that the rules were pretty stiff and the judging very thorough.

"She's a beautiful truck, Leo, but you need to come up with a name for her," Deb said. "How can you possibly expect a nameless antique Model A to strut her stuff in a serious competition like this one?"

Nearly all of our car-club members had named their vehicles and considered the names to be good-luck charms. Our own "Sadie Was a Lady" had certainly lived up to her name over the years, despite the recent busted hose, and even that had turned into a stroke of luck for Jack.

"I'm still working on a name," Leo said. "Any and all suggestions appreciated."

I was thinking that over when Jack said, "Rosie."

"Rosie? Why would I name my truck Rosie? She doesn't even have any red paint on her."

"But she does have those neat rivets along her running boards. Rosie, for Rosie the Riveter of World War II fame. Remember the posters? She was a pretty good-looking gal. And your truck is blue, just like the shirt Rosie wore on the posters."

"So she is," Leo said. "Rosie. I like it."

Deb and I exchanged looks. We'd both been born after the war ended, but we'd learned about Rosie the Riveter from Deb's mother, who'd responded to the call to help fill the workforce while the men in the area went off to war. Rosie supposedly represented all the women across America who'd answered that call. Jack's mother was another "Rosie," and my mother had volunteered at the local Red Cross. With a tradition like that to uphold, Leo's Rosie was bound to be a winner. We toasted the name with the best apple juice I'd ever tasted and wished Leo luck in the upcoming competition.

It was raining steadily by the time Leo, Debby, Jack, and I hustled out of the enormous Apple Barn restaurant. We carried the obligatory doggie bags filled with homemade apple fritters—a perfect snack for later, easily re-heated in the kitchen at our cabin. The wooden rockers on the restaurant porch moved to and fro, filled with hopeful diners taking refuge under the huge overhang as they waited to hear who would be seated next.

Debby and I crawled into Sadie's back seat, moaning and groaning about full stomachs and old bones. I was a bit nervous about seeing the Beadles' car, fearing it would be just what I'd been dreaming about for years and that Jack would decide it was too expensive.

Leo, as our official navigator, pulled a new Tennessee map out of Sadie's glove box and began seeking coordinates for the directions the young man had given us the night before.

As Jack had feared, the farm where the farmers-slash-musicians lived was located at eighth and plum—eight miles out and plumb back in the sticks. As we were about to pass the last turn for the third time, Debby spotted it. The road sign was missing, but she got a glimpse of the barn the young man had described. The barn was enormous, white-washed, oval shaped rather than square, with round white turrets topped with lightning rods.

"Wow, I've never seen anything like that, and as a farmer's wife, I've seen an awful lot of old barns in my time," I said as I dug in my tote bag for my camera.

Jack had bought me a digital camera last Christmas, and I'd been snapping pictures of all the old, unusual barns I saw in hopes of making a coffee-table book of them some day.

"Think you might put this one in your book?" Deb asked.

"Yep. It has to be the most unusual of the lot so far. Many of the barns I've photographed are well over a hundred years old, having been built to withstand just about any disaster. Many are caving in from sheer age or are being torn apart and replaced with the newer metal versions. I want to preserve as many of them as I can with my pictures. Obviously, this wonderful old monstrosity should be included."

"We should've put the fritters in the trunk," Debby said, covering a delicate belch. "I'm as full as a tick on a bird dog, but the smell is still tempting me."

I nodded. "As soon as we park, I'll move them."

The rain slowed to a mere mist as Jack rolled to a stop in front of a house that instantly had me drooling with envy. I loved our old farm house, complete with screened-in porch on the back and covered porch on the front with wicker furniture everywhere, but the porch on this place went clear around the house. I caught a glimpse of a day bed on one screened-in side.

"I bet they sleep there on hot nights," I told Debby, handing her my umbrella.

"I bet they don't even have air-conditioning," she said. "Wouldn't need it much up here in these hills. I'd like a shot at a nap on that porch, myself." She eased out of her side of the car and covered me with the umbrella as I tucked the tempting food inside Sadie's trunk.

I wouldn't have minded a short rest there either, but we were here on business, so I slammed the trunk shut and headed for the front porch. The woman we'd seen playing the washtub last night wiped her hands on a pink gingham, flour-splattered apron and introduced herself as Medina Beadle. A bit of hair sprung loose from under her kerchief and waved in the breeze. The old hound that accompanied them the night before opened one eye, dismissed us as non-threatening, and went back to snoozing in a porch chair.

"My man's out in the barn. Car's stored out there. You folks are welcome to head out that way." She wiped the back of her hand across her forehead, leaving a trail of flour. "Charlie isn't up yet. He had to work late." The ornate screen door squealed in protest as she headed back inside.

"Who is it, Medina?" a quivery female voice said from inside.

"Just someone to see about the car," she replied.

As I turned to grab the rail and ease myself off the porch I heard the elderly voice say, "Medina, I told you I don't want—"

"Hush, Mother. Not now, please."

SIX

THE FRONT DOOR slammed shut, and I couldn't hear any more conversation between the women. Leo and Jack were already halfway to the barn, wondering aloud what kind of shape the car was in. Deb and I exchanged glances. What was it the unseen elderly woman hadn't wanted? To have strangers visiting the farm? To sell a car the family had obviously owned for a very long time? To have the front door closed, preventing her from seeing what went on outside?

Debby shrugged, and we moseyed toward the barn, with me snapping pictures all the way, her holding the umbrella, and all of us dodging a flock of chickens hoping for a mid-morning snack.

Not far from the house, we passed one of the most unusual flower beds I'd ever been lucky enough to cast my envious gaze upon. The entire area was larger than the nearby farm house and consisted of a multitude of raised beds held in place by old railroad ties. Each one of the beds was built nearly as high as my hips, which meant the savvy gardener didn't have to weed on bended knee, and each held many different types of plants, some I'd never seen in all my gardening years. Flowers of every color and variety were still in bloom, with several gone to sleep until next spring.

Mingled amongst the beds, the wonderful herbs gave off their scents. Enough variety there to please any cook. I paused to touch my favorite, a huge rosemary bush, wondering what magic Medina Beadle used to grow it this large. I snapped a few pictures and admired the planning that went into this layout. The sun slid out from behind a cloud and lit up the area while I stood and gawked. Deb gave my umbrella a shake and quizzed me as to the identity of some of the plants. I had to admit I didn't know a lot of them.

The tallest bloomers were carefully placed in the back rows, and the shortest in the front. Plants were scattered in such a way that there would always be something to feed the soul all across the area, keeping it from looking barren unless and until a hard freeze put them all to sleep for the winter. Which might not always happen, given that the area was located in the south. Snow on the higher hills, yes, but not always hard freezes on the lower ones, like this. My fingers itched to dig into the rich earth and work with the plants.

"Wow," Deb said at my elbow. "Must be a full-time job keeping this garden up. My flower bed isn't a tenth of this size and I have to work at it nearly every day. How does she do it?"

I shook my head, took a last long sniff of the wonderful fragrances, and headed for the barn.

I'd ask for permission, of course, before using any of the pictures I'd taken, but this ugly old building was one of the most unusual barns I'd ever seen and might even qualify for a spot on the front cover of my book. And the chickens scratching the ground and chasing each other around in front of the barn added to the ambiance. Assuming, of course, I ever got the barn book published.

As we passed a large, rickety outbuilding situated beside the barn, the door squealed open, and a young man stepped out, spotted us, and quickly stepped back inside.

"I thought she said her son was still asleep," Debby said.

"That wasn't Charlie Beadle," I said, viewing his picture again on the camera screen. "That kid is much heavier, and his beard is shorter than Charlie Beadle's. But that was odd."

"What was?" Deb asked. Jack and Leo were several feet ahead of us, still deep in conversation.

"When he saw us, he scooted right back inside, like he didn't want to be noticed. Didn't even wave. Folks in rural farming areas always wave at other folks, even strangers."

"I'm a city girl, even if the city is as small as Metropolis, but you're right, he did seem startled to see us. Maybe he just didn't want his picture taken."

"Maybe. But I can easily delete that one because I have plenty of others."

I wiggled my shoulders in an effort to stop the sudden sensation slithering up my spine. Deb hadn't seen the purse snatcher last night, since he'd hit her from behind, but I had. The young man who'd stepped out of the doorway just now looked taller and slimmer than Deb's attacker, but something about him made me uneasy. Okay, so I was paranoid since the purse snatching. I still felt guilty for not dropping the jerk in his tracks.

Jack reached the barn and turned to see if I was still following. I moved to just above turtle speed to join him. "Remember, now, Kitty, we aren't—"

"I know, buying the first car we see." I stepped inside the barn, and my heart lurched.

There she sat, surrounded by hay and dust, a calico cat asleep on her wide front fender. My dream car. The tires were flat from dry rot and the paint was a bit faded, but she had all her necessary parts, at least those on the outside. Suicide doors—doors that opened backward—a running board that went almost past the trunk, a huge spotlight just in front of the driver's door, and windows everywhere.

Jack shook hands with the owner, and while introductions were swapped, I tiptoed up—well, as easily as I could tiptoe with a cane—and peeked inside. The seats were intact. Could've stood a good recover job, but at least they weren't all mouse eaten.

"Mose Beadle," I vaguely heard the farmer tell Jack and Leo. He took off a faded baseball cap as he nodded toward Debby and me.

The body of the car seemed to be a grimy, old, dark blue color. Old blue. Like our old blue-tick hound, this car had hunkered down and napped here in the barn for who knew how long. But she'd be ready for action once Jack and I were done with her. If I could just convince him to buy her.

Old Blue. We still missed that dog ever since she'd dropped down for a nap on our hooked rug one rainy afternoon and never gotten up again. I'd name this car Old Blue, in her honor. I'd bet the car was just as dependable and eager, once the grime was washed away and she'd had a good polish job.

I moved forward to check the windshield for cracks and startled a stray rooster near the front tire who flapped his way to a beam above our heads and proceeded to make his displeasure known in loud tones. The cloud of dust he stirred up set me to sneezing. Deb passed me a tissue.

"She's a beauty," Deb whispered. I nodded and blew my nose, all the while trying not to get my hopes up. Yet.

I limped to the driver's side of the car. Debby joined me there as I peeked in the window. Floor shift. I'd learned to drive in a similar vehicle, so no problem there, even with a fairly bum leg. Surely my leg would heal eventually, despite the fact that I had early signs of osteoporosis and had broken that leg twice in the past year.

I checked out the dashboard. All those wonderful old gauges behind glass. I could hardly believe my eyes. I was

willing to kill for this car. Namely, I'd kill Jack Bloodworth
if he didn't buy her for me. Assuming she was priced somewhere under the size of the national debt.

"How much did you say you wanted for her?" Jack
asked. I held my breath. Before the older Beadle could
speak, a voice from behind us quoted the same heart-
stopping figure as he had last night. We all turned to see
young Charlie Beadle looming in the large doorway to
the barn.

"I'm afraid that's more than we're prepared to pay,"
Jack said.

What was this "we" stuff? Did he have a mouse tucked
in his pocket? Yes, the price was a bit stiff, but the good
shape the car was in would help trade off for repairs that
wouldn't have to be made. There wasn't a noticeable bump
or scratch on the body of the car, so far as I could see. A
good polish job would fix her up just fine. I didn't want
to show her or win trophies; I just wanted to drive her. I
swallowed hard again.

"I'm afraid we can't take any less than that."

A shadow passed over the older man's face as the boy
said it. I couldn't tell if he was angry or relieved.

I wondered how badly the Beadles needed the money.
They were already working outside the farm, playing
music to passing tourists. And the only money they seemed
to get for that was tips. I doubted they'd been hired for the
job by the restaurant. Most street musicians worked that
way, independently, getting only what the hearts of their
listeners dictated, and that usually wasn't a large amount.

On our way out to the barn I'd glanced around at the
nearby fields. Best I could tell, they'd already harvested
what looked like a very small summer crop of soy beans,
and I'd seen no evidence of winter wheat, which I would've

expected if they were short of money and needing another crop this year.

Jack turned and headed for the barn door. "I appreciate you letting us take a look, and she is one sweet car, but I've got some others to look at before we decide."

I figured he was doing his usual drop-the-price-before-I-get to-the-door-and-I'll-deal routine. If he was, it didn't work.

"No problem," Charlie Beadle said, "but I've given our address to several other interested buyers in town for the car show this weekend, so she might not be here when you come back."

"I understand," Jack said.

And, much as I hated to admit it, I understood, as well. As badly as I wanted that car, we did have to see what else was available before we bought one because whatever we brought home was going to have to last me a very long time. Like until I was too old to drive any longer and my daughters pried the keys out of my tightly clenched fingers.

Deb and I followed Leo and Jack back toward Sadie. I paused as Medina Beadle opened the front door and stepped out onto her porch again. I saw Mose Beadle give a small, negative head shake in her direction. She started back inside.

"I'd like to ask you something, Mrs. Beadle," I called out to her.

She turned back to me, looking a bit alarmed, as if I was about to inquire into their private finances or something, so I hurried on. "I took some pictures of your barn just now. And some of your outbuildings. And that wonderful flower garden."

I was dying to ask her about the raised beds, but I didn't

want to seem too nosey. Besides that, permission for use of the pictures was the important question of the moment.

I pointed to the barn roof. "I've never seen one shaped like that. Would you object to me using the pictures I took in a book I'm thinking of doing on old barns and outbuildings?"

She opened her mouth to speak, but the answer came from somewhere behind her waist. "What would you want to put pictures of our old barn in a book for? And who'd read it?" said the elderly woman in a wheelchair.

She looked to be at least as old as the house, maybe older, and she looked as if she'd blow away if I huffed and puffed at her, until I saw her eyes. Bright and shiny as a lump of Southern Illinois coal, and just as hard. The wooden ramp at one end of the porch must have been built for her.

"Mother, I'm not sure—"

"It's still my barn, Medina. I have the right to ask. Come on up here, young lady."

Mercy, nobody had called me "young lady" in, well, I couldn't say how long. Deb and I moved to the porch. The hound dog's ears twitched, but he didn't bother barking at us. As Jack backed Sadie around to head down the long driveway, I eased my way up the steps. Medina Beadle moved aside, and her mother joined us.

"My husband and I are retired from farming," I said. "He rents our land to a neighbor. I—"

"You all didn't sign up for one of those government programs, did you?" the old lady interrupted. "The ones where they pay you not to raise any crops?"

"No, ma'am. Those are excellent programs, but Jack and I feel the land should be put to use and not left to lie fallow."

"My name's Sassy Bentley." She reached out and shook

my hand with a firm grip that belied any weakness living in a wheelchair might have suggested. "You and your husband are my kind of farmers."

"I'm Kitty Bloodworth, and this is my friend Debby Evans." I saw Deb wince at the firm handshake.

"Is that your garden?" Deb asked, tipping her head toward the profusion of flowers and herbs beside the house.

"Yes, it is," the old lady said. "I spend most of my days out there, sitting in the warm sun, feeling the damp earth in my hands. It keeps me alive."

Deb grinned down at her. "It's wonderful. I've never seen anything like it."

"Don't let this chair fool you," Sassy Bentley continued, patting the chair arms as she spoke. "I have a long-handled spade to work with, and the beds were built just high enough for me to reach them. I can still work in the garden most days, if the weather is good. Medina helps me when she can."

The old woman shaded her eyes with a thin hand and glanced up at the cloudy sky. "Won't get much of anything done out there today, I'm afraid. Too much rain this morning. My chair would likely get stuck."

She turned her attention back to me. "Now, what good do you think a book about old barns will do?" She gestured toward the barn. "The old days are gone, not likely to come back around again." She frowned up at me, her twisted fingers kneading at the bright lap quilt covering her legs.

"Yes, ma'am, I feel the same way, but these old barns are beautiful, and before long they'll be lost to us forever. I want to preserve them in a book. Maybe no one will look at it but me or my family, but I want to try."

She nodded. "As I said, it's my barn. The whole farm is mine. Mose and Medina work it for me, and it'll be theirs when I'm gone. But for now, I have the say-so over it. You're welcome to take a few pictures."

"Of the barn and outbuildings," Medina Beadle put in. "I'd rather you not take pictures of anyone in our family." She glanced down at her mother, who quickly nodded her agreement.

I thanked Sassy Bentley. "And I'll give credit as to who owns the farm in the book, but I won't list any locations, so no one will bother you."

She thought that over and nodded. "Send me a copy of the book," she said over her shoulder as she turned her wheelchair to go back into the house. "If I'm still alive and kicking, I'd like to see it."

I promised to do that, and Debby and I headed down the steps to the car.

I slid into Sadie's back seat beside Debby, and she patted my good leg. "Don't worry, we're bound to find you something while we're still in the area," she whispered. "There are certainly enough antique cars to look at."

SEVEN

AND BOY HOWDY, did we look. And look, and look. Jack quickly discovered we could actually drive through the parking lots of the businesses situated along the highway rather than having to park and walk for two or more miles to view the cars on display there. We must have eased through thirty blocks of parking lots, strung together like a long, beaded necklace, all the while craning our necks to spot a bargain and climbing out now and then for a closer look.

I was amazed at the variety of vehicles. Everything from an ancient Hudson, which the owner swore was one of only two known to still exist in America, to the ever popular Fifty-Five, Fifty-Six, and Fifty-Seven Chevrolets, abundant in every color imaginable.

Of all the cars for sale, my personal favorite was a Thirties' roadster with no door handles. The owner had replaced them with an automatic release that popped the doors open when he pushed his keyless entry. Cute, and very different, but I had to wonder how one entered or exited the car if the battery on the key chain suddenly died. And the orange paint job was a bit bright, even for me. I'd be happy if other drivers admired my car as we cruised around Metropolis, but I certainly didn't want to blind anyone.

Along with all the fully restored cars there were fixer-uppers needing complete overhauls and flatbed trailers covered with parts most fixer-upper owners usually had to scour their local junk yards or the Internet to find. The only thing we didn't manage to locate was my dream car. Certainly nothing like the car the Beadles had tucked away in their old barn. By the end of the day I was tired and discouraged. So was the rest of our group.

"I need some ice cream," Leo said.

"We haven't even had lunch, Leo," Deb said. "Not to mention supper, and it's getting close to that time."

"Why can't we do both meals and ice cream at the same time?" Jack suggested. "I spotted a place a block or so back. Then we'll change clothes and check in with the car club. See how everyone's doing."

I quickly agreed. I didn't want Jack to see how disappointed I was. Yet. There was still time to get back to the Beadles' and buy that car, assuming they'd be willing to lower the price and I could get Jack to go back out there. For now I'd wait.

As usual, Jack's restaurant-scouting abilities were right on the mark. Greasy burgers, hot, salty French fries, and chocolate shakes to top them off. The meal restored my spirits, and we headed up to our cabin to dress for the car-club meeting.

I was pulling my hair into a ponytail when my cell phone rang. Jack quickly dumped the contents of my tote bag onto the bed and answered the phone without pushing the wrong button and cutting off the call, for once. He exchanged pleasantries with our daughter Maggie while I tied a ribbon around my ponytail to hide the rubber band.

"Tell Tori I hope she's feeling better real soon," he said and handed the phone to me. Tori, my granddaughter, sick?

"What's wrong with Tori?" I demanded of my daughter, stuffing the contents back into my tote bag.

"She's had the sniffles for several days. Now she's coughing a lot. Joe's gone to the drugstore to pick up her medicine. Don't worry, Mom, the doctor says she'll be fine."

"Keep an eye on her. There was a lot of pneumonia going around town last week. The Bakers' grandson wound up at Massac Memorial with it. Is everybody else okay?"

"We're all fine, Mom, really. Stop worrying and enjoy your trip."

"How are the wedding plans coming?" I asked, mentally crossing my fingers.

"Trust me, Mom, you don't want to know."

She was probably right. Most of the mothers of brides I knew wanted the entire expensive shebang for their daughters, but Jack and I had eloped, and we'd never regretted our simple wedding. I'd tried to teach my daughters to focus on the importance of the marriage, not just the wedding day itself. I'd succeeded with Maggie, whose wedding took place at the lovely gazebo in a small park in Metropolis, but I wasn't so sure about Sunny, who was considering a ten-foot-tall ice sculpture, a very expensive orchestra, and live swans floating on a pond—said unnamed pond yet to be designated—not to mention the dreaded chartreuse.

"Gotta run, Mom, Tori says she's going to be sick. I'll call you later."

"Take good care—" I said to dead air.

A HALF HOUR LATER we arrived back at the bottom of the mountain to find the car-club meeting in full swing, literally. Fifties rock-and-roll music poured out of every window of Philby and Reva Mason's cabin, located about a mile or so below the place we'd rented. The Metropolis Cruisers had agreed to meet at their rental cabin after supper. As president of the club, Philby would have all the information on the upcoming competition, and he might have information on any cars we'd missed. Club members were great about helping car enthusiasts find their dream car.

At least the Masons didn't have to navigate those hair-pin turns up the mountain to reach their cabin like we did. I wasn't sure Philby's old car could have made it. Or that his heart could have stood the altitude. Model T owners tended to be older than other antique-car owners.

In the middle of the living room, those car-club members who were still physically able were jitterbugging or twisting, depending on which decade they'd grown up in. The heavy wooden furniture had been pushed against the log walls, and Deb and Leo were quickly swept onto the dance floor, Deb's turquoise poodle skirt floating above her Oxfords as Leo twirled her around. Normally I was a Twister when both of my legs were in good working order, but my red felt poodle skirt wouldn't get much of a chance to float or twirl to this fast music. Maybe when my leg fully healed.

Philby was manning the record player, and I wondered how he'd managed to stuff it inside his small Model T in order to bring it here. I plopped into the large leather chair beside Reva and tapped my good leg in time with the music. Jack stood beside Philby, flipping through albums most of today's teenagers had never heard of, much less danced to.

"Kitty, I haven't had a chance to call you," Philby said, sliding his portable oxygen tank to his other hip. "We've had two applicants apply for the automotive scholarship we sponsor at Shawnee College for next semester. This is the first time anyone's been smart enough to even ask about our scholarship much less apply, much as we've tried to get the word out, and I hate to turn either one of them down. Did we, by any chance, put enough into the fund to grant scholarships for both students?"

"More than enough, Philby." I reached into my tote bag and pulled out the car club's checkbook. "And even if we hadn't, the last fundraiser really pumped life into our checking account, in case we need more." I quoted him our balance and he whistled.

"Do we know these kids?" Jack asked.

"Yep, the Lofton twins."

"Lori and Lana?" Jack smiled. "Well, it certainly serves the male college students right for letting the ladies get the jump on them in applying for the scholarship. And you can bet those two gals will make terrific auto mechanics."

Philby nodded. "How did the great car search go? Find anything yet?"

"Yes," I said as Jack said, "No."

Philby looked back and forth between us. "Well, which is it?"

Jack ducked his head. "We found the car Kitty's always wanted stuck in the corner of an old barn out in the country, but the price was a bit stiff."

"But we didn't find anything cheaper this afternoon, and we checked practically every car from here back to Sevierville," I said.

"We looked at a lot of cars, too," Philby said. "Meaning the whole group. Nobody reported spotting a car that fit the requirements you mentioned. How much is the owner asking?"

Jack described the car and related the price.

Philby whistled again. "That is a bit steep, but given the condition she's in, I'd say it sounds fair. Did you make him a counter offer, Jack?"

"I didn't dare. I wanted to look around first, and if he'd accepted my offer or a counter offer, it would have been a done deal for Kitty."

Jack looked down at me and smiled. "I think maybe we

should pay another visit to the Beadles' farm tomorrow. See if they're willing to deal."

I knew there was a reason Jack Bloodworth was my hero.

"Now you're talking sense," Reva Mason put in.

Philby put a slow dance song on the old record player and somebody turned the lights down low. Jack pulled me to him and slowly guided me out to the floor. This I could manage, with his arms around me. For the rest of the evening we were lost in the Fifties.

EIGHT

"The wedding is off!" Sunny shouted into my cell phone.

"Wha—?" I said, fumbling on the nightstand for my glasses. Late-night phone calls were always bad news. I knew I should have turned the ringer off and left my cell phone buried deep inside my tote bag.

"Craig is a beast. I can't possibly marry him."

"Slow down, Sunny. Take a deep breath and tell me what happened?"

"Craig insists that his best man wouldn't be caught dead in a chartreuse cummerbund. I mean, really, Mother, it's only for a couple of hours, and they've been best friends since third grade."

"Tell her I'm not being caught dead in one either," Jack whispered into my shoulder. Then he turned over and pulled the blanket back up to his nose. Before I could even respond to my frantic daughter, he was snoring again.

"Is that Daddy muttering in the background, as usual? What did he say? Is he taking Craig's side against his own flesh and blood?"

Planning the wedding had been a sore spot ever since Craig had dropped to one knee beside our living-room fireplace and proposed to our youngest daughter last Christmas Eve.

That was several months ago, and he'd spent the intervening time trying to talk Sunny into a simple ceremony, without all the "falderal," as he put it, and her father always backed him. And I'd have to lower the volume on my cell phone if I didn't want Jack to be able to listen in and make a running commentary on every single one of my phone calls.

"Sweetheart, isn't there some other color you could use in order to placate the best man?" I said as quietly as possible in an effort not to wake Jack again.

"What? Mother, I can't hear you. Why are you mumbling?"

I sighed and slid out of bed, heading for the bathroom. Maybe I could take care of two tasks at once. Now fully awake, my bladder was in need of relief. "Hang on a minute."

Safe inside the master bathroom I turned on the light, gently closed the door, and perched on the throne. "Okay, we can talk now. I didn't want to keep your father awake. Why can't you choose another color that's more in tune with the best man's delicate sensibilities? Trust me, Sunshine, by your tenth anniversary you won't remember what color anybody wore."

"Keep Dad awake? Mom, it's only nine thirty, what are you guys doing in bed this early? Never mind, I probably don't want to know." She sniffed.

I glanced at my watch. "Sunny, it's ten thirty where you are. You really need to buy a watch with a face large enough to read and get rid of that itty-bitty excuse for a time piece. And it's eleven thirty here. We're an hour ahead of you. We crossed a time zone, remember? And we never stay up past ten o'clock if we can help it. Your father is a retired farmer, for crying out loud. Early to—"

"Sorry, Mom, I forgot. I just—" She burst into tears.

I made the appropriate motherly noises. When the

waterworks on the other end of the phone slowed up a bit, I ventured a question.

"This isn't really about chartreuse cummerbunds, is it?"

"No." She sobbed harder.

"Sunny?" All of a sudden that old song Johnny Mathis made into a hit floated through my mind. Something about a Sunny who got blue. By now I was really tired and afraid I'd fall asleep and slide off my uncomfortable perch onto the cold tile floor.

"Craig said he'd make Barry wear it, but I can tell his heart really isn't in it. Mom, what if his heart really isn't in marrying me, either? What if he's getting scared? What if he wants to back out? What'll I do?"

Great, her last question brought to mind another old tune asking the same question. At this rate I was likely to burst into song and wake up the entire mountainside. I stood and hoisted my flannel pajama bottoms back into place, then hit the flush knob, hoping the noise didn't wake Jack. The last thing I needed was him joining me in the small bathroom, telling me what to say to our daughter while I tried to think of something to say to her that wouldn't set her off again. I was rarely able to have a simple phone conversation with anybody without having to listen to and answer Jack at the same time, and it was extremely distracting.

"Sunny, Craig would walk barefoot on flaming glass shards for you. And standing up in front of the huge crowd you are bent on inviting to the wedding is pretty much the same thing for him. He's willing to do it for you. But when you start planning the minute details of the wedding, it scares the daylights out of him and he balks a bit. He'll be fine, but I suggest you worry out the finer details with your sister and me and leave him out of it. He doesn't have to know every single thing up front."

He really didn't need to know the details of the wedding at all. Craig would show up at the church in a daze and be happily on his way to some romantic honeymoon spot before he knew what hit him. And while chartreuse wasn't my idea of a wedding color, either, I didn't dare tell the bride that. Not if I wanted to be included in the wedding.

"What's really going on, Sunshine?" I ventured.

"Oh, Mom, Craig isn't really being a beast, I am. I want everything to be perfect and so many things can go wrong. I can't think of a single one of my friends who hasn't had a disaster at her wedding. Casey's bridesmaid threw up five seconds before they started down the aisle. Sandy's cake collapsed under the weight of the upper tiers. Meredith and Jay forgot to hire a pianist and there was no music. Her father hummed as they walked down the aisle. It was horrible. Everybody laughed. What if something like that happens to me? I mean to us?"

I leaned into the mirror to examine my graying hair and nearly lost my balance. I yawned as quietly as possible, but it was late and I was wearing down more and more by the minute.

"Sunny, there is always a disaster of some sort at a wedding, and the bride and groom usually survive to live happily ever after, or as near as possible. I've told you girls, the marriage isn't even legal if something doesn't go wrong at the wedding. Now is this really about the perfect wedding or the perfect groom? Are you having second thoughts about Craig? Because if you are—"

"No, Mom, I promise you, this isn't about Craig. I've dated a lot of guys..."

"And?"

"Craig is the man I've always dreamed about. But he thinks I'm perfect. So what happens when he figures out I'm not? Which he will. Probably on our honeymoon."

I was going to have to sit down again for this one. My leg was beginning to complain about me standing at the sink for so long. I lowered the toilet lid and eased down onto it. Thankfully, it had one of those warm, furry covers.

"Sunny, Craig is very bright and very down to earth. And he knows women aren't perfect. He was raised by one of the crankiest women ever born. He knows the perfect woman doesn't exist. He thinks you're perfect for him. So do I. He loves you and you two fit well together. Now, please, let me go back to bed, and you get some rest before we tackle the cummerbund question again. Okay?"

I could hear her sigh. But at least she wasn't still sobbing in that heartbroken way that made me want to sob with her.

"Okay, Mom. I'm sorry if I woke you and Dad up. And you're right about Craig."

"I love you," I assured her.

"Love you, too. And, Mom?"

"Yes, dear?"

"The chartreuse cummerbunds stay."

I eased back into bed as quietly as possible, but Jack was a light sleeper.

"Straighten Sunny out?"

"No, the chartreuse cummerbunds are still in."

He groaned and turned over to face me.

"Care to try to straighten me out?"

"I've been at it for over four decades with little success, but I'll keep trying."

"That's not what I meant."

"I know."

NINE

I THINK IT FINALLY dawned on Jack just how serious I was about that car the next morning when I refused all offers of breakfast at the Apple Barn and for him to cook up one of his special omelets. I swallowed a bowl of cereal practically in one gulp and headed for the shower.

Deb tossed the paper bowls in the trash and nudged Jack's arm. "You best have your checkbook handy. Kitty's on a mission."

As I went through the bedroom door, I heard him say, "We'll see." Yes, indeedy, we would see.

The trip to the Beadles' farm was much quicker, now that we knew which turns to take and which to ignore. When we pulled up in front of the old farm house, I could see Medina Beadle on a side porch, giving her husband a haircut. Mose Beadle yanked the towel off his shoulders, pulled his baseball cap back on, and headed out the side door to greet us, with his wife close behind. I crossed my fingers, hoping Charlie Beadle had again worked late and was still in bed. Perhaps his father would be more inclined to deal with Jack if the boy wasn't around.

"Heard you folks coming up the driveway." Charlie Beadle stepped out of the front door, shrugging his overall straps up onto his shoulders. I gritted my teeth. Okay, Master Charlie, you aren't the only one who knows how to drive a hard bargain. If you and Jack can't strike a deal, I'd go over your heads.

"Sweet set of glass packs you have in that car," Charlie said.

Jack grinned. He was extremely proud of the low rumble Sadie made wherever she went. Come to that, so was I since I'd helped him install them. Raising our daughters and teaching at the local elementary school weren't the only valuable skills I'd acquired in my lifetime.

"We'd like to take another look at your old car, assuming she's still for sale," Jack told Mose Beadle as they shook hands.

"She's right where she was yesterday." Beadle gestured toward the barn, and the four men headed that way. I reached into my tote bag.

"I have a digital camera and one of those little portable printers, so I printed out some of the pictures I took of the barn yesterday, for your mother." I handed the pictures to Medina Beadle. "And there are some of her flower garden. I thought she'd enjoy looking at the blooms when she can't get outside on cold winter days."

I hadn't printed the shot I'd taken of the young man by the outbuilding, not wanting either woman to know about it. But I hadn't deleted it, either. I wanted a chance to study it closer.

"Mother's resting at the moment, but I'll make sure she sees them." Medina turned toward the door then turned back. "Thank you for thinking of her. You're very kind."

I smiled and started for the barn, my stomach churning. Jack had been in the barn with the male Beadles for a bit too long without me there to encourage him to buy the car. And when Deb and I stepped inside, the bartering wasn't going as well as I'd hoped. Jack appeared to be in the middle of pointing out every single thing he could find wrong with the car in order to lower the price, and

Charlie Beadle was quickly assuring him that any flaws could easily be fixed. Easy for him, maybe.

The bright sunlight outside filtered through the spaces between the old barn boards, revealing my dream car still squatted in a dusty corner. I looked her over to be sure I hadn't dreamed her. I hadn't. She was as lovely, even if a bit rough, as she'd been the first time I'd seen her. What a fun vehicle she'd be when restored to her original glory.

I turned back to the conversation just as Jack did his heading-for-the-door routine again.

"Sorry, but that's too much to pay, considering the shape she's in," he said.

It was all I could do not to trip him with my cane. He was letting the two men think he was willing to leave once and for all this time without the car, in the hopes they'd quote a lower price, even though this price was a bit high but doable. He always wanted to bargain and get a bargain. I gave him a look that said he should be expecting "cold shoulder" for dinner for the next few months.

As Jack reached the barn door, Charlie Beadle called out to him. "Make me an offer, and we'll see what we can do."

Jack shot back a price that was ridiculously low. I gripped my cane to keep from whacking him upside the head. No way would they accept that offer.

They didn't. The young man quoted a figure halfway between his original price and Jack's counter offer. If Jack didn't take that one, I most certainly would kill him and pay for the car out of his life insurance money. Yes, I'd be in jail, but the car would be mine when I got out. And what was twenty-to-life for a dream?

I was trying to decide whether to throw myself at his knees and beg or simply beat him senseless with my cane when Jack pulled out his checkbook and asked if the elder Beadle would take a check.

"Sure, but I'll have to run your check to the bank for my dad before we can sign off on the pink slip," Beadle the younger replied. "I'll get a receipt and meet you up at the house."

I was beginning to wonder if the older man had any say-so in the transaction. So far he hadn't said much of anything beyond a couple of mumbles and grunts.

"No problem," Jack said. "I'll have to rent a trailer to take the car home with us. We're planning on staying in Pigeon Forge a few more days, so I'll be back after the car when I find one. Meanwhile, take good care of her," Jack said. "My wife will kill me if we don't get home with her all in one piece."

I gave Jack a bear hug, the likes of which he hadn't received in a while, at least not in public. Debby was grinning like a possum in the background. Leo snorted. I knew he thought Jack was crazy, but then, he'd paid a pretty hefty price for Debby's beautiful turquoise Mustang, and without batting an eyelash I might add. Guess it depended on who was doing the buying, and for whom.

"What happened to 'I'm not buying the first car we look at'?" Leo asked when the Beadles walked out of ear shot. "You crumbled like a stale cookie."

"I remembered that bumper sticker on the back of your family car. The one that says 'We're spending our children's inheritance.' Our kids very nearly got their inheritance when that so-and-so tried to kill us last year. I promised myself right then that Kitty would have her car before too many moons passed."

I'd have kissed Jack right then and there, but I knew it would only embarrass him. And the check wasn't written or cashed yet. No use pushing my luck, so I yanked my camera out of my jacket pocket and snapped a couple of "before" pictures of my new car. With any luck, I'd be able to take some "after" shots in a few months.

I dug for my cell phone in order to share the good news with my daughters. Unfortunately, Sunny wasn't home. Most likely out having the bridesmaids' shoes died chartreuse. Maggie answered on the third ring.

"Mom, that old car sounds like a beauty. I can't wait to take a ride with you. The kids will love her, as well. Can you send me a picture with your cell phone?"

"I would, but I haven't taken the time to figure out how the camera part works yet. I've always used the camera your dad gave me, instead. I'll e-mail you a picture tonight. But remember, no sippy cups allowed in my new car," I warned. "And absolutely no animal crackers." I wasn't nearly as big a pushover as she thought.

"I'm sure we can handle that. What are you naming her?"

I looked at the car. "I'm not sure yet. Maybe Old Blue, in honor of the dog. I'll have to give it some more thought. How's Tori feeling today?"

"Not much better. The cough medicine kept her comfortable all night, but her fever is a bit higher this morning and I can't seem to bring it down."

"Have you tried a tepid bath?"

"She's in the tub right now. Tori, stop splashing so much. You're getting Daisy all wet," Maggie said. "And Daisy's shaking it out on me."

"You're bathing the dog with her?" I asked, shocked.

"Of course not, Mother. Tori first then Billy then Daisy. I don't multitask that much. But I've got the children and the dog locked in here with me so I don't have to chase anybody down when it's their turn."

"I hope the bath works. If not, try feeding her some

chipped ice. Maggie, I've got to hang up. Your dad is about to write the check for the car, and I want to make sure there aren't any glitches with the sale. Kiss the children for me. Oh, and would you try to ever-so-casually broach the subject of a wedding in the Smoky Mountains to your sister?"

"A wedding in the Smoky Mountains? Hmm, sounds romantic. Of course, the mere thought of a car trip that lengthy with the kids in the back seat gives me the heebie-jeebies, but for my sister, I'll risk it. Particularly if it means a simpler wedding and no chartreuse."

"It would mean a quick return trip here for us in a few months as well, but I'd walk all the way, if it meant a simpler wedding," I said.

Maggie laughed. "I'll see what I can do. Love you, Mom."

As I hung up, I tried not to picture an overgrown Labrador retriever splashing around my daughter's bathtub, most likely covered in lilac-scented bubble bath.

TEN

THE FOUR OF US ambled on back to the Beadles' front porch, and Charlie Beadle invited us to have a seat while he filled out the receipt for Jack's check. Medina Beadle offered us a glass of lemonade. Deb and I stepped around the old hound, now lying on his back, apparently hoping for a belly scratch, and headed for the rocking chairs.

"Lemonade is a great idea, my dear." Mose Beadle plopped onto a nearby porch rail and wiped his brow with a handkerchief.

"I'd love some lemonade, too," Debby said, pausing before sinking into the comfortable-looking chair, "but could I possibly use your bathroom first? All that breakfast coffee just went right through me."

I coughed to cover a snicker. Debby Evans had cast-iron kidneys, and she could hold her liquid longer than any woman I'd ever met. She wanted inside that farm house to see what it was like. She'd said as much when we'd first come here. Truth to tell, so did I, so I didn't protest when she grabbed my arm and pulled me inside with her. Medina Beadle looked a bit alarmed, but she led us inside. Probably afraid we'd spot a speck of dust on a tabletop or something. At least that was what usually worried me when unexpected company showed up on my doorstep.

The front parlor—for those were the only possible words to describe the first room we came to—boasted the most beautiful old pump organ I'd ever laid eyes on. At least a hundred years old, it was embellished with hand carving, and not a speck of dust could be seen there or anywhere else in the room. The rest of the furniture was sparse, but old and quite beautiful. Obviously worth a lot of money, but most likely belonging to an old lady who wouldn't allow a single item to be sold. So the rest of the family sang for their supper outside a busy restaurant.

Instead of the usual couch, there were four antique wooden chairs with lovely tufted fabric seats and backs, all grouped around the fireplace. Each chair was very different and very unusual. I could imagine long winter evenings in those chairs, watching the fire and listening to music or reading a good book.

We followed the lady of the house down a long hallway, just past a narrow staircase that probably led to the bedrooms upstairs. We'd seen an ancient outhouse behind the farm house, but by the looks of it, it hadn't been used in quite some time. I supposed that was what had given Debby the courage to ask to use the bathroom in the first place, her assumption that there would be one located inside. I'd gotten accustomed to using an outhouse when Jack and I lived with his parents on our farm. Not one of my favorite memories, and we'd installed indoor plumbing right after we'd inherited the farm from them.

The bathroom Medina Beadle led Deb to had been built underneath the tall staircase. Great use of space. I peeked inside just before Deb closed the door. What the room lacked in size, it made up for in charm. A small clawfoot tub, a pedestal sink, and an ancient toilet, the internal workings of which were located somewhere near the ceiling instead of just above the bowl. And I was willing to bet that, unlike Daisy, the old hound on the front porch had never been bathed in that tub. He'd probably never even seen the inside of the house.

At her invitation, I followed Medina Beadle to the

kitchen, located just beyond the staircase, sniffing the aroma as I went. Fried chicken, if I knew my kitchen smells, and something with a lot of cinnamon. Apple pie, perhaps? Despite a stomach still full of cereal, my mouth watered. I stepped through the huge kitchen doorway and stopped to gawk. It was huge and square and there was a fireplace large enough to roast a whole pig in, if the cook had a mind to.

On the other side of the room stood an antique, green enamel Copper Clad stove with a pie warmer near the top. And there, warming for lunch, was the pie I'd smelled. Originally a wood-burner, the old stove had been converted to gas somewhere in its history, and grease popped and splattered in the huge iron skillet on the flame, browning a chicken. I wondered if said chicken had recently resided with the others we'd dodged around during our trips to and from the old barn.

I could see potatoes bubbling on another burner. That stove had to be nearly a century old, and Medina Beadle was still cooking on it. And it looked as clean and new as the day it had been installed. I wasn't a poor housekeeper by any means, but I certainly wasn't that clean. This lady must've worked from daylight to dark to keep the house so spotless, not to mention helping with the farm chores and playing music at the restaurant on weekends. I didn't envy her schedule.

I pulled out one of the old wooden chairs at the huge farm-style kitchen table and eased into it, wondering if Medina Beadle had sewn the fluffy dotted Swiss curtains at the huge, eight-foot-tall kitchen windows. Unless maybe her mother had made them? Rows of freshly canned green beans cooled on a table beside the window. I heard the familiar ping and hoped for Medina Beadle's sake it meant a jar lid was sealing itself rather than unsealing, as often happened to me when home canning.

Was the elderly Sassy Bentley still able to help out with the housekeeping, or was she too frail, adding to the day's list of chores to be done? If she could work in the garden much of the day from her wheelchair, surely she helped out elsewhere. But caring for an aging parent had to be one of the world's toughest jobs. One I hoped neither of my daughters ever had to tackle. The sharp voice behind me brought me out of my musings about the farm house and its occupants.

"Are you folks a buyin' that there old car?" Sassy Bentley asked as Deb slid into the chair opposite mine.

"Yes, ma'am," I answered. "My husband is writing your son-in-law a check right now."

"Son-in-law. Humph. Never raised any boys, but if'n I had, he wouldn't be such a—"

"Hush, Mother, these folks don't need to see our family laundry aired," Medina Beadle said.

Sassy Bentley gave her daughter a look that said she didn't appreciate being corrected, but she changed the subject.

"Can your man fix up that old car?" she asked, rolling her wheelchair up to the table. "Hasn't been driven in a mighty long time. Not since I broke my hip a few years back. Been in this chair ever since." She smacked her hands on the arm rests for emphasis.

"Yes, ma'am, Jack can fix up just about any old car. It's the new ones with computers that give him fits," I said.

"Humph, computers. And the young kids who drive those cars these days aren't worth a nickel, either, particularly—"

"It's time for you to rest, Mother." Medina Beadle reached for the handles on her elderly mother's wheelchair, but the old lady's iron grip on the wheels prevented the chair from moving. She focused her dark gaze on Deb and me again. And hadn't she been resting when we'd arrived? Was her daughter trying to prevent her from talking to us? Maybe to keep her from somehow stopping the sale of the car?

"In a minute, Medina. I want to talk to these lovely ladies first. That's a beautiful cane." Sassy Bentley nodded toward me. "Did your man carve it?"

I passed my cane to her so she could see up close the delicate flowers and leaves carved into the shaft and the names underneath the handle.

"No, ma'am, Jack didn't carve it. I found the cane in an antique shop after I broke my leg. It says 'To Jewel from Joseph, 1925.' I guess he carved it for her. It was hidden behind a jelly cabinet at the store, and I just couldn't leave it there. Artwork like this should be used and enjoyed."

She nodded again, running her hands over the words carved underneath the handle.

"I sort of figured maybe you were battling arthritis like me," she said. "I've got the kind that grows big knots on my joints. That's what's kept me in this chair after my hip healed. You say you had an accident?"

"Kitty's car went off the road, and she was trapped in a deep gulley all night and part of the next day," Deb said. "She's lucky to have survived. About the time her leg healed, it was broken again in a tractor accident on their farm. She's still healing up from that one."

"Old bones don't heal none too quickly," Sassy Bentley said, looking at me. "But I can see you are a woman of courage. And you appreciate the old days. So do I. Back then, folks treated each other with respect."

I wondered if she meant her daughter and son-in-law or

her grandson. Young Charlie hadn't struck me as overly respectful.

"Youngsters nowadays expect everything to be handed to them," she continued, answering my unasked question. "They don't know how to work for it. You and I, we know what hard work is, from living on a farm."

Sassy Bentley held my cane out to me. As I reached for it, she squeezed my hand.

"Thank you for bringing me those pictures. I can't navigate my wheelchair much beyond my flower bed anymore, so your pictures let me see that the outbuildings are still in pretty good shape. You're a good woman, and so's your friend here." She nodded at Deb. "All right, Medina, I'm ready for my rest."

Medina Beadle pushed her mother's wheelchair toward the back of the kitchen. When they reached the doorway, the old lady put her hands on the wheels, stopping the forward motion, and turned back to Deb and me.

"Don't ever let yourselves get old, like me."

Now why did elderly people always say that to anyone more than a decade younger? And what alternative did she think we had?

Sassy Bentley looked Deb over then swung her gaze back toward me. "You girls read your Bibles regular like?" she asked. We both nodded and she continued, "You remember what the Good Lord said to the apostle Peter about growing old?"

I guess we both looked blank because she sighed and rubbed her hands together. "Read Luke's account. 'Most assuredly, I say to you, when you were younger, you girded yourself and walked where you wished, but when you are old, you will stretch out your hands, and another will gird you and carry you where you do not wish.'"

"Actually," Deb spoke up, surprising me, and from the

look on her face, Sassy Bentley as well, "it's recorded in John chapter twenty-one, and the Lord was warning Peter about how he would die one day."

Sassy Bentley smiled her approval at Deb. "You do know your Bible. And you're right, but the Biblical warning applies to all of us old folks. Comes a time when others make our decisions and carry us where we don't want to go, whether we want them to or not."

She let go of the wheels, and her daughter pushed the chair through the doorway. I assumed it was her bedroom. Many older farm homes had rooms downstairs converted for the use of elderly relatives who couldn't make it up a steep stairway any longer.

"What do you suppose she meant by all of that?" Deb whispered to me.

"Beats me. I wonder what else Sassy Bentley wanted to say to us earlier, in regard to young people, before her daughter interrupted her."

"Maybe she doesn't like Medina's husband. But he seems like a nice guy, if a bit quiet. More likely she meant her grandson."

"It's really none of our business, but parents do have to treat their children's spouses with some respect, and vise versa, if they want to have any peace in the house. Joe always treats me with respect, and I'm expecting the same from Craig. But I certainly didn't hold with parents badmouthing their children's spousal choices. Even if said choice later turns out to be a huge mistake."

Debby nodded. Thankfully, our daughters' choices hadn't been mistakes, so far as I could tell. And my wonderful mother-in-law had been like a mother to me, certainly far more than my own mother had ever been.

"If either of my girls were to make a wrong choice in a

mate, I'd only allow myself to complain if he was abusive to my babies or grandbabies. Then there'd be trouble."

"And, most likely you'd wind up in jail," Deb said. I didn't deny it.

"Neither Medina Beadle nor her mother look abused, and Mose Beadle appears to be a mild-mannered kind of guy," I whispered.

I could generally—though not always—judge a book by his or her cover, having taught school for so many years. Teachers learned an awful lot about character by watching their students.

"Maybe Sassy Bentley thinks her son-in-law is a wimp," Deb said, "and he just might be, judging by the way he lets his son do all the talking. Young Charlie completely took over selling the old car to you and Jack."

I thought that over. Apparently the car, like the rest of the farm, actually belonged to Sassy Bentley, since she mentioned she'd driven it last. But had she really wanted to sell it? I hoped so because I wanted that car, badly, but if she was selling it under pressure from her family, I'd have no choice but to leave it here with her. I didn't subscribe to the notion of dispensing with anyone else's belongings when they were still alive and had a mind of their own as to how things should be done.

"I apologize for Mother," Medina Beadle said, breaking into my thoughts as she returned to the kitchen. "She lived alone here for many, many years before we moved in, and she doesn't always cotton to strangers."

But she seemed to like us well enough, so what was this all about? I took a deep breath. "Look, that car obviously belongs to your mother, and if she isn't ready to sell it, I'm willing to wait. I don't want—"

"Oh, no, that's not the problem at all. The car has to be

sold. It's just sitting out there in the barn, rotting down. And we need the money, so don't give it another thought."

She sounded sincere, so why didn't I believe her? I was afraid I was going to be giving this a lot of worry time.

"Was that your other son we saw outside yesterday?" Deb asked.

"Other son? Oh, no, Charlie is our only son." Medina Beadle swiped at the already spotless table top with her apron. "You must have seen *him* out there. There's no one else here."

Odd, I was sure the young man at the outbuilding hadn't been Charlie Beadle. Good thing I'd kept that picture. I'd examine it again when we were on our way back to the cabin.

As if reading my mind, Charlie Beadle came into the kitchen and said, "You probably saw my cousin, Jerry. He sometimes comes over to help out, or to borrow our equipment for his place. He lives the next farm over."

He handed his mother his lemonade glass and asked for a refill. I wondered why he didn't just get it himself. Most farm kids were taught to wait on themselves. And why did Medina Beadle look so surprised at the mention of the cousin?

ELEVEN

THE NEXT FEW HOURS after we left the Beadle farm were spent searching for a trailer to tow the car home. Naturally there were none to be had. There weren't that many U-Haul offices located in the area, and those that were there had been hit by eager buyers ahead of us wanting to trailer newly bought cars home. We wound up leaving our name and cell number at each place, and we exited the last office tired and discouraged.

"Let's head on over to Dollywood," Jack suggested. "That is, if Kitty feels up to it." He gave me his very best lost-puppy look, and I caved. My leg was aching from being on it so long, but no way could I resist.

"Sounds great to me," I said. "We've got those free tickets, so why don't we share one with Deb and Leo? That way, we'll all get in for half price."

Everyone was happy with that plan, so we piled back into Sadie and headed down the highway. The four of us couldn't squeeze into Rosie, the small Model A truck Leo and Debby had driven here to enter in the competition, so Sadie was doing double duty on this trip.

"We can probably get a great country-style lunch at Dollywood as well," Leo said.

"Lunch?" Debby asked. "It's only been a short time since we ate breakfast."

"Yeah," Leo agreed, "but I walked that all off at the Beadles' farm, not to mention the unproductive trailer search. I need something to keep me going. Besides, if we happen to run into the amazing Ms. Copper Penny, you wouldn't want me fainting on you."

Debby snorted. "I doubt we'll see her, Leo. She likely doesn't hang out in the amusement-park area. She'll be busy rehearsing her show or trying on new penny-covered outfits or something. But feel free to dream."

"I most certainly will. I still haven't forgiven Jack for meeting her without me," Leo said. "It's going to take a very long time for me to get over that one."

"I promise, the next time I meet up with Copper Penny, I'll make sure you're along," Jack said.

"Right now, I'd just be satisfied with lunch," I said. "I have to agree with Leo, hunting cars and trailers to pull them home with is hungry business." I was regretting the hurried bowl of cereal, wishing we'd had something more substantial.

I reached for my cell phone. Time to check in with our daughters. Sunny would be in class, so I'd have to catch her tonight, but Maggie and the kids would be at home until Tori recovered, and I wanted to see if Tori's temperature had lowered. Unfortunately, Billy answered, and he wasn't exactly the best answering service around.

"Hi, Grandma, what are you bringing back for us?" Billy wasn't one to beat around the bush. Personally, I found bush-beating to be quite a lot of fun, as long as I wasn't on the receiving end.

"A new suit and tie for you to wear to church. And some spinach-flavored candy."

"Grandma!"

"I don't know yet, Billy. I haven't had a chance to check out the stores. I promise I'll find something you'll like."

He giggled, knowing I could be trusted to bring home something he'd love and his mother wouldn't love. I was still in the dog house with Maggie over the battery-operated, remote-control airplane complete with strobe lights and an eardrum-popping engine roar. A grandmother's payback for her own children's youthful misdeeds could be deadly.

"Grandma, we miss you. When are you comin' home? I got drowneded for bringing a baby snake into the house, but it wasn't my fault. Daisy dug it up, and Tori's frowing up."

I assumed he meant he'd been grounded, not drowned, given that he was still breathing and able to talk to me. I also assumed he meant the dog had dug up a rather large worm, not a baby snake, but with Maggie's bunch, you really never knew. But Tori was rarely sick. That part of the dialogue did worry me.

"Where is your mommy?" I interrupted his narrative, needing to get to the heart of the matter.

The resulting *kerplunk* indicated that Billy had dropped the cordless phone down on the kitchen counter rather than taking it along with him to locate his mother. And who knew if he'd even remember to tell her she was wanted on the phone when he finally located her? Or if she could untangle herself from the current crisis long enough to answer it?

I listened to several seconds of silence, followed by scraping and banging as Billy picked up the phone again and delivered it to his mother.

"Mom, you there?" Maggie huffed into the phone.

"I'm here. What's going on? Billy said Tori is still sick."

"Tori has been throwing up since just after I talked to you. She can't keep anything down. I'm taking her to the doctor in a few minutes. How are you and Dad doing? Find a trailer to bring the car home with yet?"

"No luck on the trailer. They're all rented out. Look,

do you want me to come home and help with Tori? I can catch a bus or maybe even fly in."

"No, Mom, you stay right where you are. I'm sure the doctor will give Tori something to settle her stomach and bring her fever down. Where are you, by the way? I hear horns honking."

"We're on our way to Dollywood. Copper Penny gave us free tickets."

"Wow, Dad must be in heaven, meeting Copper Penny in person and seeing Dollywood. I'd love to visit there sometime with the kids. Assuming Tori ever stops throwing up."

"What did the doctor say when you called for the appointment?" My worry meter jumped up several points.

"To bring her in as soon as I could. I'll let you know what the doctor says. Why is everyone around you honking? Is Dad shifting from lane to lane, as usual?"

"No, not this time. We're stalled at a traffic light. Irritated drivers are honking at each other. I've never seen traffic move this slowly, not even when we've driven in Nashville during rush hour. Any more word from your sister on the wedding plans?"

"Well, Sunny didn't ixnay your suggestion of a wedding in the Smoky Mountains right away when I broached the subject to her, so I'd say there's still a small ray of hope. In fact, she actually said she'd consider a wedding in the Smoky Mountains, but I think that was for Craig's benefit. I doubt she really means it. And she's still firm on the chartreuse."

"I'll call her tonight and see if I can gently push that plan." Maggie's resulting snort didn't encourage me.

"Gotta go, Mom. We appear to be between pukes, I've rounded up a bucket and Tori's favorite stuffed animal, and Billy is standing by the door, so I think we might be close to a lift-off."

"Call me later and let me know how Tori is."

I leaned back in the seat and dropped my cell phone into my tote bag. My grandchildren were generally healthy, but sick kids could dehydrate quickly. I knew Maggie would do all she could to ensure her daughter got the best of care, but I hated being this far away from home if she might need me.

"Problems?" Deb asked.

"Tori is still very sick, and Maggie is taking her to the doctor. She wouldn't do that if she wasn't worried. Which worries me. I hope we can find a trailer soon. Once the contest is over, Jack and I can head on home, if need be."

Deb nodded and pointed out the window at a large parking lot full of antique cars. Who knew there were this many still around from the Twenties, Thirties, and Forties, not to mention all the Fifties models—some fully restored and ready for tomorrow's show, others with hefty price tags on the windshields, and still others in rough condition, waiting for someone to love them back into proper shape. And that took a lot of love, time, and money.

We picked up our free tickets at the entrance to Dollywood, split the difference for two extra people, entered the park, and looked for a place to eat. It didn't take us long to find one, and soon we were all happily full again. Ham and beans, all we could eat and then some. Thus fortified, we were ready to see the sights.

"I'd like to visit the shops first and buy something for Tori and Billy. Probably my best chance to find our grandkids something to make them squeal and mommy frown, and I might not have to venture out into traffic again, trying to get into the shops on the Pigeon Forge main drag," I suggested to the group.

The main drag, of course, was still currently flooded by the antique cars and the visitors drooling over same. Come to that, Dollywood wasn't exactly deserted. The lines to the rides and shows were likely to be long.

"I'm very much afraid Leo and Jack are going to have a crick in their necks by the time we leave here," Deb said as we navigated from one store to the next.

I had to agree. They'd both been craning their necks since the moment we'd entered the theme park. "Never say die," I said.

"Or, hope springs eternal in the male breast, no matter the age?" Debby misquoted. I laughed.

Not only did I buy extra gifts for the kids to assuage my guilty conscience, but the traditional craft artists got my attention as well as Debby's, and I'm afraid a couple of them wound up with a rather large amount of my spending money. Well worth it, though. True craftsmanship beat the daylights out of factory assembly-line goods every time.

I did have to take a stand, or rather a seat, when Jack and Leo got in line for some of the scarier rides. Deb joined me on a nearby bench.

"Rides that take you that high off the ground that fast or get you that wet should be off-limits to the over-sixty crowd," I said. "The kiddy rides look to be more my speed, but I'm a bit too tall to qualify for a spot on board. Maybe I can sneak onto one of the tamer rides with my grandchildren some day."

"I'm with you. That ride would make me dizzy in seconds, especially after a huge meal," Deb agreed.

I thought of Tori and said a quick prayer that she'd recover quickly. And that Billy wouldn't catch whatever bug she had.

We watched in perfect comfort and safety as Leo and Jack shouted and hollered with their fellow riders and got nice and wet. I was thankful Sadie's seats were vinyl, in case the guys didn't dry out by the time we left the park.

When the males had at last satisfied their lust for speed and danger, we headed over to the area where the shows were held. Unfortunately for the guys, Copper Penny's popular show wasn't scheduled for that day. Despite their disappointment, the shows we had time to see were terrific, and we all had a great time humming along with the music. By the end of the day I was exhausted and not sorry to see the exit gates looming in front of us.

"Hey, y'all, didja have a good time?" that extremely famous voice called out from somewhere just behind us. Jack and Leo froze in their tracks, nearly causing Debby and me to trip over them.

"Y-yes, ma'am, um, a great time, th-thanks to you," Jack said.

"Leo, close your mouth before you swallow a bug," Debby ordered under her breath. Leo didn't move. I wondered briefly if he'd turned to stone.

"Y'all take care, you hear?" Copper Penny shouted, waving over her shoulder as her golf cart swung to the right and shot out of sight behind a large wooden gate.

I shouted "Thank you" to her retreating back and grabbed Jack's arm, dragging him along toward the exit gate. Debby was pushing Leo behind us. I was very much afraid if we didn't keep the guys moving, we'd be stuck in that same spot for days, waiting for Copper Penny to reappear through that gate. Which might've been okay if it hadn't started raining.

We reached the car and Jack fumbled with the keys for several minutes while we all got damp. Finally, comfortably seated in the back with my ever-present soft flannel blanket over my legs, I leaned back, said another prayer for Tori, then relaxed as we headed for the cabin.

"Time to decide where we're going to eat dinner," Leo said.

"Is that all you think about, Leo?" Jack asked.

"Yes, it is," Deb answered for her hubby. "Well, nearly all," she said and flicked Leo on the back of the head.

"Hey, someone has to be in charge of sustenance. All the rest of you want to do is look at old cars."

"Easily said by someone who has an outbuilding full," Jack reminded him. "You practically have your own museum."

And so Leo did. At last count there was the Model A truck he'd driven here, a coupe, Debby's turquoise Mustang, and his pride and joy, a 1956 black two-door Chevy, the car he'd won the most trophies with. It was anybody's guess who'd spent the most time spit-polishing an antique vehicle before a show, Jack or Leo, but Leo had definitely cornered the market on trophies. And it kept them both off the street and out of trouble, most of the time.

"How about we slide through a drive-in and pick up something simple to eat at the cabin?" I suggested. "I'm really not up to standing in a long line again tonight."

"Suits me," Jack said as he quickly moved Sadie to the outside lane. "There's one just ahead."

You'd think we hadn't eaten in days instead of hours, given the size and cost of the to-go order. But I had to admit, my stomach began to grumble when I got a whiff of the food.

Twenty minutes later we arrived at the top of the hill, hauled ourselves and our supper to the front door, and found the door frame splintered and our rental cabin ransacked.

TWELVE

"LOOKS TO ME LIKE a bear broke in," the rental company's security guard said after surveying the damage and scratching his stubbly chin. His name tag read J. Conklin, and if he had more than a week left toward his retirement, I'd be surprised.

"Yes, it looks like a bear tossed the place," Deb said, a bit testily, "but would a bear be able to manage that zipper? I have trouble with it myself." She pointed to her red suitcase, wide open and upside down on the bedroom floor.

Conklin shrugged. "Maybe you forgot to close it, ma'am. You said nothing was missing but a jar of peanut butter and a loaf of bread. So it still looks like a bear raid to me."

"And what did the bear do with them?" Deb demanded. "Make a sandwich? I don't see a bear waltzing off with a loaf of bread tucked under his arm. Don't bears usually eat where they find food? And there aren't any bread crumbs scattered anywhere, just the smeared peanut butter. Why smear it? Why not eat it?"

Conklin shrugged again, unwilling to commit himself. I didn't know what to think. We'd kept our valuables with us at all times, so there really hadn't been much to steal. And thankfully, Leo's ancient, beautiful truck was still safely tucked inside the locked garage. I didn't want to think about what would've happened if someone or something had gotten in there.

I'd worked my way upstairs with the rest of the group

to check out Leo and Deb's bedroom, refusing for the moment to take a closer look at mine, after one quick peek at the damage in there. Most of Deb's clothing had been yanked from her suitcase, ripped to shreds, and strewn around the room, which lent a smidge of support to the security guard's theory. Obviously, an emergency shopping trip was in order if Deb and I were to appear fully clothed in public tomorrow. Jack and Leo's suitcases were untouched, naturally.

I leaned over and picked up the pretty sweater I'd given Deb for her last birthday. It was nearly un-recognizable. I could've cried. Deb's loud squawk startled me, and I dropped the sweater on the floor as she raced toward her closet. I followed her around the foot of the bed as fast as I could, my heart in my throat. Before Conklin arrived, we'd all been too upset by the obvious damage to the other rooms to check either bedroom closet closely.

"Oh, Kitty, I'm so sorry," Deb said, holding up the remnants of the outfit she always wore to car shows and contests. "All your hard work—"

I hobbled back downstairs to our bedroom and yanked open the closet door. My red felt poodle skirt—chosen to match Sadie's paint job—as well as Deb's turquoise number that matched her Mustang, were now in tatters. Ditto for my little white angora sweater set, though I confess, I wouldn't miss that much. Certainly not in July. But I'd hand-sewn the poodle skirts for each of us, sitting up well past midnight before our first car competition where both Leo and Jack had taken home trophies. They'd become our good-luck charms, and now they were gone. If the damage had been done by a bear, he'd better be long gone.

"At least the guys' leather jackets are still in one piece," Deb said from behind me, peeking deeper into the closet Jack and I were sharing. "Good thing we stuck them in the back of the closets. I hate to think what it would cost to replace them, even from eBay."

I took a closer look into the closet. "Where's my little black case? I put it up there on the shelf."

Deb reached up and fumbled around on the shelf. Extra blankets and pillows came out with a sweep of her arm, but no black case that housed my tiny printer, ink, paper, and my extra camera equipment. "Not up here. Let's look under the scattered clothes. Maybe it's covered up."

I hoped she was right, but the knot in the pit of my stomach told me she wasn't. I always kept my tiny camera with me, usually in my jacket or jeans pocket, so it was safe, but the printer had been a recent birthday gift from my daughters, and I couldn't stand to lose it on top of everything else.

We carefully felt over and around the items tossed about the bedroom then Deb bent over and checked underneath the bed.

"Here's your black bag, but it's empty. Did you zip it shut this morning after you printed out the pictures for Sassy Bentley?"

I shook my head. "I don't remember, but I usually do zip it closed to keep the dust out."

She handed me the bag and dove under the bed again. "Your printer is under here, Kitty, or at least what's left of it." She pulled out several chunks of grayish plastic, dropped them on the rumpled bedspread, and put her arm around my shoulders.

"C'mon, let's show the damage to Conklin. Your homeowner's insurance might replace the printer if the rental company won't. And I promise I'll help make us new skirts."

I nodded, not trusting myself to speak.

Conklin was at the kitchen sink, rinsing something

sticky off his hands. The cabinets had all been ransacked and what little food we'd brought with us was scattered on the floor, on the furniture, and on our belongings. Jack's favorite sugar cookies I'd yanked out of the freezer for the trip were smashed. Thankfully, we'd intended to eat most of our meals out, or our situation would've been even worse.

Conklin seemed to read my thoughts as I glanced around. "I suggest you call the rental company's emergency number again and see if they'll send a cleaning crew up here right away." He pointed to my cane. "It's certainly not your job to scrub syrup off the fireplace."

I gratefully agreed. By now my bum leg was giving me fits for standing on it so long, but there wasn't really any place to sit, what with the kitchen chairs smeared with who knew what and the living-room furniture flipped in all directions.

"Maybe they'll give us another cabin," Deb suggested. "I'm certainly not comfortable spending the night here. Bear or burglar, neither option appeals."

She flipped open her cell phone with one hand and rummaged in her purse with the other for the rental company's number. I shoved the damaged outfits and the empty printer case at Conklin and beat it out to the terrace to find a seat and prop up my leg. Jack followed. I could practically hear the wheels spinning inside his head.

"What?" I asked, sniffing the pine scent in the air in an effort to slow my heart rate to somewhere near normal.

"Nothing. Just that I hope the security guard is right and it was a bear. Because if it was a burglar, this was beyond burglary; it was downright vicious."

"And it was mostly aimed at Deb and me. That's what you're thinking, aren't you?"

He nodded. We lapsed into silence, listening to the birds chat before their bedtime and pondering our situation.

The rental-company employee arrived fifteen minutes later and joined us out on the terrace, her face pale after surveying the scene of the crime. She handed Jack keys to a cabin further down the hill, not far from Philby and Reva Mason.

"The view won't be nearly as good, I'm afraid," she said, "but it's all we have empty at the moment. There are more houses nearby, so it isn't likely a bear would visit you down there."

"Or a burglar?" Deb asked, coming up behind her.

She blushed and quickly switched subjects. "There is a lovely hot tub outside on the ground-floor patio. You'll really enjoy that."

Naturally, the rental company didn't want to be responsible for any loss to us. They'd have a tough enough time cleaning up the mess. I felt sorry for her, but not quite as sorry as I felt for myself.

Jack hustled to fetch our cabin keys and hand them over to her while Leo felt in various jacket pockets for his. Deb searched her purse and discovered her key was missing. It wasn't in the little zippered pocket where she'd kept it. Jack, Leo, and I all had ours. So where was hers?

The color slid out of Deb's face. "I'm really sorry, you guys, I guess I didn't check my purse carefully enough when that jerk knocked me down at the restaurant and grabbed it. My cash was gone, but my credit cards were still there, so I assumed everything else was, too. I guess this break-in was my fault." She dropped into a chair and began to cry.

Leo rubbed Deb's shoulders to comfort her. "Since the door was broken open, no one used Deb's key, did they?

Why damage the door if you've got the key?" he asked. No one seemed to have an answer.

"We have had a few break-ins in the area recently that involved tourists' belongings," Conklin said to no one in particular, "but most of those were stolen hotel-room keys, not cabin keys, and no damage was done, just personal property missing. Break-ins this high up and with this much damage usually involve a rogue bear."

He turned to Deb. "I'm sure the two incidents are completely unrelated, but I'll call the local police in to investigate. Just in case. Good thing you're moving elsewhere. Was your purse out of your sight at any other time?"

Deb sat up and dried her eyes. "No. I kept it under the seat or hooked on my chair at the restaurants and on my shoulder everywhere else. At Dollywood, it was locked in the trunk. And the trunk hadn't been disturbed when we got back to the car."

She looked up at Leo. "Kitty and I stayed in the car while you guys tried to rent a trailer. The only other place we've been is out to the Beadles' farm to look at their old car. It was in the trunk then, as well."

"Mose Beadle's place?" Conklin asked. "I live the next valley over from them."

"Yes, we bought their old car," Jack answered.

"The ancient Chrysler they keep out in the barn? Didn't think Miss Sassy Bentley would ever sell that jewel. I figured they'd just let the old car rust down. But they've had a real rough couple of years. Probably need the money. That boy has pretty much kept 'em broke with his legal troubles."

I swallowed hard on that one. "Legal troubles?"

"Fine people, the Beadles," Conklin said, "and so's Miss Sassy, her momma. But that boy of theirs ain't worth shootin'." Conklin spit over the wooden deck rail to emphasize his point. "Got hisself arrested for joyriding in a stolen car a couple a years back. There was an accident, and one of the boys died. Mr. Charlie and the rest of his friends earned themselves some serious jail time. I haven't seen him since he got out, and far as I know, he hasn't been in any more trouble. I just hope it stays that way, for his momma's sake."

Deb carefully checked her purse again, dumping the contents out on the picnic table while Jack followed the realty-company lady back inside, presumably to make sure she gave us a discount on the new cabin.

"Nothing else is missing except the cabin key," she assured Conklin.

Conklin thought that over, rubbing his chin. "My money's still on the bear, and I bet you just misplaced your key. Likely the company won't charge you for it."

"They most certainly will not!" Deb said, with a look that let Conklin know there'd be trouble if they even thought about it.

"I'll be in touch," Conklin said, heading back inside the cabin.

AFTER GIVING STATEMENTS to the police officer responding to Conklin's call, the four of us headed into town to buy Deb and me some new unmentionables and something to wear on top of them. Bear or burglar, there wasn't anything left of our clothes worth salvaging. Not to mention our sense of safety.

I generally wore jeans or comfy sweats, but I was happy to note that what we called pedal pushers in the Fifties were now known as capri pants, and they were back in fashion, having gone out of style sometime before Nehru jackets. This meant Deb and I could still dress in the style of the Fifties for the upcoming contest, even without our lucky poodle skirts. And we each found outfits to match the colors of our cars.

Our new cabin was lovely, if a bit sterile compared to the old one at the top of the mountain. The fireplace in the newer one was gas rather than wood, which meant we didn't have to buy or haul any more firewood, and that was a distinct improvement. The fall evenings had been decidedly cool since we'd arrived. Leo lit the fire while Deb and I sorted our new clothes, folding them into new suitcases. We didn't talk much during the operation.

Conklin's money might be on the bear, but mine was on the purse thief. He'd had at least a few seconds before Charlie Beadle caught up with him. He could easily have removed Deb's key along with her money in order to gain entry into our cabin. Then, not finding anything worth stealing, he could've trashed the cabin and splintered the door frame to make it look like a bear attack. And to make life difficult for us.

Charlie Beadle recovered Deb's purse mighty quickly— not to mention easily—after the culprit stole it. Could he have been in cahoots with the thief? Why? For an easy introduction to us? To get us to come out to the farm and buy the car? And if so, why break in and trash the cabin, stealing only bread and peanut butter? Was the elusive young man I'd taken the picture of at the farm the purse thief? Was the break-in merely a cover for making sure there were no pictures of him on my camera?

I hoped Jack found us a trailer soon. Partly so we could pick up my car and partly so I could keep an eye on Charlie Beadle. Maybe even gently quiz him. Or his family.

I finally managed to snuggle down beside Jack after a late-night call from Maggie assured me the doctor had changed Tori's medicine and she should be fine in a day or two.

"Talk to Sunny since we got back from shopping?" Jack asked.

"No, I'll call her in the morning. Right now I just want to try to put the day behind me."

Besides that, I considered no news from Sunny to be good news and decided not to tell either of the girls about the break-in and change of cabins. One disaster at a time was enough to deal with, thank you very much, and there was no use worrying either of them when they both had plenty of worries of their own.

I prayed Tori's new medicine would work. And why in the world was Sunny so bent on chartreuse for her wedding? As far as I knew, she'd never even worn anything that color. Was it some sort of test for her husband-to-be? If so, he might very well fail. In which case, I was going to have to run some serious motherly interference with my daughter.

But first we had a car to load up and a young man to take a closer look at. And if I got even a whiff of proof that Charlie Beadle was involved in the theft of Deb's purse or the trashing of our cabin, I'd haul his sorry backside out to his father's woodshed in a heartbeat.

THIRTEEN

AFTER A FAIRLY RESTLESS night and another too-large break-fast, we headed out for the morning's competition, stopping at a car wash on the way. We arrived at the county fair grounds, and Jack propped open the hood and the trunk and slid a long mirror under the car so the judges could see Sadie's pristine undercarriage. I busied myself inside Sadie, making sure every surface was dust free while he elbow-polished every single speck off her paint job.

Leo had to park Rosie two rows over and a bit up from us since she was competing in a different category, but I could still see Deb wiping the inside of the windshield while Leo squatted on all fours in the bed of the truck, polishing for all he was worth. If neither of our men won a trophy today, it certainly wouldn't be from a lack of elbow grease.

I crawled out of the front seat and eased myself into one of the comfortable fold-out lawn chairs we always carried. Jack popped a Fifties tape into the portable player he used for such occasions and dropped into the seat beside me. I handed him a glass-bottled soda with the requisite straw, and we toasted each other for luck, clinking the bottle-necks.

"Thanks, babe. You think we'll win?"

I glanced around at the other cars. "Well, Sadie's got some serious competition here today, but that's never bothered her before."

"Yeah, but you don't have your lucky poodle skirt on."

I thought that over. "I can't help noticing it was much easier to navigate today without that stiff crinoline underneath my skirt, scratching my legs. There's a good reason those things were called horsehair petticoats. I never liked them when my mother made me wear them to school, and growing up didn't change my mind about that."

"Maybe the bear," Jack said, making quote marks in the air around the word, "did you gals a favor. If the capri outfit is more comfortable, it could become your new lucky duds, assuming we win."

"I'm sure Sadie will do her very best. And hopefully the contest will be over before my ponytail gives me a serious headache."

Smarter than me, Deb always kept her dark curls cropped short with a headband reminiscent of the Fifties for decoration. Shorter than me, her felt skirt usually reached the top of her oxfords. I was willing to bet she'd wimp out on helping me make new felt skirts if the guys won a trophy today.

"The judges are moving down Leo's row," Jack said. "Wonder how long it will take them to get to us."

I shook my head. Despite the heavy competition, I'd be surprised if Jack didn't win something. He'd painted every single nut and bolt when he'd restored Sadie—including those the judges couldn't even see—after finding her slouched behind an abandoned gas station and tracking down the owner so he could rescue her. I seriously doubted she looked this good the day she first rolled off the factory assembly line.

"Might as well relax, Jack. They have an awful lot of cars to look over. I've never seen a competition this big."

Silly me. Jack was always on the edge of his lawn chair at a competition. He'd only relax when we were driving out of the fair grounds, if then.

Several sodas later, the judges arrived at our location and looked Sadie over from stem to stern while I bit off the few fingernail tips I had left. Yeah, it was a habit I needed to lose. Jack leaned back in his chair, folded his arms, and whistled softly as if he didn't have a care in the world. Great acting.

I was dying for a bathroom break, no matter that the bathrooms were portable, but I stayed put, hoping to guess from the judges' faces what our fate might be. Not a chance, these guys were far too professional at judging. I'd have to wait until they looked over, under, and around every single car on the place. At long last they moved to the next car, and I made tracks for the nearest porta potty.

I stopped on the way back and chatted with Deb. "How's it going?" I asked.

She was biting her nails, as well. "Dunno. But I feel sorry for any sucker dumb enough to play poker with those judges. I couldn't tell a single thing from their faces. Leo's as nervous as a long-tailed cat in a room full of rocking chairs." Deb always resorted to some of the oldest clichés when she was nervous.

"I couldn't tell anything, either. Guess we'll have to... Wait, it looks like they're done." I craned my neck over Leo's truck and watched as the judges picked up a box of trophies and headed back toward the vehicles, reversing the route they'd taken before. I scooted across the rows to Sadie, dodging a couple of moms with kids headed toward the potty area.

I reached Sadie just as the judges blew by a Nash Rambler belonging to someone we didn't know, placed a small trophy on the hood of Joe Hosman's Studebaker and another on Philby Mason's Model T, each parked a few spaces above ours in the quay. I held my breath as the head judge paused in front of Sadie, smiled at Jack, and

me, and plopped the enormous First Place trophy for our
category on the grass near Sadie's front bumper.

Forgetting my delicate state, Jack grabbed me up and
swung me around. "I just knew those cute little pedal pushers were gonna be lucky!"

"Capris," I corrected, praying he wouldn't plunk me
down hard enough to break another bone. Jack eased me
back to the ground and waved the trophy at Leo. He and
Deb were jitterbugging a victory dance for us in front of
their truck. Now, if only they'd win something. I crossed
my fingers.

The judges meandered up the next two rows, passing out
small trophies and plaques for the various categories while
I held my breath again. At long last they reached Leo's
truck…and passed him by. My heart sank. Leo shrugged
and waved at us.

As WE WERE PACKING UP our chairs, the loud speaker
squawked and a man's voice announced, "Ladies and gentlemen, we have just one trophy left to bestow on one lucky
winner, but it's the biggest trophy of all." He held it up. He
was right, that sucker had to be four feet tall. Jack's eyes
were as large as Sadie's hubcaps.

"This is the trophy for Best of Show over all the categories, and it comes with a grand prize of one-hundred
nice American green backs. All the cars shown here today
are truly prize winners, and we thank you all for entering them. But the beautiful vehicle that earned this prize
deserves an equally beautiful presenter to hand over the
trophy." He pointed to his left, and I stretched my neck in
that direction.

"Here to present this prize to the lucky winner is the
one and only Miss Copper Penny!" He held out the trophy,
and Copper Penny stepped out of the cluster of judges and

took it. I swear the sun reflecting off all those shiny pennies made me reach for my sunglasses.

The male population in the crowd went wild, whistling and clapping. And I noticed a lot of the females cheering along with me. Copper Penny began the long walk down the center of the lined-up cars while everyone held a collective breath. Personally, I didn't see how she could navigate with those high heels and carrying that monstrosity of a trophy, but she moved right along with the head judge trailing worshipfully behind. When they reached the center of the vehicles, not far from where Jack and I stood, the judge took her elbow and guided her to a row away from us.

He led her straight to Leo and Deb's truck, where she placed the big trophy in front of the truck and planted an equally big kiss on Leo's reddened cheek. Leo clutched his chest and staggered back dramatically, whether from the size of the kiss or the trophy, I couldn't rightly say. Copper Penny laughed and started back toward the entrance with her judge as escort. Leo recovered and began doing another jig around his truck, with Deb following. I'd bet his whoops and hollers could be heard all the way back to Metropolis, Illinois. The rest of our club was cheering and dancing, as well.

Jack gave Leo two thumbs-up then gently scooped me up into his arms for another swing around.

"Aren't you a teensy bit jealous?" I asked. "His trophy is twice the size of yours, and the one and only Copper Penny actually kissed him."

"Nope, not one bit. Leo deserves that award. And like they say, 'Some days you get the bear, some days the bear gets you!'"

And with that he kissed me right on the mouth, for all the world to see.

The car-club members quickly gathered at Leo and Deb's truck for a gander at the huge trophy and congratulations for all the winners. Philby arrived with his trophy tucked under one arm and his portable oxygen tank under the other. I'd always admired how he never let his breathing problems hold him back from enjoying life.

"What say we celebrate at the Country Cowboy tonight, everyone?" Philby suggested.

"I've heard about it," Leo said, "but Deb and I have never been there. Is the food good?"

"The food is great," Reva Mason answered, "and the show is even better. You'll love it!"

We hadn't been there, either. "Sounds great. What time?" Jack asked.

"Six, and don't be late, or I'll eat your food," Philby threatened.

"We'll be there," Jack promised. Philby headed for his Model T then turned back to Jack. "Say, did that young fella find you?"

"What young fella?" Jack asked.

"Some kid in his early twenties, sporting a scruffy beard I wouldn't be caught dead in, looked like he'd had a few too many meals. He didn't give his name, just said he was looking for Jack Bloodworth. I pointed him in your direction. You weren't that far up the row from us, so I figured he couldn't get lost. Guess I should've brought him over to you."

Jack scratched his neck. "Wonder who it was?"

I had a pretty good idea who it might be. Charlie Beadle or his cousin. But neither had stopped by to talk to Jack while I'd gone to chat with Deb or he would have mentioned it. Had one of them been here at the competition, asking about us? And if so, why?

FOURTEEN

JACK AND LEO dropped Deb and me off at our cabin while they scouted the area once again for a trailer. The competition now over, chances were good people wouldn't still need rental trailers once their cars were safely stored in their garages again.

Deb and I spent a couple of hours sipping tea and shooting out e-mail announcements on Deb's laptop about our wonderful trophies until the guys returned, towing a trailer behind Leo's truck. Sadie was taking a well-earned break, locked securely inside the garage.

"At last," I said, "and now that we've come, seen, and conquered, we can pick up my new/old car at the Beadles' sometime tomorrow, and we can think about heading home."

"Hey, what about Cades Cove?" Deb asked. "It was at the top of our list, remember? Leo and I never had time to drive through there and see the old homesteads when we visited the area before. If we're leaving soon, I'd like to see it before we rush home with the spoils of victory. And we still haven't been to the outlet mall for our wedding outfits. That's gotta be done soon. I'm not about to cross a cranky bride."

"Right. The wedding outfits," I said. "Something not chartreuse. Let's go to the outlet mall first," I said. "Then to Cades Cove. We've been out there, but it's always worth another look. What about the trailer?"

"We'll leave it and the truck here and go in Sadie,"

Jack said. "I don't want you ladies to miss a single sight. But we'd best leave the mall until last. The park closes at dusk."

I figured Jack was trying to make up for the cabin disaster, even though it wasn't his fault. I knew he felt a bit guilty because he'd been the one to insist we rent a cabin clear at the top of the mountain, well away from the other tourists.

"On the way let's pick up a to-go box at a local chicken place for a late picnic lunch," Leo suggested.

We all quickly agreed to his plan, switched vehicles, and headed for the countryside.

"Look at that," Deb said, pointing out her car window at the mountain stream rushing over the large rocks alongside the highway leading to Cades Cove. I fished in my tote bag for my camera.

It seemed as though there were rushing mountain streams everywhere we looked. Jack stopped several times so I could take pictures. The sound of the water over the rocks very nearly lulled me to the point of needing a nap. And the wind sighing through the trees had me turning in slow circles, trying to capture the colors on my camera so I could enjoy them at home.

Back on the road after another quick stop, Leo said, "Are you speeding, Jack?" He pointed to the passenger-side mirror.

I turned around in time to see an official car, lights flashing and siren blaring as it whizzed around us. Jack pulled to the edge of the road as best he could, and traffic in front of us parted like a pond wave as an ambulance slid by. The sirens were deafening. I counted a fire truck, another ambulance, a police car, and several other official vehicles as they flew by, and said a silent prayer for whomever those vehicles were racing to rescue.

"Wow, must be something big going on," Deb said. She'd roused herself from a brief back-seat nap long enough to see what all the ruckus was about. Jack inched his way nearly into the intersection that split off toward Cades Cove, and for a few seconds I feared we'd be flattened in the crush of cars scuttling out of the way. Fortunately, the emergency vehicles zipped by us and continued on.

Jack turned onto the loop that meandered through the historic Cades Cove area, and the next few hours were spent admiring the amazing fall colors or hiking up the short walks to some of the older cabins, like the old Oliver place where we saw a momma deer and her twins snacking on a low tree limb. She sniffed at us as we sniffed at her.

"Even though deer pass through the pasture behind our old farm house nearly every day, I never get over the thrill of watching them up close," I whispered to Deb.

"Believe it or not," Deb whispered back, "I saw one not long ago in our backyard. They didn't used to venture inside the city limits, but I suppose the way Metropolis has spread out into the country is eating up their space."

"And that growth will likely increase the number of face-to-face encounters between the deer and the local residents, and nobody ever came out ahead in those events," Leo predicted.

We left the deer family to their meal and hiked the rest of the way to the old Oliver family log cabin, settling in for our own picnic under a nearby tree.

"I always try to imagine the people who once lived in these old cabins and what their lives might have been like," I said, carefully gathering up the leftovers and cartons. I certainly didn't want to leave any litter behind in this lovely place.

"The view from the porch is so beautiful it takes my breath away," Deb said.

I nodded and glanced around inside, marveling at the small size of the rooms and lack of privacy for family members. Many of the old cabins had one central room where the family did household chores, ate, sat by the fire, and sometimes even slept.

"I'm thankful the locals somehow managed to preserve this historic area. It's something future generations need to see, how people lived in pioneer days," I said.

I'd nearly filled an entire memory stick on my camera with pictures of the homes and the woods and fields surrounding them. At this rate, I'd need to buy another memory stick before we left the area, even if they did cost the earth. And I'd have to replace my little printer, without letting my daughters know what happened to the one they gave me.

"Let's take a different route home," Jack suggested as we passed through the exit gate. "See what we can see." Words that always made me cringe.

"Can you read that sign?" Jack asked, after we'd ridden in silence for several miles. Thankfully, I could still see distance better than he could, even from the back seat.

"Yes, it says 'Weddings in the Woods. Get married among the beautiful trees of the Smoky Mountains.' Hmm, I wonder if Sunny and Craig would consider having their wedding here. It certainly would be far less expensive than the extravaganza she's planning, and the area here is beautiful."

I snapped a couple of quick pictures, in case Sunny showed some interest. Never mind that we didn't know exactly where "here" was. I'd keep my eyes open and see how we got back to where we were supposed to be, assuming Jack didn't get us permanently lost.

We were haggling over whether or not to have a quick snack of ice cream to tide us over until we met the car club for dinner as Jack fiddled with the radio knob.

"I bet they've got a great oldies station around here," he said.

"Yep," Leo said, "they don't make songs like that now-adays."

"Like what?" Deb asked. "'Purple People Eater'?"

"Actually, I was thinking about the one where the momma doesn't rock and roll," Leo said.

"You've got it backward," Deb argued. "The momma don't dance and—"

"Hey, listen!" I pointed toward the radio. "They've found a dead body in a ditch. Just up the road from the Cades Cove entrance."

FIFTEEN

"I REPEAT, a dead body just turned up in a ditch out on, uh, well, seems it was on Highway 321, near the Cades Cove Loop early this noon time," the radio announcer said. "Victim was a young male wearin' blue jeans an—"

"Must've been the reason for all those official cars swooping around us earlier," Jack said. I nodded, straining to make sense of the announcer's southern twang.

Leo chuckled. "That news guy must be a real country boy. Even I know it's Tommy Hilfiger, not Hil-finger."

"Listen to the rest of the description," I said.

They listened. The guys looked puzzled, but the light began to dawn with Debby. "From the announcer's description, it sounds like Charlie Beadle," she said.

"Particularly the part about the ugly eight-ball tattoo on the victim's hand. But surely it couldn't be him," I said.

"Of course it isn't him, Kitty. Don't get your girdle in a wad or your overactive imagination in high gear," Jack cautioned. Sadie's speed slowed considerably, and I figured that was Jack's way of telling me we weren't going to the Beadle farm to check out my theory.

"How many times do I have to remind you, Jack Bloodworth, that I haven't worn a girdle since the early Seventies?" Nor had any other sane woman I knew. "And Deb's right. Despite the announcer's lack of ability to pronounce the name of a very well-known clothier, the description certainly fits that young man. It wouldn't hurt to just drive out there and—"

"Kitty!" Jack's warning was a bit louder this time.

"I, for one," Leo said, quickly cutting off any further marital spats, "am ready for a nap before dinner. Exploring Cades Cove wore me out."

"Truthfully, I could use a rest as well," I admitted. "My bum leg is tired. If it was Charlie Beadle, we'll find out soon enough." Sadie resumed the posted speed limit and Jack winked at me in the rearview mirror.

Soon enough turned out to be too soon. A couple of Pigeon Forge police officers were waiting for us at the cabin door. The dead body was indeed that of the young man who'd first offered to sell us the antique car. The officers insisted on taking Jack to the station despite my protests.

"Ma'am, your husband is not under arrest. We just need him to come with us and answer a few questions," the first officer, name of Scoggins, explained. "We haven't even read him his rights."

I wasn't buying it. "We're visitors here, as I'm sure you know. Therefore, we don't have a lawyer stashed in the trunk of our car. Poor planning on our part. Therefore, Jack is not going anywhere with you without me."

Jack started to protest, but I cut him off. "You go nowhere without me. I want to be sure your rights are protected."

And I wanted to be sure Jack didn't say anything stupid. The more nervous he got, the more he tended to ramble. Sitting with two hulking police officers at an unfamiliar police station was likely to cause him to confess to kidnapping the Lindbergh baby, despite the fact that Jack was just a twinkle in his father's eye at the time.

The larger of the two large officers, Franklin, nodded,

obviously a married man who knew when to stand up to a woman and when to cave. Leo and Deb drove me to the police station while Jack rode in the back of the police car.

Our most loyal friends, Leo and Deb, had hung with us during the toughest times of our lives, losing our newborn son the first year we were married, struggling to make a living and raise our two girls on our farm, the recent murder of my cousin, the problems that disaster caused our family, and me nearly dying in two separate accidents. And we'd returned the favor whenever we could. But lately it seemed the scales had been tipped heavily in our favor, a fact I wasn't particularly proud of.

We arrived at the police station just as Mose and Medina Beadle exited, passing near us in the front lobby. Medina Beadle leaned over and whispered to me, "I'm so very sorry about this. Hopefully we've straightened it all out for you."

Her husband turned to Jack. "If you no longer want the car because of this mess, I'll understand."

Officer Franklin took Jack's arm to move him through the next door. Over his shoulder Jack said, "My handshake is my bond, so I'll take the car unless you want to back out." I was too upset to even contribute to the discussion.

Mose Beadle shook his head. "A deal's a deal. Come after her whenever you're ready."

"What on earth was she talking about?" Deb whispered in my ear just loud enough for Officer Franklin to overhear.

"Please do not attempt to discuss this case, or I'll have to ask you to leave," Franklin ordered her.

Deb glared at him but didn't argue.

We each took seats in uncomfortable metal chairs in front of the chief's desk. Franklin again ordered us to remain silent, and he and his partner left the room. Before we could decide whether or not to comply, the chief of police entered the room. He carried a file, and my heart sank.

This kid would make any professional wrestler look weak and undernourished, and if there was a wrinkle in his uniform, I sure couldn't find it. Blond hair was buzzed so close to the scalp I had to look twice to make sure he wasn't bald. He dropped straight into the chair behind his desk without appearing to bend any part of his body.

"Mr. Bloodworth, I'm Chief Wilburn. I apologize for my officers interrupting your vacation to our lovely area, but we do have our duty. Are you here for the car show?"

I relaxed a bit. Anyone with a voice that gentle couldn't be all bad, could he? Unless they taught that method at the local police academy.

"Yes, sir, we are. And I came down here to buy a car for my wife. But I'm sure you knew that from the Beadles." Jack's tone was just a smidge left of sarcastic, so I gave him a slight kick while smiling innocently over the desk at the chief.

"We passed the Beadles on our way in. Medina Beadle said they'd straightened everything out. What did she mean?" I said, hoping for good news.

"When I sent Officer Franklin out to their farm to break the news about their son's death, Mr. Beadle's nephew…" Chief Wilburn paused to glance at the papers in front of him. "Mr. Beadle's nephew, Jerry, told the officer he'd seen you hanging around the barn yesterday afternoon, Mr. Bloodworth, and that you'd argued with his cousin. That's why I had my officers bring you in."

"What time yesterday afternoon?" Jack asked.

"About two or so. We do seem to have differing witness accounts. Mrs. Sassy Bentley assured my officer that the boy had been plowing one of the fields at the back of their farm and couldn't have seen you or anyone else at that time. However, the boy claims the older woman has Alzheimer's. We'll check both stories carefully, but it would help if you could tell us where you were."

Jack sat up straighter. "I was at Dollywood all afternoon with my wife and our friends."

"Copper Penny saw us," Leo said, "if you need another witness."

The chief leaned forward, obviously fascinated. Score another conquest for Copper Penny. "Would Miss Penny actually vouch for you?" he asked.

Before Jack could speak I assured Chief Wilburn that Copper Penny would recognize both Jack and me as we'd ridden with her in the limo to the auto-parts store. And I swear his face actually turned green with envy at hearing that story.

"Well, I guess we won't need anything further from you right now, until I call Miss Penny and confirm what you've told me. Just be sure you leave your contact information at the front desk. And don't leave town right away. I may want to talk to you both again."

"I trust you're also going to talk to the Beadles' nephew, Jerry, again," I said. "I'd be interested to know why he said Jack was at their farm, arguing with his cousin, when he wasn't."

The chief didn't bother to answer my question, too busy reshuffling the papers on his desk. We hadn't planned on leaving town until we had the car loaded on the trailer, which I'd hoped to do tomorrow. But now I was anxious for a chance to actually chat with Jerry Beadle. Why would he say he saw Jack at the farm arguing with his cousin when we were miles away? And why weren't the police more interested in interviewing him instead of us? Something was fishy here, and I aimed to find out what.

"Could you tell us how the young man died?" I asked. Nothing ventured, nothing gained, my momma always said. "The radio announcer said it looked like he'd been in a fight with a bear and lost."

"The body did have several severe cuts and bruises. We won't know if those injuries killed him until the autopsy. Or if a bear was even involved. Beyond that, I can't say anything more."

The chief rose, and we were dismissed. I was dying to pump him for more information, but Jack took me firmly by the arm and led me to the door. One of the difficulties of being married to the same man for most of my life was that he knew me too well. But there was more than one way to skin a cat, as long as I held the right knife to the right end of the cat. If at all possible, I'd find out what I wanted to know about Charlie Beadle's death and his cousin fingering Jack.

By the time we arrived back at the cabin, it was far too late in the evening to join the car-club members at the Country Cowboy, and I was plumb out of the celebrating mood anyhow. So was everyone else in our cabin. I called Reva's cell phone to let her know. No use everyone worrying about us because we hadn't shown up. We were doing enough worrying all on our own. Since we weren't going to dinner, we weren't going to make it to the outlet mall, either. My dress for the wedding would have to wait.

Jack and Leo opted for short naps before we reheated the dinner we'd picked up on the way home from the police station. I headed out to the porch to get a better signal on my cell phone in hopes of calling Maggie. I had to find out how Tori was feeling and do it without letting Maggie know what was going on here.

I was debating how to handle my daughter when Deb

stepped out on the porch with a tray full of coffee and cookies. Just exactly what I needed—a hot cup of coffee to warm my hands as well as my insides before dialing Maggie.

"Thought this might help calm you down," Deb said.

"I hope so. How am I going to talk to Maggie without her figuring out what's going on with us? She'll want to drive right down here, and Tori's far too sick for such a trip."

Before Deb could answer, my phone announced a Merry Christmas and Maggie began firing information at me.

"Mom, I just wanted to let you know, the doctor is sending Tori to Massac Memorial for tests. We're on our way there now." Maggie's voice broke on the last couple of words.

"Hospital? I thought you said the new medicine would take care of her illness. What does the doctor think is wrong with Tori?" Great, I was six hours from home, and a young squirt of a police chief had just ordered all of us to stay put. Well, if anything was seriously wrong with Tori, I was going over the wall and heading for home, even if I had to walk. Just let Chief Wilburn try to stop me.

"The pediatrician isn't sure. Tori is very congested. Might be pneumonia. The heavy congestion is what's causing the vomiting. I'll let you know as soon as we get her settled in. I just needed to hear your voice."

Now, that one really got to me. Adult children guarded their independence as if it was all the gold in Fort Knox, until there was an emergency with their own children. Then all bets were off.

"I'll get home as quickly as I can."

"Don't you dare, Mother, or I'll never call you again when anything happens. You're hours away. By the time you get here, Tori could be fine. Just please pray for us and stay in touch. If we need you to come home, I'll let you know."

I glanced at Deb, who mouthed the words, "Bus or plane?" I shook my head.

"Mom? Are you listening to me?"

"Yes, Maggie, I hear you. We'll stay here for the moment, but if you need me, I'm on the first plane. I don't know where the airport is, but I'll find it. Most likely I can fly into Paducah, and Joe can pick me up."

"I'm sure that won't be necessary, Mom, but I love you for offering to cut short your trip. I just wanted you to know what's happening."

"How is Tori now?"

"She's asleep for the moment, in the back seat of the van. Billy's watching a movie. We should arrive at the hospital in a couple of minutes."

"We're hoping to pick up the car we bought in the morning. After that, I should be able to come home just about any time." If necessary, I'd leave Jack behind to deal with everything here and hop on a plane. With or without Wilburn sending out the search dogs for me. "Call me the second you know something."

She agreed, and I snapped the lid shut.

"What are you going to tell Jack?" Deb asked.

"Nothing for the moment, until I hear from Maggie. Then we'll decide what to do. If I tell him now, he'll insist on heading for home this instant, and Maggie made me promise not to come there until she knows what's wrong with Tori."

"What exactly is wrong?" Deb asked.

"The doctor suspects pneumonia. She's sending Tori to Massac Memorial. Tori's having problems breathing. Apparently, none of the medicine worked."

"If they need you, I'll get you on a plane and we'll stay here to deal with Wilburn and the cars."

"Somebody will have to sit on Jack. He'll insist on going with me or driving hard for home with Sadie."

"Leo and I can handle Jack. You worry about Tori and Maggie."

I nodded and took a sip of coffee. I was already doing a very good job of worrying. This entire trip had turned into a disaster the likes of which I hadn't been involved in for quite some time and had hoped to avoid forever. If only we always got our druthers.

SIXTEEN

THE GUYS EMERGED from their naps and demanded dinner, so we re-heated the two large pizzas we'd picked up on the way home from our chat with Chief Wilburn. A hot card game was most likely on the agenda for later, with snacks to round out the evening and keep our minds off our recent brush with the law. Not to mention my private fears for my granddaughter.

Jack hadn't even asked if I'd spoken to our daughters today, something he usually did frequently, and I didn't know whether to be thankful or worried about that. His distraction meant he was really upset about Charlie Beadle's death and the police chief questioning him.

"I do wish you'd talked us into making this trip a bit sooner," Leo said, reaching for his fourth piece of meat lover's pizza. "Philby says the entire car club is going to see Copper Penny perform tomorrow night, but he only got enough tickets for those who signed up at last month's car-club meeting."

"You two have seen her up close and personal," Deb reminded the guys, "and so have Kitty and I. You'll have to be satisfied with that. It's too late to get tickets now."

They both nodded, but it was obvious their hearts weren't in it. Leo's sigh was truly heartbreaking to hear. So was Jack's.

"I know," Leo said, "but as long as we're stuck here, I'd like to see her perform on stage."

Jack scooped up the paper plates and headed to the

kitchen with Leo right behind. They were going to give us a break on clean-up yet again. Fine by me because I had an idea. I was about to put it into action when my cell phone wished me a Merry Christmas.

"Mother, what's going on?" our youngest daughter demanded. I swear that girl had ears longer than a donkey, not to mention a nose that could smell trouble a mile away, usually mine.

"Well, it's true your dad was taken—"

She didn't let me finish. "You were supposed to call and let me know if you bought the car. Did Dad manage to talk the guy down? Did you get the car? Can you e-mail me a picture? I can't get Maggie to answer her phone. Is Tori feeling any better?"

I breathed a sigh of relief. I was sure Sunny had somehow figured out Jack had been hauled to the police station for questioning. Maybe from someone in the car club who'd called home to check in. It was downright impossible to keep anything secret in a small town like Metropolis, even if you were miles away when it happened to you.

Once either of the girls heard about everything, they'd demand we return home immediately, or worse yet, threaten to join us here. And Maggie couldn't possibly leave home right now.

I hadn't realized just how much I'd missed our grandkids, even though we'd enjoyed a few days of peace and quiet while we were here. No boisterous bucking bronco rides on grandpa's back in the middle of my living-room floor, no pleading for cookies, no pulling my cat's tail, and no arguing over toys. Well, okay, the thought of all that made me even more homesick, and I couldn't wait to see my family again, particularly Tori. But I also wanted to solve this mystery and get my new car safely loaded for the trip home.

"Mother? You're not answering me. I knew something was wrong."

I managed to drag myself back into the conversation before disaster struck. "Honey, Tori is feeling worse, and the doctor is admitting her to Massac Memorial for tests. They think she might have pneumonia."

"What? Mom—"

"Sunny, I wanted to come home immediately, but Maggie wouldn't hear of it. Could you please drive down there and check on Tori for me? Let me know what's going on and whether or not I should come home anyway?"

"I'm on my way out the door, Mom. You can talk to me while I head out of town. I should be at the hospital in an hour. I'll be so glad when I'm living in Metropolis again and not over an hour away from all of you."

I'd be happy about that, too.

Several seconds of scraping and shuffling sounds was followed by, "Okay, Mom, I've got my headphone on, so tell me, did Dad find a car for you?"

"Yes, he did, and she's a beauty. Suicide doors and everything. We had to rent a trailer to bring her home with us. As soon as she's loaded up, we'll be on our way. But it's going to take another day or so before we can do that."

No way was I telling her the real reason for our extended stay. "And I did send you a picture of the car. You should check your e-mail more often. We want to see a few more of the sights before we take off, assuming everything turns out okay with Tori. I'll call you again when we're leaving town."

"Not so fast, Mom. I've got a long drive to Metropolis. Tell me more about the car. What does she look like? How much did Daddy cough up for her? What kind of shape is she in? How long before we can ride in her?"

"Honey, I'll e-mail you with all the details tonight, I promise. You have your hands full there with the wedding plans. How is that going, by the way?" Silence on the other end of the line. "Sunny?"

"Craig has given in on just about everything I want. Which should make me happy, but it doesn't. Oh, Mom, I wish we'd just run off and gotten married like you and dad did."

"It's certainly not too late for that. Just don't leave me out of the plan."

Silence again. I waited several seconds. "Sunny?" No answer. I looked at the screen. Call dropped. Which was fine with me.

I leaned over the table and whispered to Deb, "I need to send Sunny a quick e-mail. She's worried about us. We got cut off, and apparently the wedding negotiations still aren't going well. She must be driving through the dead zone outside of Carbondale. At least she'll be with Maggie at the hospital."

Deb nodded. I grabbed up her laptop and plopped in the chair by the fireplace, giving Jack a brief version of our youngest daughter's phone call.

"Perish the thought of her dashing down here," Jack said. "You didn't say anything to her about the Beadle boy or our trip to the police station, did you?"

I gave him a look. How dumb did he think I was?

When the guys graciously volunteered to fix some popcorn to snack on during the upcoming card game, Deb and I moved out to the terrace again for a few minutes, watching the moon rise and talking in low tones about the murder of the young man we'd known so briefly and why Jack had been pointed out as a suspect.

The terrace of the new cabin the rental company had provided us with was perched on far more level ground than the other cabin we'd rented, and built on a site well below the top of the mountain, but the view here was still spectacular. We could see not only the smoke-covered mountains on one side of the terrace during the day, but the bright lights of Pigeon Forge at the other side of the valley, popping on one by one at dusk, as well.

A cool breeze whispered over the porch railing, and I snuggled deeper into my jacket, listening as a couple of birds chattered back and forth in a nearby tree.

"Sassy Bentley no more has Alzheimer's than I do," Deb insisted. "She's no spring chicken, but she's got more energy than many people we know, including her poor dead grandson."

I nodded. "Obviously, that boy Jerry didn't want what she said to be taken seriously so he claimed she was losing it. But why? Because he might be involved in his own cousin's death and he's trying to blame it on Jack? I wish we'd had a chance to talk to him that day at the farm. I can't seem to get a fix on him."

"Me, neither," Deb said. "But I'm guessing he's at least involved somehow in Charlie Beadle's death."

"I can't wait to get out there again and talk to the family. Particularly Jerry Beadle. See what we can find out."

Time to bring up what really bothered me about the whole mess. "I find it odd that the Beadles were not only anxious to clear Jack with the police chief, but also concerned about the sale of that car. If—heaven forbid—one of my babies had just been found dead in a ditch, those items would be at the bottom of my worry list."

"I have to agree, but I don't necessarily see Jack and Leo letting us out of their sight long enough for a chat with the family again. Particularly now."

"Except we do have the trailer," I said, "and the car does have to be loaded onto it. That should keep the guys busy for several minutes while we figure out a way to get back inside the house and talk to the women of the family. Assuming I don't have to fly home first thing in the morning."

"We should find out why Sassy Bentley was willing to thwart Jerry whatzizname when he accused Jack of fighting with Charlie Beadle," Deb said. "Again, that's assuming our husbands even let us climb out of Sadie long enough. But Sassy Bentley did seem to take to you when we chatted with her in the kitchen. Still, families generally stick together against strangers. This whole situation is odd. So how do we get back inside their house?"

I thought about that and came up with what I hoped was a fool-proof plan.

"We can always try another run to the bathroom, if Medina Beadle lets us in, and if the guys believe us, and that's a couple of big ifs. And if all that fails, I'll try a bit of blackmail."

"Blackmail?"

"When I used your laptop just now to e-mail Sunny, I did a quick bit of surfing and managed to snag four tickets to see Copper Penny perform tomorrow night. Leo said the rest of the club already had tickets. Either they let us go inside the Beadle house or I tear up the tickets, which I've already paid for."

Deb's mouth dropped open. "Wow, quick thinking. No way the guys will want to lose those tickets. My suggestion is you try the threat first. Divide and conquer. If Jack doesn't cave, Leo will."

"Good point," I said. "I just wish…"

"What?"

"I wish Maggie would call back and let me know how Tori is. I hate to bother her by calling."

The balcony door slid open, and Jack stepped out. "You gals coming in, or are you staying out here all night?"

"Send her a text message," Deb said, turning to Jack. "If that's buttered popcorn I smell, I'm coming in. Hope we have plenty of soda to go with it."

"We do," Jack assured her. "Besides, it's about time for the bears to start hunting for supper. This part of the terrace is on ground level, and I don't want you gals tangling with a big black bear. I wouldn't want the bear to get hurt."

"Very funny, Jack," I said. "This lower area is fairly well populated, and there is a lot of traffic on the road, so I don't see a bear checking us out."

As we moseyed over to the sliding glass door, a large black bear rounded the back corner of the cabin, moving toward us on all fours. The bear stood on its hind legs, grunting displeasure at meeting us.

My heart jumped into overdrive as Jack, Deb, and I beat a retreat to the other side of the terrace. Jack danced around, scrabbling for a weapon, but this side of the terrace was completely empty, and the table and chairs were now well beyond our reach. I'd calculated the height of the terrace railing and was about to risk jumping over it when the bear suddenly hauled himself across his side of the railing and lumbered off into the dusk, leaving a rather unpleasant odor trailing behind. Who knew bears passed gas when frightened? Crisis averted. But I'd certainly be more careful out here from now on.

Was it at all possible that Conklin had been right about a bear breaking into our other cabin at the top of the mountain? And could the radio announcer have been right about a bear killing Charlie Beadle? Somehow, I didn't think so.

Time to learn how to send a text message. I'd heard they

were expensive. Maybe, maybe not, but I'd send one if it cost the farm.

I was pouring our soft drinks when the cell phone beeped and I read Maggie's message:

> *Tori and I staying overnight. Pneumonia. Doctor says not to worry. It'll clear up in few days with IV. Sunny here, insist you stay put. Thanks, hugs, Maggie.*

Don't worry? Yeah, right. A grandchild in the hospital. My husband possibly suspected in a murder case. Several hours away from home. Sure, I wasn't worried. Not one weensy little bit.

SEVENTEEN

OVER BREAKFAST the next morning at a pancake house, Philby Mason—seated at the head of our table—tapped a spoon on his coffee cup and called a quick meeting of the Massac County Cruisers, in order to offer congratulations once again to the club members who'd snagged a trophy at the competition. Our group had done quite well in the judging.

"Since we only meet once a month," Philby continued, "and we're all together now, we might as well take care of some important new club business. The Lofton twins have applied for our scholarship fund for next semester at Shawnee Community College. Kitty assures me we have enough in the scholarship fund to cover both girls, and some extra in our club checking account, should we need it. Could I please have a motion and a vote on the issue? Unless you want to discuss it further."

I was happy to see that the motion was quickly presented and seconded, with no discussion, and it received a resounding "aye" vote from everyone.

"We're covered for the rest of this year, but I need some suggestions for tours, beginning in January," Philby said. "The weather may hold us back, but in case it doesn't, where would you folks like to go?"

Next thing I knew, I'd actually volunteered us to host a "garage tour" at our farm. Jack's huge barn housed not only Sadie and her necessary accoutrements but all of his collectables like antique gas pumps that cost the earth, his hubcap collection, old license plates from across the country, and many old metal signs. Of course, the building was climate controlled, probably better than our farm house. And he'd created an eating area at one end that looked a lot like a 1950s diner.

Car-club members enjoyed touring each others' garages and barns and having a potluck dinner to chat over. Jack had wanted to invite the group, but with my bad leg we hadn't been able to host them in a while. Jack's wink let me know I'd just scored major points with him.

"Okay, that takes care of the January meeting," Philby said. "And we have a tentative plan for February's meeting place. I'll let you all know if that works out. Now to the really important business of the day, Kitty and Jack's difficulties."

I'd overheard Jack telling Philby about our recent roadblocks when he'd called to let us know about the breakfast meeting this morning.

"Most of us only planned to stay in Pigeon Forge over the long weekend for the car show, but in light of Jack and Kitty's problems with the law and the task of getting their new car towed home, I think some of us should stick around and help out. After all, it's not like any of us have to be anywhere in particular for the next few days since we're all retired."

The group nodded, and my heart swelled with gratitude for our friends. Most of them did have somewhere to be in the upcoming days. If not to work, then certainly to play with grandchildren, or senior aerobics, or bridge games, or volunteer work, or houses to dust, or lawns to mow. But they were all willing to stay here longer to help us out of this mess. I nudged Jack and he wiped syrup off his mouth, dropped his napkin on the table, and stood.

"Philby, and all of you, Kitty and I appreciate your

friendship more than I could ever say. But we don't want to put anybody out. Leo and Deb are staying over, and they can help us get the car home. If anything changes between now and the time you were planning on leaving, you can be sure we'll ask. And please, if at all possible, don't let your families back home know what's going on with us. Tori has pneumonia, so our girls have enough to worry about right now as it is."

Blushing—for he wasn't much of a public speaker— Jack dropped back into his seat and grabbed for his fork. After I'd kept him awake with my belly-flopping on my side of the bed most of the night, Jack had demanded to know what was bothering me, and I'd told him about Tori. He knew me far too well to accept that I was only worried about Chief Wilburn. He'd insisted on taking off for home right then and there, until I showed him Maggie's text message. But it wouldn't take much to make him change his mind. Or mine, for that matter.

"You're not getting rid of me that easily, Jack Blood-worth," Philby insisted. His wife, Reva, nodded. So did several others. Well, at least if the police came for Jack again, we'd have some backup.

Jim Modglin, seated next to Leo, pushed his chair back and stood. "It appears to me that somebody should do some detecting. Maybe visit the local newspaper or library and check out this Beadle family a bit closer."

Jack shook his head, but I jumped in. "Great idea, Jim. Deb and I can search the local newspaper files this morning from the nearby library while Jack and Leo contact Mr. Beadle and set up a time to pick up the car. I'm sure Jack will want to secure the car with extra straps or chains or whatever else they sell at the nearest car-parts store."

I thought about Philby Mason. Helping us had been his suggestion, and I didn't want to hurt his feelings by leaving him out. Some of our group had been friends since first grade, if not earlier.

"Philby, could you and Reva check out the title to the car at the Sevier County courthouse? I love that car, but there was something a bit odd about the sale. Maybe Jim and Wilma can go along with you to check out any other records. The rental company's security guard said the Beadles' son had been in jail."

I addressed the groups at the other tables. "Maybe some of the rest of you could do some Internet surfing, if you brought along laptops?"

I was rewarded with a chorus of "Sures" and "You got its." Philby saluted in my general direction. He and Reva and their team would know what to look for at the courthouse. So would the rest of the group, via the Internet.

"And don't forget, everybody," Philby warned the group. "Not a word to our families back home about Jack and Kitty's problems, or Maggie will pounce. And she's liable to bring all of our kids along for the ride in order to help her straighten us out." A visible shudder passed through the group.

Breakfast ended, and Jack snatched up everyone's tickets at our table, intending to buy the breakfasts of all those who'd volunteered to do the actual footwork of detecting. The rest of the men followed him, rushing to get a place in line at the cash register and argue over who was paying for what. Most of the wives made a bee-line for the bathroom. I decided I'd rather wait until we arrived at the library. The line there was bound to be shorter and the bathroom larger.

As I placed my tote bag onto my shoulder, someone cannon-balled into my back, knocking me to my knees. Deb, Reva, and Wilma reached down to peel me off the floor. Thankfully, this particular breakfast place kept their floors spotless. I dusted myself off and struggled to stand upright, praying I hadn't re-injured my bad leg. A quick self-exam told me most of the damage was to my other knee, and while I'd be a bit stiff for a couple of days, nothing seemed to be broken.

"Anybody get the license number of that truck?" I asked.

Wilma and Reva shook their heads and continued dusting my slacks off. Deb looked around, her mouth set in a line that warned the wary she was about to explode.

"It was the bus boy. And I'm going to give that guy a well-deserved lecture. He didn't even stop to see if you were hurt or apologize, Kitty. He bent over for a second then tore off toward the kitchen. The manager is going to hear about this, just as soon as I get that kid's name."

Before I could stop her, Deb pushed her way through the kitchen door. I felt sorry for the hapless bus boy...almost. Like Deb said, he could have apologized. The manager seemed to be busy taking the tickets and money from our group, and as we'd been in a back room, probably usually reserved for meetings, no one else seemed to have noticed my fall.

Deb came back, her mouth set even tighter than before.

"What?" I asked, but I had a feeling I didn't really want to know.

"I could have sworn it was the bus boy who mowed you down. I couldn't see his face under the huge ball cap, but he was wearing a white jacket. Unfortunately, the head cook swears the only bus boy on duty today is a girl, and she was on a bathroom break when you fell. She came into the kitchen drying her hands just as I was leaving."

"Couldn't it have been her?" Reva Mason asked.

"Not unless she lost a hundred pounds or so between here and the bathroom. And about a foot of height."

"Nobody else in the kitchen looked like the guy who ran into me?" I asked.

Deb shook her head. "It's mostly women working in there. The only guy was about half the size of the guy who knocked you down. And they said no one else came through the kitchen. There is a side door before you reach the bathrooms."

"Kitty, what's taking you gals so long?" As usual, Jack had a toothpick dangling from one side of his mouth, and he was reaching into his wallet for tip money to drop on the table.

I gave the girls a warning look. "Um, nothing. We were just chatting."

If Jack knew about my fall, he'd likely drag me off to the nearest emergency room for a once-over, and I wasn't badly hurt beyond a sore elbow and kneecap. And I had things to do, not to mention people to investigate. I scrounged my tote bag off the floor, and we headed out to our destinations.

We found seats at the library computer station, with Debby searching for anything of interest on the Beadles and me searching the birth and death records. After what seemed like a decade or two but was actually only an hour, we took a break and split a can of diet soda. My elbow throbbed. I fished in my tote bag for an aspirin. Debby handed me her printouts.

"Nothing too spectacular here. Mose Beadle wins an award at the local county fair almost every year for his prize bull. That animal must be old enough for Social Security. And Sassy Bentley's jams and jellies—not to mention her pickled peaches—took first prize every single year clear up to 1995. She must have retired from the competition back then. There's no more mention of her entering or winning after that. But I'm surprised the other contestants didn't pool their money and hire a hit man somewhere along the line to take her out. Obviously, they didn't stand a chance whenever Medina Beadle's mother entered the fray."

Deb reached for the soda can and took a sip. A true competitor, I wasn't surprised by her sympathy for the other ladies who'd gone home losers year after year. I'd won a couple of ribbons for my quilts at the Massac County fair over the years but I'd certainly never been able to "own" a competition the way Sassy Bentley apparently had. I couldn't see how that would've made her real popular with her peers.

"I found a mention of Medina Beadle's birth and Mose's," I said. "He was born in the adjoining county. Probably moved here when they married. And I found his parents and her father's obituaries. Nothing else on either of them."

"What about their son, Charlie?" Deb asked, glancing up at a teenage girl and boy meandering by, hand in hand. My guess was they weren't here to research anything beyond whether or not the librarian could see clear to the back shelves if someone happened to engage in a little bit of romance. As I recall, Jack and I had done some of same research at the Metropolis Public Library many moons ago, and the head librarian had sent us home after a lecture.

Back to the business at hand. "I found his birth record and a mention of his high-school graduation, complete with pictures of the class." I pointed him out on the monitor and clicked "print."

"He's put on a lot of weight since then," Deb said, squinting at the monitor. I knew better than to suggest she might need reading glasses.

"And no beard back then. It really didn't do a lot for his appearance, but I suppose he thought he needed it to make himself look more countrified when the trio played at the restaurant," I said. "No tattoo, so he must've gotten that done in jail."

"I found an article about his foray into a life of crime," Deb said. "Like Conklin said, he went joy riding with some other teens in a stolen car on graduation night. There was an accident, and one of the boys died. The judge handed down some pretty stiff sentences to all of them, but Charlie Beadle apparently got out early. He must've been a really good boy."

"Find anything about the family's little band? Maybe some appearances they made besides outside the restaurant?"

"They did a few gigs for the Odd Fellows several years back, but it was just Mose and Medina. No Charlie. Maybe he was away in jail at that time. And there is absolutely no mention of a Jerry Beadle."

"If he's related through his mother, not his father, then he'd have a different last name."

"Probably. Well, this has been a washout."

She tossed the empty soda can into the nearest trash bin. I gathered up all the articles we'd printed out, stuffed them into my already stuffed tote bag, and slung it over my shoulder.

"Let's catch up with Philby's team at the courthouse and see what they've found," I suggested, reaching for my cell phone. "It isn't far."

"Great, we can have lunch with them."

I stared at Deb's pencil-thin figure. "But we just ate."

"That was over an hour ago. It's time for a snack."

And she accused Leo of thinking about nothing but food? I shook my head and dialed Maggie's cell-phone number.

"How's my granddaughter this morning?" I demanded

when her sleepy voice answered. It was nearly lunch time, so obviously Maggie hadn't slept much last night or she wouldn't be napping now.

"She seems a bit better this morning. Her temp is lower and she's asleep right now. But it was a long night. She's never been in the hospital before, and she's terrified. Sunny and I took turns rocking her. Not easy with an IV in place. How are you guys?"

"Just fine," I lied. "We've had breakfast, and we're checking out some of the local sights." Deb raised her eyebrows on that one but didn't speak.

"Well, don't rush home. Sunny's going to stay with me. Joe took time off to be with Billy, and I've got things covered here. Enjoy your trip. Did you load the car up yet?"

She wasn't fooling me. Her oh-so-casual question about loading up the car let me know she was anxious for us to come on home. No more anxious than I was to be home. Which made me more determined to help out the police chief in solving this case so he'd let us go.

"We found a trailer, but we can't load the car today. The family we bought it from had an emergency. We'll get out there as soon as we can, and then we'll head home. I promise." And I sincerely hoped I could keep that promise.

Maggie and I said our goodbyes, and Deb and I moved toward the check-out desk to pay for our copies. Arriving there, we ran smack dab into Copper Penny.

EIGHTEEN

"WHAT ARE YOU lovely ladies up to?" Copper Penny inquired. "My, you folks certainly do get around this area."

"Um, just a little research," I answered. Deb appeared to be as dumbstruck as Jack and Leo in Copper Penny's awesome presence. I tried not to stare at her jeans, covered in shiny pennies, just like her jacket. Could she actually sit down in those things?

"Say, I heard about Charlie Beadle's death from Chief Wilburn," Penny said, "and I was happy to vouch for you folks when the chief called me. Such a shame. Charlie hadn't been home from jail all that long."

I was fascinated. "You knew Charlie Beadle?"

"Not really. But Mose Beadle helps take care of my place when things are slow on his farm. He brought the boy along once or twice after he finished servin' his time. Kid gave me the willies. And he was disrespectful to his daddy. My daddy wouldn't of put up with that for five seconds. I'm surprised Mose did. But him and Medina will take their son's death real hard. I'm sending a basket of food over."

"That's very kind of you," Deb said, finding her voice at last.

"Folks around here stick together," Penny said. "Life's too hard without friends to help out. Now, if you'll excuse me, I need to speak to one of the librarians. Get some advice on genealogy."

"You're researching your family tree?" Deb asked. "For a biography?"

"Well, yes and no," Penny said. "Some of my people lived in the Cades Cove area. I didn't realize that until I was approached to help raise money for the preservation of the area. When I saw a familiar name in one of the history books, I decided I needed to know more about my family."

"We toured the area," I said. "I wish my students could have experienced it. I used to show them pictures from my previous trips, before I retired. Much better for them than reading a history book."

"Yes, indeed," Deb said. "I wonder what those Cades Cove folks would think if they could see how we live today, with cell phones and all the other electronic devices."

"I suspect they'd think they were better off without them," Copper Penny said. The pennies dangling from her ears sparkled in the sunlight streaming in through the nearby window. "Since you obviously love the area like we do, would you ladies be interested in helping us raise money for the preservation effort?" Penny pulled a couple of brochures out of her large penny-covered tote and gave one to each of us.

"I'd be honored," I said.

"Love to," Deb said. "Um, would you mind signing this?"

I was afraid Penny would refuse, but I shouldn't have worried. She whipped out a pen, signed both our brochures, smiled her thanks, and headed toward the head librarian's desk.

"She is gorgeous," Deb said. I nodded and paid for the copies we'd made.

"Let's give the guys a call and let them know what we found out," Deb suggested, digging for her cell phone.

"Suits me. Wonder if they found everything they think we'll need to get the car home safely."

"I don't know, but when they find out we chatted with Copper Penny again, they'll be mad."

I couldn't disagree with that. I fished in my tote bag for my camera. "Every single time we've seen Copper Penny either my camera hasn't been handy, or I thought it would be intrusive to take her picture at that particular moment. Maybe she wouldn't object to a picture taken with me here in the library since we've agreed to help with a project she's so interested in."

"Great idea," Deb said, punching keys on her cell phone.

My camera wasn't in my tote bag.

"When did you have it last?" Deb asked, snapping the lid shut on her cell phone. "When you uploaded the pictures of your car to my laptop?"

I shook my head. "I e-mailed those pictures right after we bought the car. I charged the battery up again last night, so I know I had it then. I usually keep the camera in my pocket, but like a dope I dropped it into the bag when I took it off the charger."

"And the bag hasn't been out of your sight, right?"

"Nope. The bag was on the back of my chair at the restaurant and here in the library. Anyone passing by might've been able to sneak the camera out, assuming they were quick enough to dive to the bottom of the bag and snatch it out without alerting me. But I don't see how even the most experienced pickpocket could do that." My stomach rolled over, and I swallowed hard. My lovely little camera, gone?

"I vote for the elusive bus boy," Deb said. "I saw him bend over when you fell. I thought for a second he was going to pick you up. When he took off without apologizing, I was so mad I didn't even stop to wonder what he was really doing when he dropped down beside you."

Now I was getting mad. "I was so busy trying to figure out what hit me that I didn't even look up at him. And I didn't see him touch my tote bag, but it was behind me, so he could've made off with the whole thing and I wouldn't have noticed right that minute."

"Yet he didn't take your wallet, which most thieves would assume held cash and credit cards. Is anything else missing?"

I stepped to a nearby table and carefully checked the contents of my tote bag again. "Only my camera is missing. And the memory stick that held all of the pictures I haven't had time to upload to the computer." I felt like crying. "Now I won't even be able to take a picture of Copper Penny to show our grandchildren."

"I'll take the picture with my cell phone. But, Kitty, I think you should report this theft to the police as soon as possible."

My first reaction was to argue, but common sense kicked in and I agreed.

"I don't have the serial number of the camera with me. It's stashed in my desk at home, but I can send it to Chief Wilburn after we get back."

"Maybe the police will find it and you'll get it back," Deb said, giving me a hug. She knew how much that camera meant to me, not to mention the pictures stored on the memory stick.

"Maybe." But I didn't hold out much hope. Why take my camera and not try for my money or credit cards? Was there something on the memory stick that was important to someone besides me? This seemed mighty coincidental to the destruction of my printer.

When we finally gathered for pie and coffee and to exchange information, the other car club "detectives" hadn't unearthed any more clues than we had. The title search on Sassy Bentley's car proved she'd been the only owner, and the small amount of yearly taxes and license fees were paid up-to-date, which meant no legal hassles for us to worry about. But with so little time left of our trip here, I didn't see how we'd ever figure out what really happened to Charlie Beadle.

NINETEEN

"WHAT WAS THAT?" Deb asked. She leaned over the cabin's deck railing and peered into the nearby woods.

"Hopefully not the bear again," I replied, though it did sound like a rather large animal moving through the brush. The grassy area beyond the cabin deck was quite long and the deck was short, so if there was a bear nearby, we'd be able to scoot back inside before it reached the railing. Otherwise I wouldn't have ventured outside after the last encounter. But the clouds were so beautiful at sunset, I couldn't resist.

"I feel like a total dunce at this detecting business," Deb said. "Did we learn anything at all today that would help us figure out who killed Charlie Beadle? Assuming it wasn't a bear like the radio announcer mentioned."

"Nothing I can think of."

"Somehow I can't picture Charlie Beadle alone out there on that highway, all dressed up and no place to go. And apparently no vehicle to go in, so how did he get to that spot in the first place? What was he doing way out there all alone?"

I thought that over and shrugged. "Quite possibly we did learn something, but not from our snooping this morning. When we were checking the newspaper files, I sort of figured if Charlie Beadle was murdered, it was someone with a grudge, maybe related to the accident that sent him to jail. Or maybe even somebody he ran afoul of while he was in the pokey."

"In which case, we'd never be able to figure it out."

I nodded. "But the more I think about it, the more I'm sure his family is somehow involved. Now that my camera is missing, I believe it's someone we met on the farm. Someone who knew I'd been taking pictures there. Why else steal my camera and not my wallet? Maybe when we go back—"

"What's up, ladies?" Jack stepped through the sliding glass door.

Deb took a seat at the far end of the deck, still keeping her eyes on the wooded area. I sighed as the last of the sun dipped behind the trees. "Deb and I were discussing our detecting efforts from this morning. We've got a trailer, but I hate to disturb the Beadles by picking up our car at this point. But mostly there's just something really odd about this whole thing."

"And you're dying to get out there and see what you can find out, right?"

"Of course, and I hate it when you do that."

"Read your mind?"

"Yes."

"You read mine all the time. Fair's fair."

I ignored that.

"We'd have to stay a couple more days, anyhow," Jack said. "The chief was quite firm about that. Might as well deal with the car while we wait."

"Maybe we won't have to stay that long. When we ran into Copper Penny at the library, she mentioned vouching for us to Chief Wilburn, which means he now knows you weren't at the farm when that boy said you were, arguing with his cousin. Chances are Wilburn will let us go any time now. But we do have to get the car. Then we can head home and check on our babies."

When I'd finally told Jack about Tori's illness and hospitalization this morning, he'd agreed that we should abide by Maggie's wishes and stay here until we'd finished our business. Of course, he called her every couple of hours to check on Tori. As did I. So our cell minutes had likely turned into hours. Well worth it.

"The only problem is, I don't know what to do about the car," I said. "Do you really think they'll still want to sell it? Maybe they were just in shock when we saw them yesterday. And won't it bring some bad memories with it for us? Maybe we should just forget about it and ask for our money back?"

Jack shrugged. "Mose Beadle said the deal was still on. And that's exactly the car you've always wanted. Might be a long time before we find another one like it. I'll give him a call and see how he feels about the sale now."

"Before you go back inside, I have a surprise for you." Jack's eyebrows stood at attention.

"I managed to get us four tickets to Copper Penny's show tonight." The eyebrows wiggled. Which, of course, made me feel guilty.

"I'd planned on using them as a bribe, so you'd let me chat with Medina Beadle again. I'm sorry."

Jack hugged me. "I think you're the nicest wife I've ever had. And you don't have to bribe me. I'm fine with you talking to Mrs. Beadle and her mother again. Just be careful around the men. After all, it was their nephew who tried to say I argued with Charlie Beadle. He must be involved somehow. But I can't figure out why he'd do that to his own cousin."

"Then you and Leo need to be careful, as well." I told Jack about my missing camera. He glared at me.

"Kitty, you have to be more careful. And no picture taking with your cell phone at the farm. Don't even let the

Beadles see that you have a cell phone. Did you report the camera missing?"

"Yes. Deb called Chief Wilburn's office for me and left a message. They said they'd look into it. I doubt they'll ever find out who took it."

"After I call Mose Beadle, I'll hunt up Leo and we'll get ready for our date with Copper Penny." He wiggled his eyebrows at me, knowing I was too far away to do him any physical harm.

I turned to the sunset again as Jack headed inside. Leo was grabbing a quick nap. Deb swore her husband could sleep standing up if it came down to it.

"You don't seem very happy about picking up the car," Deb said, joining me at the railing. "I thought you were dying to get out there and quiz the Beadles."

"I thought so, too. But I keep thinking about how tough this must be, especially for Medina Beadle. Losing an only child. She must've been in shock yesterday. I can't imagine any other reason for her attitude."

Despite the mild evening, Deb rubbed her upper arms as if trying to keep warm. "I can't imagine a loss like that."

"Neither can I, but you're right. I do want to find out why Jerry Beadle said he saw Jack on their farm arguing with his cousin when he couldn't possibly have. And why Sassy Bentley contradicted him. If she was inside, she probably wouldn't know who was where."

"I don't know," Deb said. "Wheelchair or no, she seems to be pretty aware of what's going on in and outside of that house."

Jack stepped through the door again. "Still tempting the bears, ladies?"

"I'm about at the end of my patience with bears and burglars," Deb said. "If that bear has any sense, he'll steer clear of this cabin. Ditto for the burglars."

Jack smiled. "Nobody home at the Beadles'. Or they're not answering the phone. I left a message with my cell number and asked if we could pick up the car early tomorrow morning, assuming they're okay with that."

"Suits me," I said. "Much as I love the Smoky Mountains, I'm starting to get homesick for the kids and my back porch and—"

"And sick and tired of murder, right?" Jack said.

"Yeah, sick and tired of murder."

"We can't leave until Chief Wilburn gives the okay, but I'll check in with him tomorrow and see if he'll give me a better time frame now that I have an alibi. And the instant Maggie gives the word, I'll put you on a bus or plane and send you home."

He put his arms around me, and we hugged. Over his shoulder I saw Debby slip back inside the house, giving us some private time. I really thought I'd been handling this whole fiasco well, but suddenly I started sobbing into Jack's shoulder. Maybe Charlie Beadle had been in prison after a stupid stunt. Maybe he hadn't been a perfect son, but no one deserved to wind up in a ditch alongside the highway, looking like chopped liver. From what the radio announcer said, the boy had taken a serious beating in the process.

Finally Jack said, "C'mon, Kitty, it's getting cooler out here, and I don't want to meet that bear again."

I knew he was just trying to get my mind off murder. I dried my eyes. "I suppose you'd rather meet Copper Penny?"

"Yeah, but she's too busy to show up on our back porch. The bears have more leisure time. Besides, she's waiting for me at the theater."

I turned my head at the renewed sound of thrashing in the woods. I peered at the foliage, but from this distance

I couldn't see anything moving between the trees. But I was more than happy to go inside and sit by the fire for a few minutes, until it was time to dress for Copper Penny's performance. I hoped the rest of the audience was into casual because Deb and I hadn't thought to buy any evening clothes when we'd had to replace our traveling wardrobes.

TWENTY

COPPER PENNY STEPPED OUT on stage covered in bright shiny pennies from head to toe. I very nearly reached for my sunglasses in spite of the dark auditorium. Instead I reached for my cell phone and snapped a couple of pictures to go along with those the obliging librarian had taken of Deb and me and the lovely Ms. Penny earlier. And how did the woman stay that slim? Running from admiring fellas, most likely. She began belting out songs that even I recognized. It occurred to me that I'd listened to Jack's CDs more often than I'd realized. And I loved her voice, soft and pure country.

I leaned over to Deb and whispered, "Hard to realize there's also a very savvy businesswoman under all those coins, isn't it?" We'd watched the Biography Channel last night during the card game, and they'd been showing a repeat of Copper Penny's rise to fame. I doubted very many people could have written as many songs as she had and made them into huge hits. I was amazed by her humility and determination not to let fame or fortune swell her head. She was reputed to be friendly and helpful to strangers, which explained her willingness to stop on the side of the road and help Jack and me.

"She must be a genius, just keeping up with her daily schedule," Deb whispered back. "Can you imagine exercising before the sun comes up?"

I nodded. My schedule paled to nothingness in comparison, as did most women's.

Jack elbowed me from the other side. "Shhhh, she might hear you gals chatting and think you aren't enjoying the show."

I snickered. If Copper Penny could hear herself think above the band behind her, I'd be surprised. Not to mention the audience clapping in time with the music. I wondered just how many country-music worshippers this auditorium could hold at one time. I hadn't seen any empty seats, but then I couldn't turn around once we were seated and look, not without being rude. I'd paid quite a bit extra for the front-row seats available due to a last-minute cancellation, as a special treat for Jack. Expensive but well worth it as nothing blocked our view and I fully intended to remind him of my largesse when my next birthday rolled around.

Deb snickered as well, but we stopped chatting and watched the show. And what a show! I thought I'd faint when Alan Jackson stepped out on stage, surprising everyone, including Copper Penny. She kissed him on the cheek in mid-song as he blended his wonderful voice with hers and I turned green with envy.

After the song ended, Jackson leaned over the edge of the stage to shake hands with those of us lucky ticket buyers seated nearby. Who knew women could move that fast to reach him? With Deb's help, I made it to my feet in time to gaze worshipfully into his eyes as he grinned down at me. I thought I felt a tug from Jack's direction on my jacket lining, but I swatted his hand away. Luckily for Alan Jackson, my bum leg prevented me from climbing up on the stage, and he escaped before any of the other front-row fans thought of trying it.

"For a minute there I thought I was going to have to drag you off the stage, Kitty," Jack mumbled in my ear. I decided to let him worry about that for a while. He wasn't the only family member who knew how to make a total fool of himself in public over a country-music star, and it was high time he recognized it.

At intermission Jack refused to move from his seat, whether from an irrational fear that someone might take it over in his absence or that he might be late getting back to it when Copper Penny re-appeared, I couldn't say. Unlike Deb, I didn't possess unlimited kidney space, so I worked my way up the aisle with her in tow and we made for the bathroom.

"I hope this isn't an urgent stop for you," Deb said, pointing to the line at the bathroom door.

"It isn't, but I hate waiting in line."

"We could always sneak into the men's bathroom," she suggested. I knew she was joking, but I was tempted. The line there was never as long, as most males seemed able to take care of business and move on much quicker than we females.

The line moved at last, and Deb and I exited the bathroom. "How much time do we have left?" I asked.

"Five minutes, according to that blinking sign. I've got a bottle of water in my purse. Want some? I should have thought to bring a snack."

My whistle was a bit dry, too, so we shared the water, saving room for calories later.

"I expect the guys will want to go out for dessert when we're done here," I said. "Let's hit the T-shirt and CD table on our way out. I might squirrel a couple of items away for Jack's birthday while he and Leo retrieve Sadie from the parking lot."

"Don't look now, but do we know him?"

"I hate it when you ask about someone and tell me in practically the same breath not to turn around and look. How am I supposed to know who you're talking about?"

"I meant be discreet, don't gawk. He's at two o'clock,

wearing a blue denim jacket. I can't see much of his face. He's wearing a baseball cap, inside the theater. Can you believe it?"

"Two o'clock? You've been watching too many old war movies with Leo. It's high time you introduced him to something more sophisticated like *Pride and Prejudice* or *Emma*." While I lectured Deb, I slowly turned around and scanned the crowd. "I don't see anyone in blue denim."

Deb stopped pretending to study the posters and looked around. "He's gone. He was right there by the water fountain, and he kept staring at the back of your head. Creepy."

"Maybe it's my fatal charm? It always worked with my students."

"Well, he looked old enough to be out of high school. College age, but somehow he didn't look like a college student. He looked…oh, I don't know, creepy."

"You already said that. Repeating yourself is a sign of aging." I took another sip of water. "You sure he was staring at me?"

"Yes, and when he saw me looking at him, he quickly turned away."

"Well, he's gone now, and the guys are waiting. We'd better get back before the show starts."

We headed back to our seats just as the lights began to dim. I glanced at the crowd, but with so many people and such little light, I couldn't spot any blue clothing, denim or otherwise. We slid into our seats and leaned back to enjoy the rest of the show, though I didn't see how Copper Penny could possibly top the first half. I should have known better. By the end of the evening she had the entire crowd on its collective feet, singing right along with her.

I thought for sure Jack would faint this time when she came down the steps and headed straight for him. He wobbled a bit, but stood firm as Copper Penny squeezed his hand and said something I couldn't hear over the noise of the crowd and the music. Then she headed up the aisle, shaking a hand or giving out a hug now and then. At last she threw a kiss to the crowd and disappeared through a side door, Jack still sighing in her direction.

Leo had been the first of our group to grab a seat, placing himself four seats too far away from Copper Penny to get such attention. "Jack, you have more luck than a field of four-leaf clovers," he said.

"Did you see that?" Jack asked as we all gathered up jackets and other paraphernalia and prepared to stand in the aisle forever to exit the theater.

"Jack, if you're going to try to tell us that last kiss she threw to the crowd was aimed straight at you and/or Leo, you'll get no argument here. I agree she looked right down here in our direction when she threw it."

Jack looked as if I'd let the air out of his balloon for a few seconds, then he puffed his chest out even further than usual. "Mighty fine woman, Miss Copper Penny," he said.

Deb and I nodded. No need to argue.

"What did she say to you when she stopped?" Deb asked Jack. "I couldn't hear a thing."

"She thanked us for coming to the show. And she said it was a pleasure to meet us. I didn't have brains enough to tell her it was my, uh, our pleasure, as well." He gave me a guilty glance. I grinned to let him know the hero worship didn't bother me. At least not as long as he stayed right by my side and didn't try to follow Copper Penny home.

By the time we reached the lobby, most of the fans were gone. Ditto for the souvenirs of the show, but I did manage to nab a couple of T-shirts and a CD I knew Jack didn't own, and Deb and I went outside to wait for the guys to pick us up.

Deb rubbed her arms and stepped back inside the doorway. "What's taking them so long? I know we had to park a ways out, but they've had time to walk practically back to our cabin by now, never mind the end of the parking lot."

I scanned the lot, but with so many cars still trying to get out of there, I couldn't distinguish one from the other.

"Must be the traffic. They should be here soon. And you know how Jack is. Sadie has to have plenty of space around her to avoid nicks and dings from other drivers, so he parks as far away from any building as he can."

Most of the antique-car owners did that, but Jack always insisted it was to give us the needed exercise, not to protect Sadie. He wasn't fooling me.

But the parking lot was now practically empty and neither Jack nor Leo was answering his cell phone. I was about to beat on the locked theater door and ask for help when they finally arrived.

"What in the world took you two so long?" Deb demanded through chattering teeth. I was busy trying to keep Jack from seeing that my tote bag was extra full with birthday gifts for him and slide into Sadie's back seat to browbeat him myself.

"Leo and I caught someone trying to break into Sadie's trunk," he said. "We chased him quite a ways, but he was too young and too fast for us."

"Did you get a good look at him?" Deb asked.

"Just from the rear," Leo said. "He was wearing jeans and a blue jacket. Had on a ball cap, but he was running away from us so I didn't get a look at his face."

Blue jacket? I shivered.

TWENTY-ONE

"Mose Beadle returned my call while you were in the shower," Jack said the next morning.

Suddenly nervous, I dropped the mascara wand into the sink, narrowly missing my soft, new cream-colored sweater. "What did he say?" Whatever it was, I figured it wasn't good.

"He asked if we'd found a trailer yet. I said we had, but I hadn't picked up the car because I didn't want to intrude on their sorrow."

"And?" I prompted. I swear, sometimes Jack Bloodworth danced all the way around a subject before he got to the point.

"He asked if we could pick it up this morning. Said he'd like to clear that part of the barn out before the next harvest."

Which sounded good on the face of it, except he didn't have any crop out at the moment that I'd seen when we visited the first time. So why the rush to empty the barn when they'd just lost their only son?

"We'll go right after breakfast," Jack said. "And, Kitty, go easy on interrogating the womenfolk. Be subtle. Leave your bright light and rubber hose here."

"Jack, I wouldn't dream of bringing up the subject." Of course, if they brought it up, that was a different matter entirely. Assuming Deb and I could get ourselves invited inside the house again.

We decided to eat breakfast at the cabin because we'd

been stuffing ourselves at restaurants. Not that it made much difference since there was a ton of food on the table when we sat down to eat. Bacon, eggs, canned biscuits, gravy, and fried potatoes. Deb and I had the mess to clean up, but to give the devil his due, Jack and Leo did the cooking, saying they wanted this to be a real vacation for Deb and me by relieving us from stove duty. And we used paper plates, so clean-up was a bit easier. Deb hauled the trash out to the Dumpster, with Jack reminding her twice to make sure the lid was secure from bear raids. While Deb took the trash out, I dialed Maggie to see how Tori was doing.

"Not as well as I'd like, Mom," Maggie said. "Her fever is nearly gone, but she's so listless. I swear, I'll never complain again when she and Billy race through the house, him chasing her with a worm, and her screaming loud enough to loosen the outdated popcorn finish on our ceilings. She's just too quiet."

Fat chance of Maggie not complaining about the noise, but I let it pass. "Honey, she's been pretty sick. And children generally hate hospitals. I'm betting you'll see a huge difference as soon as she heads out the front door of that place. Anything we can do for you until then?"

"Just keep praying. I can't wait to get out of here and back to normal, noisy and busy as that is."

"I'll check on you later. Meanwhile, get some rest. You'll need it when things do get back to normal. Any word from your sister?"

"She stayed here with us last night, but she had to run home early this morning. I managed to grab a couple hours of sleep while she held Tori. It seems that Craig is going along with whatever she wants for the wedding, but she still doesn't seem happy about it. You don't think—"

Maggie stopped, as if afraid she'd been about to add to

my worries. I was already carrying that one anyhow, so I reassured her. "No, I don't think she'll cancel the wedding or break it off with Craig. She's having a severe case of pre-wedding jitters, most likely caused by taking almost an entire year to plan the enormous event. With any luck, she'll realize that and calm down."

"I hope so. I like Craig, and he's perfect for her. Calm in the face of her panic, sure of what he wants."

"I couldn't agree more. We just have to keep an eye on her. And on the chartreuse swatches."

Maggie laughed, and we hung up. Deb came into the kitchen, looking sick. "I'm going to need some help cleaning up outside. The noise Kitty and I heard on the terrace last night must've been a bear. Our garbage is scattered all over the side yard and the terrace."

We all grabbed trash bags and headed to the disaster area.

"This looks deliberate to me, not the work of some random bear," I said, positive Jack had tightly secured the trash can's lid.

"Kitty, don't go all paranoid on us," Jack said. "A farm wife knows how wild animals eagerly hunt for a cheap supper."

"Yes, Jack, but I've never seen an animal smear liquids on the back side of our house or porch. And there are chunks of food in this mess. A hungry animal wouldn't have left those behind."

Jack plopped his trash bag down and headed for the garage, Leo on his heels. Before I could navigate around to that side of the house, they returned.

"Both vehicles are locked up tight," Leo said, "but someone or something tried to break in. There are scratch marks around the lock. Lucky for us, the lock didn't give."

"I don't think a bear would have a need for an antique

car," Deb said. "They generally travel on foot. Or is it on paw? Anyhow, you should call Chief Wilburn."

I totally agreed.

Jack went inside to make the call while the rest of us cleaned up the mess.

"Maybe we should have left this for Wilburn's men. They might've cleaned it up," Deb said.

"I doubt that, but it's too late now. He'll have to take our word for it, and there are the scratches on the garage door to prove someone was here."

Leo took the trash bags and stuffed them into the can again, grunting like an angry hog as he hoisted a large rock on the top to secure the lid.

"Wilburn says his men are tied up at the moment, but he'll send someone out later this afternoon," Jack said as he stepped back outside. "We might as well go on out to the Beadles' and pick up the car."

As we headed inside to wash the gunk off our hands, I wondered about the noises we'd heard in the woods behind our cabin last night. Had someone been there watching while we chatted on the porch? If so, who? And why? Couldn't have been Charlie Beadle. His cousin, maybe? And why toss our trash? Why not break in? Because there were too many of us to tackle at once? Or had this been some sort of prank? And what if the prankster had gotten into the garage? *Best not to even think about that possibility.*

"This whole thing is getting pretty scary," Deb whispered as Jack carefully backed Sadie and the trailer out of the garage. "I can't wait to get home."

"Neither can I."

"Until we get back home, you gals stick together," Jack ordered. "Don't even go to the bathroom alone. You hear me, Kitty?" Like most men, Jack could hear a whisper when it was important to him and ignore a shout, pretending to be deaf, when it suited his needs.

"Not to worry, I'm thoroughly spooked. But promise me you and Leo will stick together. And if we're inside the house, call me when you're ready to load the car onto the trailer. I want to be there."

"Don't you trust me to handle your baby with care?"

Of course I trusted him. Just not the others on that farm.

TWENTY-TWO

MOSE BEADLE STEPPED OUT of his barn, wiping his hands on an old rag. He motioned Jack and Leo to meet him there. I hauled myself out of Sadie's back seat and sniffed the air. The aroma filtering through Medina Beadle's dotted Swiss curtains and out into the yard was every bit as inviting as the other times we'd been here. Pie cooling on the window sill, possibly peach this time? And a whiff of chicken frying?

"I wonder if the Beadles eat fried chicken for most of their dinners," Deb speculated when I moved to her side of the car. "Seems like we smell it every time we come out here."

"Doesn't smell like chicken this time. I haven't seen any cows in those fields getting fat for the slaughter house, so unless Mose Beadle deer hunts and freezes the meat, they probably do eat a lot of chicken." I glanced toward the hen house.

"I figured they kept the chickens just for the fresh eggs. Are you saying she kills the chickens and cooks them?" Deb looked shocked.

No doubt about it—Debby Evans had always been a city girl. "Medina Beadle probably wrings those chickens' necks with her nice, strong farmwife hands, then plucks the feathers out before cleaning, cutting up, and frying the bird in that big iron pan on her ancient stove."

"Please don't tell me you've personally wrung the necks of all the chickens you've fed Leo and me over the years."

"Rest easy on that score."

Deb didn't seem to mind that we raised our own beef for the freezer and that she'd eaten many a steak or roast from same. Guess it depended on who was doing the slaughtering.

I figured it was best not to mention that when Jack and I were newlyweds, still wet behind the ears and living with his parents, my dear, gentle mother-in-law raised her own chickens, providing large brown eggs for breakfast as well as meat for the supper table. When she'd passed away, and we took over the farm, Jack, bless him, was smart enough to sell what was left of the flock and let me buy frozen fowl at the local grocery store. I'd always wondered about his mother's ability to kill something she'd raised, fry it, and plunk it down on the supper table without turning a hair.

Apparently Medina Beadle had the same cast-iron stomach. I felt a chill in the warm morning air. Would she have been able to carry that kind of nerve even further—to the point of killing her own son? And assuming she could, why? Because of his criminal past?

Which wasn't all that bad, considering. No, I just didn't see how it could be her.

And her eyes weren't cold like a killer's were supposed to be.

But what about Mose Beadle? His hands were large and calloused from farm work, but he seemed like such a gentle man. And his mother-in-law certainly didn't appear to consider him strong enough to kill his own son. Sassy Bentley had strong hands, but how would she have gotten the body into that ditch, assuming she'd killed her own grandson?

I shook my head, unable to make sense of any of this mess. It had to be the cousin, Jerry. Or even someone else we didn't know. Well, we'd load the car up today and check in with Chief Wilburn. Surely he'd let us go home by now, given that there was no evidence to connect us with Charlie Beadle's murder except for the lying cousin, and Copper Penny had taken care of that issue for us.

My hands itched to get ahold of Jerry Beadle. Could he be the one who'd followed us to the concert and tried to break into Sadie's trunk? If so, how had he gotten into the theater, with most of the tickets sold out? Had he paid a couple of visits to our cabin? Maybe staged a "bear raid" or two? I'd see what I could find out from the women first.

Another couple of sniffs as we headed to the front porch and I decided the smell coming from Medina Beadle's kitchen this time wasn't chicken.

"It's ham," I told Deb. "Probably baking beneath a pineapple-and-brown-sugar glaze in that antique oven. And rhubarb pie, if my farmwife nose is any judge."

Jack wasn't a rhubarb fan, so I rarely used it in my own recipes, but the smell was making me nostalgic, not to mention hungry.

"Believe it or not," Deb said, "I've never had rhubarb pie."

"I'll have to see to it that your palate becomes better educated," I promised.

Medina Beadle stepped out onto the front porch, wiping her hands on the ever-present gingham apron. "You ladies are welcome to come inside and have something cool to drink while the menfolk load up the car. Seems like the weather's turned warm again."

"Love to," I said.

Deb practically ran me over getting up the steps. No moss grew on her detecting skills.

Seated at the ample kitchen table once again, I glanced around. Everything looked the same as last time. I wondered where Sassy Bentley was, but I didn't have to wonder long.

"Medina!" she shouted from somewhere near the kitchen. Medina set glasses of tea in front of Deb and me and moved beyond the doorway. We could hear her whispering something to her mother.

"I'm not an invalid," Sassy Bentley said, not bothering to whisper back. "Either you push this chair into the kitchen or I'll get there by myself."

A muffled protest was followed by a grunting sound, and I presumed the elderly woman was making good on her threat to push herself into the kitchen. Seconds later the wheelchair appeared in the doorway, pushed by Medina. I wondered if Sassy Bentley had crocheted the brightly colored, lacy shawl wrapped tightly around her shoulders. I couldn't fault her for wearing it, even in a kitchen that was quickly moving past toasty to downright hot. I'd survived menopause—complete with hot flashes and Jack threatening to divorce me every time I fanned the bed covers—only to find myself now totally unable to bear a cold draft touching me anywhere on my upper body.

"You here for the car again?" Sassy Bentley pulled the shawl even tighter as her chair reached the table.

Before I could answer, she turned to her daughter. "Medina, I told you not to raise the kitchen windows. It's plumb chilly in here. I need a cup of hot tea, not that tasteless cold stuff you and Mose drink."

"I can't cook in a warm kitchen, Mother." Medina slid the kettle onto a front burner and lit it with a long match. Sassy Bentley turned her attention back to me. "You didn't answer my question."

I didn't bother to mention she hadn't given me a chance. "Yes, ma'am, we're here for the car, unless you've changed your mind about selling it to us."

"Why do you want that old car anyway?" she demanded, leaning forward and peering at me over her glasses with the same intense look I'd given my students whenever I'd wanted to sift the wheat from the chaff of excuses they usually gave me. And obviously forgetting she'd asked me this question when we were here before.

I took a deep breath. "I love old cars, particularly the bulky, square models made back in the Thirties and Forties. I've always wanted to own one, to drive, not to show. Somehow those decades always seemed magical to me, even though I wasn't born until the late Forties."

Sassy Bentley nodded. "It was a magical time, certainly better than now, wars and the Depression notwithstanding." She reached for a handkerchief edged with a crocheted ruffle and wiped her mouth. I wondered if she dipped snuff, like so many of her generation had. She tucked the handkerchief back into her pocket and cleared her throat.

"Yes, we still want to sell the car. Mose says your check cleared the bank, and a Bentley doesn't go back on her word. The car is yours."

"Thank you" was all I could think of to say.

"No thanks necessary. That was my Herman's first car. He was mighty proud of her. Kept her shined and polished. We had us some good times in Betty. But I can't drive her anymore. No sense letting her go to waste."

"Betty?" Deb asked, glancing at me.

"Yes, ma'am, Betty for the actress Betty Grable, every man's pin-up girl in the last big war. Maybe you've seen the picture of her posing in a swim suit, showing off her million-dollar legs? Herman's crew had a copy of it painted on the side of their plane. That plane made it through many a dangerous bombing mission during World War Two without taking a single bullet. Herman's crewmen swore the enemy had too much respect to fire a bullet into a woman like her. That's men for you."

She shook her head, white curls dancing in the light from the nearby window. "But if it brought them all home safely, then that's what really mattered."

"I think Betty is a perfect name for her," I said. "Much better than Old Blue, which is what I was planning to call her."

Sassy Bentley reached across the table and took my hand. "I'm mighty happy to see her go to a woman like you, someone who will appreciate Betty and treat her with care." She turned to her daughter again. "Medina, cut these fine ladies a piece of that there rhubarb pie." She turned back to us. "Now please, don't refuse. My daughter makes the best rhubarb pie in the county. I tried for years to get her to enter one at the county fair, but she wouldn't hear of it. Too shy."

Out of the corner of my eye I saw Deb sit up straighter. I was afraid she'd blurt out the fact that we'd learned about the awards Sassy Bentley won at the county fair while reading back issues of the newspaper and give away the fact that we'd been checking up on the family. I should've known better. When she needed to be, Deb could be as subtle as a summer rain storm, covering you before you even knew you were in danger of getting wet.

"Did you ever enter anything in the county fair, Mrs. Bentley?" Even I couldn't tell Deb's smile was fake. I was impressed. She was obviously hoping to get Sassy Bentley to open up about herself, and we certainly needed to know more about this family if we were ever going to figure out why the son and heir was suddenly dead. And whether or not their elusive nephew was involved in the theft of my camera and the other odd incidents.

"I won a prize every year for my canned green beans

with ham hock, my carrot juice, and my rhubarb jelly, until I broke my hip. And people still talk about my pickled peaches."

My mouth watered. I hadn't had pickled peaches in years. And she'd canned her prize winners on that old stove? The difficulty of regulating the temperature boggled my mind. This was one tough lady.

"Most young people don't can their own food nowadays," Sassy Bentley continued. "Such a shame. Factory canning takes all the taste out. Not to mention the vitamins. What about you two ladies? Do either of you raise a garden?"

Deb cleared her throat. "I'm pretty much a city girl, so I stick to a flower garden. But Kitty and I used to work together in her vegetable garden, sharing the expenses and the chores. And I took home half of what we canned. We just couldn't manage it this year."

Sassy Bentley looked at me as if to see if it was my fault we no longer carried on the canning tradition. It was.

"I'm afraid my accident put me completely out of commission this year." I gestured at my cane. "I used to fix pickled peaches, but Jack didn't care for them, and as we got older and our girls left home, I had to cut back to preserving only the items we really needed for the pantry, like green beans and tomatoes. Thankfully, some of our friends from church shared their home-canned goods with us, which means we won't starve this winter."

Sassy Bentley nodded, so I'd passed muster on the homegrown versus store-bought-goods issue.

"Medina cans for us now. I can't stand up long enough for much of anything except the move back and forth from this chair to my bed. I miss being able to do things with my hands, though I still do a bit of sewing now and then, to help Medina out. And I can still tend to my garden, thanks to Mose building those plant beds for me." Sassy smiled at her daughter. "Mose never liked pickled peaches, either, so we don't have them anymore. Probably don't need all that sugar anyhow. Gotta keep our trim figures."

Medina Beadle smiled back at her mother, the first time I'd seen either woman do that.

"I bet she really appreciates your help," I said. "With, um, a husband working on farm machinery, and all, that takes a lot of mending." I swallowed hard. I'd very nearly said "With boys on a farm," which would have reminded Medina and Sassy of their recent loss. I glanced at Deb, hoping she'd bail me out as usual. She didn't have to. Sassy Bentley was still curious about my background.

"I seem to remember you said you were a farmwife," she said.

"Yes, but I worked off the farm, in the county school system, teaching."

"What grade did you teach?" she asked as Medina Beadle placed the delicious-smelling pieces of rhubarb pie in front of Deb and me, then returned with a piece for herself and her mother. She took the last seat at the table. Medina looked worn out. I didn't imagine she'd had much sleep lately. Yet her eyes weren't puffy from crying. Probably still in shock. I took a bite of pie, savored it then answered the question.

"I started out teaching junior high, but I spent most of my years working with the fourth-grade class. When I retired last year, I substitute taught at the high school. Whole different ball game there."

"Medina, this pie is wonderful," Deb said, cutting off a large piece of crust and sampling it. "I can never get my crusts to come out this tender."

"Probably work it too much," Sassy Bentley informed her. "Makes them tough. And cut back on the flour." She turned to me. "I don't understand young men today. Or young women, for that matter. They wear clothes my mother would have whipped me over if I'd dared step outside this house onto the front porch in them."

I nodded. "I once had a student show up for my class wearing pajama bottoms, a T-shirt, and fuzzy house shoes. I sent her straight to the principal's office. Students love nothing better than testing a substitute's mettle. The principal suspended her, and by the time her suspension was up, the regular teacher was back."

Deb cleared her throat. "Kitty had a run-in with a rather rude young man yesterday. He knocked her over when we were leaving the restaurant after breakfast. And we think he stole her camera." Score one for Deb. I hadn't been able to think of a way to bring the subject up.

Medina Beadle's mouth formed a silent O. Neither woman spoke for a moment. Then Sassy Bentley said, "I'm sorry to hear that. I suppose you won't be able to publish the book about old barns now."

I glanced at Deb. Was the older woman concerned about the proposed book or about something I might have caught with my camera? Perhaps something the family hadn't wanted me to see. What should I say? I decided to make sure they knew the pictures were safe in a place where no one here could delete them.

"I stored the first group of pictures I took in my e-mail program on the Internet, including the barn and outbuildings here, and the car we bought from you. I lost all the pictures I'd taken after our last visit here. But since those first pictures are secure, the book is still on track."

And boy howdy, was I glad my daughter had called and demanded to see pictures of the car. Otherwise, things would have been much worse.

"If you saw the thief," Sassy Bentley said, "maybe the police will catch him and get your camera back for you."

"It all happened so fast, I didn't see anything," I admitted, "and I doubt they'll ever catch him. Far too many other more important crimes to solve. But I'd sure like to get my hands on him. That camera was a gift. One I'm not happy to lose. Whoever stole it could use some good old-fashioned discipline."

Sassy Bentley nodded. "Children today don't know how to earn things. Much easier to take them from others. Don't parents teach them anything?"

Medina Beadle said, "Seems like children have to test adults, to see where the limits are. They don't realize the limits are there to protect them."

She covered her face with her apron and began to sob. Deb squeezed Medina's shoulder. I felt like an idiot for letting the conversation go in the wrong direction again. I should've been more careful. She was obviously grieving over her dead son. And if Medina suspected her nephew had stolen my camera and injured me in the process, it would only add to her burden. Sassy Bentley sat quietly, watching her daughter but offering no comfort.

"I'm sorry, Medina," I said. "We shouldn't be discussing this in front of you. Can I get you something?" I stood and made my way to the sink. Through the curtains I could see Jack easing Sadie and the trailer toward the barn, his chat with Mose Beadle over. I grabbed a clean glass out of the dish drainer and filled it with cool water. I wondered if the well water tasted as good as ours.

When I returned to the table, Medina Beadle had dried her eyes. She took a gulp of water and thanked me.

"Don't apologize," she said. "You couldn't have known. Our boy had to test the limits, too. That's what put him where he is today and—"

"Medina," Sassy interrupted, "these good ladies don't need to hear all of our troubles. Why don't you get us some more tea. Or would you ladies prefer hot coffee?"

"Not for me, thanks," I said. I didn't want to put Medina Beadle to any more trouble, and I suspected Jack would be loading the car any minute.

"Nothing for me, either," Deb said. "That pie filled me up."

Jack honked Sadie's horn, letting me know he was ready to start the loading operation, and we all moved to the front porch. I'd given strict orders that I wanted to be there to make sure my car was secured properly. And I wanted to make sure Jack and Leo were safe, just in case. I gave Medina Beadle a hug and leaned down to hug Sassy Bentley.

"You've been very kind to us," Sassy said. "I wonder... The boy's funeral is scheduled for day after tomorrow." She crooked a finger at me.

I scrunched down closer to her as best I could.

"Mose and Medina have lots of friends from their church and the community. Most of mine are either dead or so near to it that they don't get out much anymore." She looked up at me. "Would you folks mind coming to the funeral? And you'd be welcome to come back here after, for the gathering."

Attending the funeral of a stranger, a young man I hadn't liked much, was the last thing I wanted to do. But it would give us a chance to meet people who knew the family, and maybe find out some information we could pass on to the police. And no way did I want to say "no" to the look in her eyes. Sassy Bentley might be a cranky, crippled old woman, but behind that tough front there was a deep sadness in her eyes. And something else. Fear. But fear of what?

"We'll try, but we may have to leave for home right away. Family illness. I'll let you know."

"I understand." Sassy Bentley squeezed my hand.

"C'mon, Kitty," Jack yelled out of Sadie's window. "You insisted you wanted to oversee the loading operation. Make sure we don't put any new scratches on your car."

What I really wanted to do was find out what was bothering Sassy Bentley, but Jack obviously was ready to get the job done and drive back to the cabin, so Deb and I headed out to the barn.

TWENTY-THREE

INSIDE THE BARN, Mose Beadle greeted Deb and me, wiping sweat from his brow with a red bandanna. I wondered if he had as many of those bright bandannas tucked inside his underwear drawer as Jack did, and if he hung the sweaty things up to dry in the kitchen—like Jack often tried with his, rather than in the utility room where they belonged.

Someone stepped from behind the old car, startling me. It was the same young man I'd seen on our first visit, the one who'd disappeared into a nearby shed when he'd seen us. And the same one who'd tried to involve Jack in his cousin's murder.

"This here's my nephew, Jerry Beadle," Mose Beadle said.

The boy nodded but didn't speak or offer to shake hands. I saw Jack frown at that. He was raised in a time where men shook hands with other men and took off their baseball caps in the presence of ladies. This kid did neither. I looked him over carefully, but since I hadn't seen the culprit, I couldn't tell if he was the one who'd stolen Deb's purse or mowed me down at breakfast. He wasn't quite as heavy as Deb's attacker.

I glanced at Deb and saw her eyebrows go up, a sign that she might have recognized him as the guy who'd knocked me down. As soon as the car was safely loaded, I'd try to start a conversation with him, maybe get to know him a little. Until then, I'd keep an eye on him and see what sort of impression I got.

Mose Beadle stepped aside and I glanced beyond him toward where my car was stored. There she still squatted, as if she'd been waiting for me to come back and rescue her from the dark old barn. Betty Blue. The combination of the two names popped into my head. Maybe that's what she wanted me to call her. Jack would want to restore her original dark blue paint job and make her look the same as she had the day she'd rolled off the assembly line so she'd be more valuable. Which was fine with me, as long as he got the restoration done quickly so Betty Blue and I could hit the road. We had places to go and people to see.

I moved out of the way to let Leo guide Jack as he backed Sadie and the all-important trailer closer to the old car. Jack turned off the motor and the men approached the trailer to help with the loading operation. Driving up onto and/or winching a vehicle up any type of ramp always made me nervous. I worried that the vehicle would miss a lick and roll off. I tended to stay as far out of the way as possible, so I moved to stand near the large barn door. Deb joined me, and we watched as Mose Beadle and Leo began pulling the ramp from beneath the trailer. Jerry Beadle stopped imitating a fence post long enough to unwind the huge cable from the front of the trailer and back slowly toward Betty Blue with it.

"You seem more excited now that it's nearly a done deal," Deb said. "I was beginning to worry about you."

"I can't help but be excited. I've wanted a car like this for as long as I can remember. I just wish things had gone better for the Beadles."

"So do I. And I hate to say it, but that boy could easily be the one who knocked you down and stole your camera. When the car is safely loaded, why don't you—"

A shout from Jerry Beadle at the rear of the trailer followed by a yelp of anguish at the front cut off Deb's words.

I could only see a part of the boy rolling around on the ground, cradling his left arm, and using words I hadn't heard since I'd stopped substitute teaching high-school kids.

Leo moaned from the other side of the trailer, but I couldn't see him. Deb got to Leo's side so quickly, she must have leaped over the entire trailer. It took me a bit longer to get there, having to use my cane, and glancing around to make sure Jack was okay as I moved.

Leo rolled back and forth on the barn floor, covered in dust and hay bits, clutching his chest. At first I thought he was having a heart attack, until I saw the blood.

"Somebody call 9-1-1," Deb ordered.

I dug in my tote bag and came out with the cell phone. Jerry stopped swearing and began yelling in pain. His arm was bleeding a lot. So was Leo's chest. I swallowed hard. The dispatcher promised to send help right away. I shut the phone and knelt by Leo and Deb. Jack applied pressure on Leo's chest to stop the bleeding.

Mose Beadle stood frozen. He hadn't moved since the shouting began. "Help your nephew," I said. "An ambulance is on the way, but his arm is bleeding a lot. You need to put pressure on it."

Beadle continued to stare at Leo for a few more seconds before finally moving to his nephew's aide. In the background I could hear him urging the boy to lie still as he assessed the injury, but most of my attention was focused on Leo.

"What happened?" I asked Jack.

"That dumb kid let go of the cable," Jack said in a low voice, "and it flew up and hit Leo smack in the chest. He could have killed one of us. I reminded him to use both hands but he didn't listen. He should have known better than to—"

Whatever he should have known better about was lost as Medina Beadle entered the barn and said, "What on earth is going on out here? Mother said she could hear somebody yelling from clear inside the house."

Catching a glimpse of Leo on the ground and hearing her nephew squealing like a stuck pig in the background, Medina Beadle quickly took in the situation and headed back for the barn door.

"I'll get some towels to help stop the bleeding. Anyone call for help, or should I?"

"I did," I assured her. "Please hurry with the towels. They're both bleeding quite a bit."

Medina Beadle returned with several towels and the next few minutes were spent mopping blood off the injured and trying to remember what we'd learned about first aid and where to apply pressure correctly without damaging anything. Leo was in and out of focus, mostly out. Every time he shut his eyes and stopped moaning, Deb panicked and urged him to "stay with us." I knew she was trying to keep him awake, fending off the possibility of losing him, but staying alert was extremely painful for him.

My leg was killing me from squatting so long, so I lowered myself the rest of the way to the dusty, hay-strewn floor and gave Deb and Jack supportive pats on the arm every few minutes. At long last we heard the welcome wail of a siren. Help had arrived, unless they missed the turn the way we had on our first trip. Before I could struggle to my feet to hobble outside and flag the ambulance down, I heard the old farm truck wheeze to life as someone ground gears and headed down the driveway. Through the open barn door I saw Medina Beadle shoot toward the end of the long driveway to meet the ambulance.

It seemed like decades later when we arrived at the emergency room of the county hospital. Since Leo and

Jerry were transported in the same ambulance, both were fast-tracked into the ER, and within seconds a doctor was attending to them. Deb had ridden up front with the ambulance driver, and Jack had quickly unhitched the trailer from Sadie, and we'd followed closely behind.

Mose and Medina Beadle declined our offer of a ride, choosing to drive to the hospital in their old farm truck. From the looks of it, I wasn't convinced it could make the trip, but they arrived shortly after we did, without Medina's mother. Upon checking in at the ER we were all quickly ordered into the waiting room. Except for Deb, who stuck to Leo's side.

I was a bit surprised when Medina Beadle didn't go in and sit with Jerry, or at least call his parents. I supposed she might have called them at some point, but if she did, they never showed up.

The small waiting room was crammed full. I glanced around hoping for a chair. A couple of mothers comforted crying children and exchanged symptoms that sounded like strep for one of the children, chicken pox for the other. A pretty young woman held an ice bag on her knee, chatting loudly with someone across the room, and an elderly man looked around as if he didn't know where he was. Between the chattering and the television blaring, it was difficult to hear myself think. We were supposed to be on a pleasure trip, exhibiting our cars and buying one for me. But between the theft of Deb's purse, the murder of Charlie Beadle, questioning by the police, my fall, and Leo's accident, I wished heartily that we'd stayed home.

We found seats near the exit, and I gratefully plopped into one. The Beadles took seats nearby. I tried to read a magazine but couldn't focus on the pages for worrying. How had Leo and Jerry been injured? Jack and Leo had loaded and unloaded cars from trailers dozens of times.

They could practically do it in their sleep. So how had the winch gotten loose? I wished I'd watched the loading operation closer instead of gabbing with Deb.

Jack paced more than he sat. Mose Beadle twisted his faded baseball cap back and forth until I figured it wouldn't fit on his head anymore. Medina Beadle stared out the hospital window at the parking lot and chewed her lower lip.

At long last Deb came into the waiting room. "Leo has severe bruising to his chest and a deep cut from the winch hook, but the doctor says he'll be fine in a few days. They're getting ready to stitch up the cut."

I hadn't realized I'd been holding my breath until I heaved a sigh of relief.

"Does that mean he'll be released to go back to the cabin with us tonight?" Jack asked.

"Not yet. The doctor wants to keep him here overnight for observation. I'm going to stay with him. They're waiting for a room to be available so they can move him."

I stood and hugged her. "Deb, I'm so sorry about this. I never dreamed we'd have this much trouble over a car."

"Not your fault, but I would certainly like to get my hands on that little—" She stopped and glanced at the Beadles. Medina Beadle ducked her head.

"Can't blame you," Mose Beadle said, "I'd like to get my hands on Jerry myself, right now. I can't believe he didn't use both hands to hold on to that cable. Mr. Bloodworth and I both reminded him."

"According to the doctor, a severe blow to the chest with a large hook like that could very easily have been fatal," Deb said. "Leo doesn't have any health issues with his heart, which was a lucky break. But Jerry may have learned his lesson. The cable cut into his arm pretty deeply. The doctor says it will take quite a few stitches to sew it up."

"I wouldn't mind having a chat with young Jerry myself," Jack said. "Out behind the barn."

"C'mon, you two," I leaned over and whispered, "the kid is either backward or a jerk, but surely it was just an accident. He wouldn't intentionally injure himself along with Leo, would he?"

Deb shrugged, and Jack didn't answer.

"I need to get back in there with Leo," Deb said. "Look, this isn't your fault, and there's no use you two hanging around here. It'll be a while before they get Leo settled into a room. Why don't you go back to the cabin and rest? I'll call you in the morning and you can come by and pick us up."

"We'll go back to the cabin but not until we've seen Leo," Jack said. "I have to see for myself that he's okay."

"Ditto for me," I said. "And we'll get you something to eat. Unless you're willing to risk an unknown, untried hospital cafeteria?"

Deb smiled. "I'm not that brave. Chances are Leo will want something, too." She glanced at her watch. "Mercy, it is past lunchtime. But it seems like it should be bedtime. What a day."

What a day indeed.

TWENTY-FOUR

AFTER TUCKING LEO in and feeding Deb from a nearby fast-food restaurant, Jack and I headed back to the cabin. I'd about as soon face the bear again, rather than find Officer Franklin parked in our driveway.

"Hear you all had some excitement today," Franklin said as he stepped out of his patrol car.

"Might sound exciting to you," Jack said, "but it sure wasn't to us."

Jack's hands were stuffed in his pockets. He hadn't even tried to shake the officer's hand. I nudged him with my elbow. Jack Bloodworth was the kindest, most patient human being on the face of the earth, not to mention polite. If he was getting sarcastic with local law enforcement, then he'd truly reached the end of his tether.

"It's been a rough day, Officer Franklin," I said. And it wasn't over yet or he wouldn't be here. "I suppose you're here about my stolen camera? Or maybe the vandalism we found in the yard early this morning?"

Personally, I was ready to forget about all of it and go home. I didn't feel like helping Franklin fill out a dozen or so reports about scattered garbage after what happened to Leo. Blowing the whistle on Jerry Beadle for the possible theft of my camera I could manage, despite the kid's injured arm.

"Yes, the vandalism," Franklin said after a short pause. And I hadn't missed the odd look that slid quickly across his face before he'd responded. But if he wasn't here in response to our report this morning, or the theft of my camera, why was he here?

"Why don't we go inside and you can tell me all about it," Franklin suggested. "These fall evenings are a bit chilly for porch sitting."

He gestured toward the front door and Jack and I followed him like a couple of lost sheep. I was dying to signal Jack that something wasn't quite right, but his attention was on getting the key to the cabin out of his pocket and unlocking the door.

Inside, I dropped my tote bag on a handy chair and checked to see that everything was as we'd left it. It was, so I took a seat on the large leather couch, hoping Jack would join me there. Instead he headed toward the kitchen.

"Coffee, Officer Franklin?" Jack called over the counter. "Kitty? How about you? I need some stimulation."

I shook my head but Franklin nodded. Okay, so we were having coffee.

"I'll get us some cookies," I offered.

We were down to store-bought cookies, and not a lot of them left. Still, while I pretended to work in the kitchen, maybe I could signal Jack that something was up before he got us both arrested for who knew what. I limped to the kitchen and scrounged in the pantry. The cookies were a bit soft from the damp weather, so I checked the fridge and struck gold.

Seated again in the living room with a tray of steaming coffee and warmed-over apple fritters that I'd forgotten we'd brought home from the Apple Barn, and a fire crackling on the hearth, we got down to business.

"Tell me about the accident at the Beadles' farm this morning," Franklin said. "I've seen the report, but I'd like to hear your version."

An accident in a barn, involving one innocent bystander

and maybe one not so innocent, and the police department already received a report on it, sending someone out to investigate? So that's why Franklin was here. And what about the vandalism and the attempt to enter our garage by messing with the locks? What about my stolen camera? Why hadn't those events warranted a visit from the cops? I'd warned Jack while we were in the kitchen to watch what he said. Of course, he never listens.

"Mose Beadle's nephew, Jerry, was helping us load the car my wife and I bought from the Beadles onto a rental trailer." Jack shifted his weight, causing the cup to wobble on my knee. "Dumb kid let go of the cable. It flew up, cut his arm pretty badly, and the hook hit our friend Leo Evans smack in the chest. Luckily, Leo turned as it struck him, or it might've killed him."

"So you're saying it was the boy's fault?" Franklin asked.

"Dumb accident. At least it better have been an accident," Jack said.

"Meaning what, Mr. Bloodworth?" Franklin leaned forward.

I nudged Jack with my foot. He was gabbing way too much.

The warm apple fritter turned to stone in my throat.

"Meaning Mose Beadle and I both warned that boy to hang on to the cable with both hands, but he didn't listen. I glanced around just a second or two before it came out of his hand, and that's what's bothering me. He held it with only the one hand. His left hand. No wonder it got away from him."

"So you blame him for your friend's injury?"

"You bet I do. A kid who grows up on a farm should know how to be careful around any equipment. When I get my hands on him, I'll—"

"Jack!" This time I gave him a hard kick, hoping Franklin couldn't see my foot move behind the large coffee table.

"You'll do what, Mr. Bloodworth?" Franklin set his coffee cup on the nearby table and quickly jotted down something in his notebook. His expression reminded me of the cartoon vultures popular back in the Fifties, grinning down at their intended prey.

"Well, I wouldn't hurt him, of course, but I'd certainly give him a much needed talking-to," Jack finished lamely.

"Are you're sure that's all you'd do to him?"

"Of course he's sure," I said before Jack could dig himself in any deeper. "My husband never even spanked our girls. He wouldn't hurt Jerry Beadle, just give him an ear burning, which as Jack said, is richly deserved. Why are you so interested in this accident? How come nobody followed up on the vandalism we reported this morning? Or my stolen camera? Did someone file a complaint about the accident? Did the Beadles send you over here to find out if we plan to sue? Because if they did, there's something—"

"The Beadles didn't send me out here to talk to you. Chief Wilburn did. You'll have to come to the police station with me, Mr. Bloodworth, to answer a few more questions. We're really not satisfied about this."

"About an accident that wasn't even his fault?" I said.

Jack squeezed my hand. Now he was trying to shut me up.

"No, ma'am," Franklin said "To answer questions about the sudden death of Jerry Beadle, this afternoon."

TWENTY-FIVE

I FELT THE BLOOD rush to my face then drop clear back to my feet. Jerry Beadle was dead? What on earth had happened to him? According to Deb, his injury required several stitches, but surely it hadn't been fatal. He couldn't have bled to death. I felt as if I was in the kind of nightmare where I knew I was asleep but couldn't wake myself up.

"What happened to the boy?" Jack asked.

Franklin stood. "I think we'd best let Chief Wilburn fill you in on that, Mr. Bloodworth. Shall we go?"

I reached for my tote bag.

"No need for you to go, ma'am. I can bring Mr. Bloodworth back here when we're finished."

"Young man, my husband and I face difficult situations together, and this definitely qualifies. Either I go or Jack stays here. Take your pick."

Franklin looked me over as if deciding whether or not he could take me down, apparently decided not to try it, and we all climbed into his car.

I was tired enough to fall asleep, even on the hard back seat of a patrol car, but the way Franklin took corners and bounced up and down the hills, not to mention fear of what would happen to Jack, kept me wide awake. But how could the police blame Jack for Jerry Beadle's death? He'd been standing several feet away, watching Leo and the boy work with the cable when the accident happened.

I wished we had someone to accompany us to the police station. Our friends in the car club had formed the usual convoy and headed for home late this morning at our insistence, so it was just Leo and Deb now, and they were pretty well tied up at the hospital. I could call either of our daughters for emotional support, but I'd have to listen to a lot of hen squawking and lecture giving. Since they were six hours or better away from us, it would upset them for nothing. I might have to call them if things got any worse. But could they get much worse?

We arrived at the police station and Franklin escorted Jack into a windowless room. He left me in the room next door, promising to return shortly with Chief Wilburn. I could hardly wait. There were no large one-way mirrors that I could see, but I felt sure someone was keeping an eye on me.

After what seemed like hours, Chief Wilburn entered the room, carrying a file. He scraped a metal chair across the floor and dusted off the seat.

"Mrs. Bloodworth, thank you for coming to the station with Officer Franklin." Wilburn dropped the folder on the metal table and took the seat. "Although it really wasn't necessary for you to accompany your husband."

I didn't dignify that with an answer. Instead I said, "Why is Jack here?"

"We wanted to get his version of what happened to Jerry Beadle," Wilburn said. "And now, as long as you're here, I'd be interested in what you have to say."

"My version," I said, "is that we don't have a clue. The last time Jack or I saw that boy, he was in the emergency room, getting his arm sewed up."

"And how was his arm injured to begin with?" Chief Wilburn cocked his head to one side.

"By his own stupidity. He was supposed to pull the cable from the trailer to the car so the men could winch it up onto the trailer. Leo, Mr. Evans, had climbed up onto the trailer and began turning the handle on the winch. Mose Beadle and my husband were standing at the front of the trailer, waiting to help Leo with the winching operation. I heard them warn the boy to keep both hands on the cable, but he didn't pay attention."

"Where were you standing, Mrs. Bloodworth, when the accident happened?"

"Near the door of the barn. I didn't actually see the accident. I turned to talk to my friend Mrs. Evans. I heard someone shout, and Deb and I looked over to see what had happened. Leo was on the ground. I thought he'd had a heart attack until I saw the blood."

Remembering the blood, I swallowed hard. "Jerry Beadle was rolling around on the ground, screaming his guts out," I said. "Deb, Jack, and I went to help Leo, and I ordered Mose Beadle to help his nephew. I guess Mose was in shock. He stood there for several seconds then went to take care of the boy."

"Where were Mrs. Beadle and her mother during this time?" Chief Wilburn asked.

"Inside the house," I said. "Mrs. Beadle came out to the barn when she heard the noise. She got towels to help stop the bleeding. Then she drove the truck down to the end of the driveway so the ambulance people could find us."

"You and your husband both mentioned the injury to the boy's arm. Did you see any other injuries?"

"No."

"No swelling or bleeding around his head?

"No, I really didn't look that close. I was more concerned with our friend. But I think I would have noticed if his head was bloody."

Wilburn was silent for several seconds.

"I'm sure you've spoken to Mose Beadle about the accident," I said. "Didn't he tell you the same thing?"

"Mr. Beadle is very upset about the accident and his nephew's death. He doesn't seem to remember where anyone else was after the cable came loose, striking the two men. And neither he nor your husband can explain how Jerry Beadle came to have your husband's MedicAlert bracelet in his pocket."

That bombshell certainly made my mouth drop. "I don't know how he came to have Jack's MedicAlert bracelet, either. But Jack rarely wears that bracelet ever since it got hung on something while he was working on his Fifty-Seven engine. He's afraid it might cause him an injury, so he keeps it in his pocket most of the time and carries an alert card in his wallet for extra measure. Jack could have lost the bracelet at the farm and Jerry Beadle found it, or he might even have stolen it. It's silver, not brass, and a bit expensive. Our daughter gave it to him."

Chief Wilburn appeared to study me. I returned the favor.

"What happened to the boy?" I asked. "Stitches in his arm should not have been fatal. Why are you treating this like something other than an accident?"

"He collapsed and died shortly after returning home, according to the EMT who responded to the 9-1-1 call from the Beadles."

"But that isn't possible," I insisted. "My friend Deb was in the ER with her husband. She said Jerry seemed fine to the point of driving the staff nuts with his complaints, and his injury wasn't nearly as serious as Leo's."

Chief Wilburn shrugged. "The autopsy is scheduled for tomorrow morning. Which means I'll have to insist that you folks not leave the area, at least for now. Not until we've investigated further. The deaths of two young men in the same family in this short a time is something we can't ignore."

"We couldn't leave anyhow," I said. "Our friend is still in the hospital."

Chief Wilburn nodded. "I hope your friend recovers soon. Meanwhile, I'll be in touch."

Just what I didn't want to hear.

"Did you get the report about the vandalism at our cabin this morning?" I asked. "And the theft of my camera? Seems a bit strange that we've had problems at two different cabins since we met the Beadles."

"The security guard from the rental company checked the vandalism out and assured me the mess outside your cabin was caused by another bear raid," Wilburn said. "The neighbors spotted one that same night, and you people seem to be attracting the bears. Are you leaving your trash unsecured at night?"

"My husband is a retired farmer, so we're not that dumb. And neither one of these problems look to me like something an animal would do. For one thing, there was food in the trash and it wasn't touched. A bear would have eaten it. Are you going to investigate the camera theft? I know the deaths of the two young men takes priority and I wouldn't have it any other way, but what if these other incidents are somehow related?"

"I assure you, we will look into the theft of your camera," Wilburn said. "I have the report right here."

And I had to be satisfied with that.

TWENTY-SIX

OFFICER FRANKLIN DROPPED us back at the cabin, waved goodbye, and backed out of the driveway. Jack reached for the cabin key, but I stopped him.

"Let's go back to the hospital and check on Leo," I suggested. "I want to make sure he's okay."

"The doctor said he'd be fine in a few days," Jack said, "but I know you want to tell Deb what happened to Jerry Beadle, and I'm sure Leo will want to hear all about it, too."

Leo was propped up in his hospital bed when we arrived, and Deb was feeding him ice cream. I suspected he could've just as easily fed himself, but Leo wasn't one to pass up an opportunity to be pampered. And I was pretty sure Deb was humoring him. Close calls always seemed to wake people up to how precious life is, at least for a while.

"Come on in," Leo said, "I'm not contagious."

"You may not be, but the Beadles sure are. At least when it comes to bad luck," Jack began.

I elbowed him into silence. No sense jumping right into what happened to Jerry Beadle. We could at least take a couple of minutes to see how Leo was doing, though he looked pretty chipper to me.

"How's it going?" I asked.

Leo gently tapped the bandage on his chest. "Still mighty sore. Doubt I'll be chopping wood any time soon."

Deb snickered. "You haven't chopped wood for our fireplace in at least two decades, which is why I had a gas log installed."

Leo grinned at her. "Never know when I might need to chop some, but not tonight, nor tomorrow."

I glanced around Leo's room. Getting proper care in a rural area could sometimes be a challenge, but this small hospital was very clean and up-to-date. The staff had treated Leo quickly and courteously, and his room was large, private, and had all the bells and whistles generally found in larger city hospitals.

Deb dropped the empty ice-cream carton into the trash can beside Leo's bed, dusted her hands together, and turned to me. "Okay, what's going on with the Beadles now? And don't tell me it's nothing. You two wouldn't be here when visiting hours ended if something wasn't wrong."

Jack and I looked at each other. I nodded for him to speak.

Not one for preambles, Jack dropped his bomb. "Jerry Beadle died this afternoon."

Leo's jaw flopped open, and Deb turned pale. "What happened? He didn't appear to be that badly injured," Deb said. "Fact of the matter, I thought he was overdoing it just a tad in the ER. Yelling at the top of his lungs. I'm surprised they didn't knock him out or throw him out."

"I was wondering if he was faking, too," Jack said. "Not the cut, nor the stitches, of course. And the blood was real enough. But something about that accident worries me."

As usual, Jack was talking all around the subject. "Officer Franklin was waiting in the driveway when we got back to the cabin," I said. "We assumed he wanted to talk about the vandalism we discovered in the yard this morning, or my missing camera, but he was only interested in the accident at the barn. He asked us all kinds of questions about it. I demanded to know why he was talking to us about an accident that wasn't our fault, and he said Jerry Beadle was dead. He took Jack and me to the police station so Chief Wilburn could personally question Jack. Again."

"What did the kid die of?" Leo asked. Deb perched on the side of his bed and held his hand. I suppose it was dawning on all of us that if the kid died as a result of the accident, Leo might still somehow be at risk from his chest injury.

"Chief Wilburn didn't tell us," Jack said. "The boy collapsed and died after he got home from the hospital."

"Why did they question you two?" Deb asked.

Jack squirmed. "He had my MedicAlert bracelet in his pocket. Chief Wilburn wanted to know how it got there. I don't have any idea."

"Chief Wilburn asked me if there was any bruising or blood on the boy's head. I told him I didn't remember seeing any. Did you notice any injuries besides the cut on his arm, Deb?" I asked.

"I was pretty busy with Leo, and I really didn't look in on him at the emergency room. I was too angry. But no, I don't remember him yelling about his head, just his arm."

"I was pretty busy on the barn floor," Leo said, "holding on to my chest to keep it from falling off, so I didn't pay much attention to the kid. Later on, when the pain meds kicked in, I wanted to strangle him. Guess I won't have the chance now."

Graveyard humor. Jack and Leo both excelled at it.

"Don't say anything like that in front of the chief, unless you want to be questioned by him," I said. "And we've been ordered to stick around a few more days while they investigate further. I can't remember a vacation that turned into this big a disaster."

"Well, there was that time I accidentally got locked out of our motel room," Jack said, "and I was only wearing—"

A swift poke with my cane cut him off. I could tell Deb was all ears, but she was too good a friend to pursue the subject. At least not until she and I were alone.

"We need to try to figure this out, if we can," I said, "so we can go home soon."

"Kitty, just because we solved your cousin's murder, and we joined the Paducah Citizen's Police Academy, that certainly doesn't make us real detectives. Let the local officers solve this," Jack said.

"I just think we should make a trip out to the farm and sniff around," I said. "And we still have to load up my car."

"I agree," Leo said, "but that 'we' needs to include Deb and me." He pointed to his chest. "We've earned it, and you two would surely get into trouble out there without us."

Deb nodded.

"The nurse said the doctor will release me tomorrow afternoon if I'm still doing okay," Leo said. "I know I'm not going to feel up to a six-hour ride home, and since you've been ordered to hang around here anyhow, why not spend the time checking out the Beadles again?"

It was three against one, so Jack caved. "But we stay together at all times while we're out there," he said. "And Mose Beadle and I will load the car while you three keep a safe distance."

Leo and Deb nodded; my head didn't move.

They might agree to keep a safe distance, but I planned to be close enough to see that Jack didn't have any "accidents" while loading the car. And did I even still want the thing? Betty Blue was beautiful, and the thought of leaving her behind to rot in that old barn made my head hurt, but she represented a lot of bad luck that had happened to her owners. Did I want to bring that reminder home with us?

As usual, Jack read my mind. "We're keeping that car, Kitty. Old Blue no more carries ghosts in her trunk than Sadie does in hers. And Mose Beadle said a deal's a deal, so she's ours."

"Sassy Bentley said her name is Betty, not Old Blue," I informed Jack.

"Whatever. But you will keep a safe distance while Mose Beadle and I load Betty. The two of us can manage, assuming he hasn't changed his mind and wants to cancel the deal this time."

I didn't know which possibility to pray for. But I had to agree, a group visit to the Beadle farm was the obvious move for our new detecting team. And if Jack wanted me at a safe distance, that was fine. I'd spend my time talking to Medina Beadle and her mother. After chatting with Sassy Bentley several times, I knew for a fact that she wasn't nearly as confused as Jerry Beadle had wanted the police department to believe. And I'd bet she knew a whole lot more about the deaths of her grandson and great-nephew than the police discovered to date.

We were headed back to the cabin when I got Maggie's phone call. I was beginning to dread these calls. Seemed like lately neither of us had any really good news to share, and I hated keeping things back from her. Like the murder of Charlie and Jerry Beadle's sudden death and the chief questioning her father over it. But I'd have to tell her about Leo's accident because we really couldn't leave now unless it was a severe emergency. Deb and Leo needed us. Before I could barely start a conversation, Maggie's frantic voice broke in.

"Mom, Tori's left lung collapsed. They're airlifting us to the children's hospital in Louisville in a few minutes."

"Oh, Maggie, I'm so sorry. She must be absolutely terrified."

I bit my lip to keep from bursting into tears. I knew first hand how painful a collapsed lung was, having suffered one along with the broken leg in the car accident, and it wasn't an experience I'd wish on anyone else, certainly not a small child.

"You'd be so proud of her, Mom. She hasn't cried a bit. Probably because she's too busy breathing, but she's really being brave."

"I'll be there as quickly as I can. I'll boot up Deb's laptop as soon as possible and buy a plane ticket. I can probably be there by—"

"Mother, you are not to come home right now. Joe and Billy are driving to Louisville in the van. There isn't room for them on the helicopter. But there's really nothing you can do. The doctor assures us Tori will be fine once they get her into the intensive-care unit."

"Can't they take care of her in Metropolis?" A helicopter trip to Louisville seemed like a lot of stress for a small child already having difficulty just breathing.

"The doctor said they are far better equipped to handle a case like this at the children's hospital, and the flight doesn't take all that long. I trust her judgment, so we're making the flight. But chances are, by the time you could get there, Tori will be fine. I promise I'll keep you updated every chance I get."

"But—"

"'But me no buts,' Mom, as you were so fond of saying when we girls were little. Sunny's here, and she's riding in the van with the guys. If we need you, I'll call you. I give you my word."

I didn't know what to do. I wanted to be with my daughter and my granddaughter, but I was needed here, too. Except Maggie needed me a lot more.

"Maggie, I—"

"Mother, I mean it! You are not to try to fly to Louisville. I only called because I knew you'd probably be calling me to say goodnight and I wouldn't be able to keep from telling you what happened. If we do need you, I promise I'll let you know."

And I had to accept that. For now.

"Okay, I'll wait until I hear from you. We've got a bit of a problem here, anyhow. There was an accident while Dad and Leo were loading the car, and Leo was injured. He's staying in the hospital overnight so they can check him out."

"Is Dad okay? Are you and Deb okay?"

"We're all fine. The hook on the winch slipped while they were preparing to load the car, and it struck Leo in the chest. He's got a lovely bruise and Deb is staying at the hospital to keep an eye on him, but they should let him out tomorrow. I can leave as soon as we pick him up—"

"Mother, you are to stay right where you are. Deb and Leo need you, and I'll have Joe and Sunny with me. And Billy. I'll call you every hour, if need be, to keep you happy."

I reluctantly agreed, feeling torn, needing to be two places at once, as mothers so often did.

TWENTY-SEVEN

MEDINA BEADLE MET US on her front porch the next day. "Would you like to sit on the porch for a few minutes before you load the car? I'd invite you folks inside, like always, but Mother is feeling rather poorly this morning, and I'm afraid she'd insist on getting up to visit with you, Mrs. Bloodworth. She's become quite fond of you and your friend Mrs. Evans."

"Please, call me Kitty. And I'm quite fond of her, as well. I wouldn't want her to exert herself on my account. We can't stay long, anyway. We just came to load up the car."

"My man is out in the barn, making sure everything goes right this time." Medina wiped her hands on her apron, something she seemed to do when she was stressed, and sat down in the nearby rocker, for once empty of the hound dog.

"I'll back the car around and hook up the trailer again," Jack said. I'd forgotten that he'd dropped the trailer here yesterday during the emergency. "You ready, Kitty?"

"In a minute. You and Leo go ahead with Sadie, and Deb and I will walk to the barn as soon as the trailer is hooked up. I'd like to rest on the porch for just a few minutes." Which would give us a chance to talk to Medina Beadle alone and assure Jack and Leo that we wouldn't go inside the house without them.

Jack gave me a look, but he and Leo climbed back into

Sadie and headed her toward the barn without arguing. Deb eased into the chair next to me.

"I know your family must be terribly upset over all that's happened. I'm truly sorry that our buying your car seems to have caused such problems."

Medina fanned herself with her apron. "You folks certainly aren't to blame, so don't give it another thought. And as I told you before, we can use the money from the sale of the car. Especially now."

I figured she meant they needed the money now for the funeral expenses to bury their son. Most families didn't take out insurance on their children, fully expecting the children to bury them instead of the other way around.

"How is your husband feeling this morning, Mrs. Evans?" Medina Beadle asked Deb.

"He's still pretty sore. And he's not allowed to lift anything heavier than a coffee mug. We're terribly sorry about your nephew. And your son."

I couldn't think of anything original to add to Deb's sentiments, so I fell back on the usual, fairly meaningless question. "Is there anything we can do for you while we're still in the area?"

Medina shook her head. "We're doing okay, I suppose. Mother did make me promise to ask you again to come to the funeral. And you're all welcome to come back here for the gathering after, unless you'll be wanting to head straight home. The service will be a joint funeral, for both of the boys. Jerry didn't have any other family."

Wonderful. No other family, so the Beadles had the burden—both financial and emotional—of getting both of the boys properly buried.

"If you're sure we won't be in the way, we'll try to be there. At least the others will. I'm afraid I may have to leave right away. Our granddaughter is very ill, and I might have to fly home. My daughter insists I stay here for the time being, and so does Chief Wilburn, while he investigates the accident, but if Tori isn't better by tonight, I'm gone."

"What's wrong with your granddaughter?" Medina asked, and I explained about the collapsed lung.

"That happened to our Charlie when he was—" Tears welled in her eyes at the memory. I squeezed her hand. She swallowed and said, "Kids are often stronger than adults. I bet your daughter calls soon to say your granddaughter is just fine."

"I hope you're right. Please have your husband give Jack directions to the funeral home. And it isn't necessary to feed us afterward."

"I'd appreciate you coming to the service, if you can, and so will Mother." She rocked and fanned for a few minutes while I tried to figure out a tactful way to question her further. Maybe I should take a farmwife-to-farmwife approach.

"Will your husband be able to find anyone to help out with the farm chores now? I mean, will the neighbors help you and Mr. Beadle get your crops harvested when the time comes?"

Jack no longer raised crops on our farm, renting the land out to a younger neighbor instead. But he always helped out when it was time to bring the crops in. Few families could do that huge job without some volunteer help.

"Mose does most of the work by himself, and he doesn't plant as many acres as he used to. I help out whenever I can. Whenever Mother doesn't need me. Our Charlie was… well, he was away from home for quite some time." She spoke so softly I had to strain to hear her. "That's when Mose had to cut back on the size of the crops, so he's used to not having much outside help with them."

I waited, not sure where this conversation was going, realizing she didn't know we knew about her son's criminal record. And I didn't want to stop the flow by asking too many personal questions.

"Charlie never was much a one for farming," she said.

I nodded. It did sound sensible and explained the lack of calluses on the kid's hands.

"I'm sure it must be difficult for you to imagine anyone wanting to hurt him," I ventured.

Time was running short for this conversation. While I was certain Chief Wilburn had asked her the same thing, a mother whose child had a criminal background would likely be far more loath to admit that child's shortcomings to a cop than to another mother, even if that information might've helped solve his murder.

She shook her head. "Charlie didn't bring his friends home much. You see, he got into some trouble a while back, and he went to jail. Maybe someone he met there wanted to do him harm."

Again, a sensible answer. But she didn't look directly at me when she said it, keeping her gaze instead toward the barn, so I couldn't judge whether I was getting the entire story from her or not.

I remembered we'd first heard about Charlie Beadle's jail time from Conklin, the rental company's security guard, and we'd gotten the rest of the details from the library computer. Conklin indicated the boy didn't seem to share his parents' morals or work ethics, but I hardly expected his mother to say the same thing about him to us.

"Were Charlie and Jerry close?" Deb asked.

The question seemed to startle Medina Beadle. "Yes, I suppose they were."

Before either of us could ask her to elaborate on that, Jack bellowed for me. "Kitty, I'm winching the car up onto the trailer right this minute, with or without you!"

"Coming," I bellowed back.

Deb and I stepped off the porch, and Medina Beadle headed toward her front door. "Funeral's at three tomorrow afternoon. Chief Wilburn said Jerry's body will be released today, and we'd already made arrangements for Charlie," she advised us. "No visitation beforehand, just the funeral."

"We'll do our best to be there." I was about to ask where to send some flowers, but she'd already shut the front door.

Thankfully, loading Betty Blue onto the trailer went according to plan this time. Mose Beadle helped Jack with the winching job while Leo oversaw the operation from a safe distance, near Deb and me. As we drove out of the long driveway and headed back to our cabin, I couldn't help wishing the earlier effort to load the car had been as successful. Jack eased Sadie out onto the highway with Leo riding shotgun, Deb and me in the back seat as usual, and Betty Blue now safely secured onto the trailer. On the way to the cabin, my cell phone rang. As I answered, I prayed for good news.

"Mom, Tori's lung re-inflated. She's feeling much better now."

I let out a long breath, as if I'd been holding it in the entire time since Maggie's first phone call.

"So she's not in any danger now? You're sure?"

"We're sure. They're going to keep her in the ICU unit overnight, but she'll go into a regular room tomorrow."

"How long will she have to be in the hospital?"

"The doctor isn't sure, maybe a couple of days. But

there is absolutely no use in your coming here now. We're all fine."

"All? How about Billy? How is he handling this, and is there a chance of him catching pneumonia from his sister?"

"Not likely, the doctor said. But we're keeping an eye on him. There's a motel close by, and a McDonald's with an indoor playground, so Billy and his daddy are in hog heaven."

I'd be in hog heaven as well if Tori continued to improve at this rate. All we had to do now was get through the double funeral and head home.

TWENTY-EIGHT

THE FUNERAL HOME was small but neat and modern. We stepped inside the foyer, and Deb and I each signed the guest book. I hated funeral homes, particularly the smell of the flowers.

Time to suck it up and move further into the chapel to pay our respects to the family.

We'd come a bit early, so there were few people milling around. One couple talked to Medina Beadle while Mose stood at attention between the caskets. Mercifully, the lids were closed so we didn't have to view the bodies.

I glanced at the caskets then glanced away, deciding to shake Mose Beadle's hand and move on over to where Sassy Bentley rocked quietly back and forth in a front-row pew. It was the first time I'd seen her out of her wheelchair. The bright pink sweater clashed with her deep purple dress, but I figured she was warding off the feeling of being constantly cold—despite the warm room temperature—that most of the elderly dealt with every hour of every day.

I worked my way over and sat on one side of her while Deb gracefully dropped to her other side. I briefly wondered if I'd ever be able to do anything gracefully again. Tall and a bit gawky, I hadn't been terribly graceful before the twice-broken leg.

I put my hand over Sassy Bentley's. "How are you?"

"I'll be a sight better when this mess is over." She sat quietly for a few minutes, so I glanced around the room.

A few more people filed in, including Chief Wilburn. He stepped around an elderly man signing the guest book, moved toward Mose Beadle, and shook hands with him. I felt Sassy Bentley stiffen beside me.

"I never know what to say at a time like this," I told her, "except I'm sorry, and I hope Chief Wilburn solves your grandson's case soon so you can all find some closure."

Unless, of course, Jerry Beadle had killed his cousin, Charlie, a fact that would hit this family even harder. The boy certainly had behaved oddly. Both of the cousins had. But in light of the fact that Jerry was now dead as well, I didn't hold out much hope for Chief Wilburn or his men to be able to solve the case. And I really hated the whole "closure" concept, but I couldn't think of anything else to say that didn't sound equally dumb.

Sassy Bentley appeared to think that over. "I've lived long enough to know that there really isn't anything to say at a time like this. Except 'sorry,' and you said that. I appreciate you and your friend being so kind to an old woman you hardly know. I may need to call on that kindness again sometime very soon. Would you mind coming out to my farm after the funeral, for the gathering after? I'd like to talk to you again."

"Of course we'll come," I said. "What can we do to help you?"

Before she could answer my question, Medina Beadle said, "I'm grateful to you ladies for being here. You're welcome to come out to the farm afterward, unless you're setting out for home today."

"I've already invited them to the gathering after the funeral, Medina, and they've accepted."

That seemed to settle the question. I wondered how much Medina Beadle really wanted us in her house again. Obviously, we were a reminder of the family's terrible

losses. Well, we wouldn't outstay our welcome, but Sassy
Bentley seemed to want something from us, particularly
from me, and I aimed to provide whatever it was, assuming I could. I'd quickly grown fond of the elderly woman,
and once we arrived back home I'd not likely see her again,
given the distance we lived and her advanced age.

"How is your family?" Sassy Bentley asked. "I believe
Medina said your granddaughter was taken ill recently."

I swallowed hard. "She's a bit better this morning or
I wouldn't be here. She has pneumonia and her lung collapsed. The pediatrician sent her to the children's hospital
in Louisville. The lung has re-inflated, and the new doctor
is confident she'll be fine soon. My lung collapsed when I
had the car accident, so I know how painful it is. But my
daughter absolutely refuses to let me fly home."

"Doctors can do wonders these days. I'll say prayers.
Don't you worry. I'll bet they're right about her being back
to normal in no time."

I squeezed her hand and hoped she was right. It was all
I could do not to run out of this place and head straight for
home, thumbing a ride if necessary, in spite of Maggie insisting there was no need for me to race there now.

The organ music died down and the minister took a seat
behind the podium, so Deb and I relinquished our spots
on the family pew and moved further back, joining Jack
and Leo. I settled into the seat as best I could, folded my
arms, and prepared to endure the funeral. I let my mind
drift, wondering who could have killed Charlie Beadle, if
it wasn't his rather strange cousin. Probably like Medina
said, someone we didn't know, someone from his days
in the slammer. So there was no way we could solve that
crime. And Jerry Beadle died from who knew what.

But could Charlie's killer be someone the Beadles actually knew? Specifically Charlie's cousin? Maybe Sassy

Bentley suspected him, and maybe that's why her daughter tried to keep us apart when she could, to keep any dirty family linen from being aired in our presence, as Medina had said on our first visit.

I mulled the situation a bit more then stood to leave the chapel after a mercifully quick service. Deb leaned over my shoulder and whispered, "I wish we could get a copy of that short funeral sermon to take home to our minister."

I nodded. Brother Maxxum lived up to his name in every service he conducted, but I doubted he'd take kindly to a suggestion that he cut his preaching to anything less than an hour. Still, if Deb was willing to brave it, I'd back her in the effort.

Seated inside Sadie, we took our place in the funeral procession to the graveyard. We'd left Betty Blue snoozing on the rental trailer inside the cabin's garage, alongside Leo's truck.

I have to admit it was worth the rather long drive along the winding country road, admiring the fall foliage and the old farm houses and barns we passed along the way. I'd have kicked myself for leaving my camera inside my tote bag to be stolen, instead of keeping it in my pocket like I usually did, if my leg would've reached that high. I should have bought one of those throw-away models, but with all that happened recently, it never even occurred to me.

The cool breeze made standing on the hillside at the cemetery challenging. We listened to the final prayer, softly spoken by Mose Beadle. Medina and her mother sat as still as large stones throughout the graveside service.

The entire group of mourners turned to glare at me as my cell phone extended its usual cheery holiday greeting to all and sundry, interrupting the minister as he spoke his final words of comfort to the Beadle family. And to think I'd actually browbeaten Jack into buying the fool thing for me. I'd really have to remember to turn the little sucker off whenever I was someplace where Christmas sentiments weren't welcome, I promised myself, as I worked my way out of earshot behind a rather large headstone and hit "send."

Maggie was checking in for the day, and of course I hadn't been able to tell her not to call because I'd be at a funeral.

"Mom, where are you guys? You sound like you're in a barrel."

"Um, we're visiting an old cemetery. Just taking some time in the country."

Well, it was mostly true, and she knew I liked to look at old headstones, trying to make up a history for the people buried there. "How is Tori this morning?"

"She's much better. Sitting up, eating some Jell-O, and demanding to know when you guys are coming home."

That was certainly good news. "Where's your sister? Is she still in Louisville with you?" Silly question. Someone would've let me know if she wasn't there, but I couldn't think of anything more intelligent to ask for the moment.

"Sunny is staying here at the hospital with me. I don't know what I'd have done without her. And I'm not saying another word to her about the chartreuse. I'll wear it every single day if need be, from now until her wedding."

"Me, too, and you can tell her I said so."

"But, Mom—"

"I know, I know, the mother of the bride is not supposed to wear any color the bride uses in the wedding. And whose dumb idea was that? I think we should all look horrible in chartreuse together. Maybe even the bride."

Maggie laughed. "Oh, Tori's asking me to make sure

you know how brave she's been. Now, why do you suppose she'd want you to know that?"

I didn't dignify that with an answer. Maggie knew I generally rewarded the children if they came through a difficult time with grace under fire. From the sound of it, this was going to take a rather large reward on my part. And I'd spotted something in a shop window not far from our cabin that I thought might fit the bill.

"Tell Tori that Grandma is suitably impressed. She'll know what I mean."

Maggie snickered. "Who are you and what have you done with my real mother?" she asked. "And how come Sunny and I never got presents for being sick? Just a thermometer stuck in our mouths or some place that was even worse."

"Don't be crude, Maggie. I'm your mother. My job was to get you well and back to school. My job with Tori and Billy is to spoil them. I take all of my responsibilities very seriously."

Her response, in the form of a rather loud guffaw, made me giggle. And it was good to laugh about something after so many tense days. If I survived this fiasco, I'd head home to my beloved back porch, gather up my grandchildren, squat down on the floor to play Chutes and Ladders, or some equally challenging game, and never leave home again.

"How much longer will Tori be in the hospital?"

"At least a day or so, just to be on the safe side. Then Joe will drive us all home. Billy adores staying in a motel and eating at his favorite place, so getting him home may be a challenge, but Tori is more than ready. When are you guys coming home?"

When Chief Wilburn gives us the okay, but I didn't dare

say that to her. "Soon, I hope. When Leo feels more up to it. I'm as ready as Tori."

"How is Leo?"

"He's much better, but still a bit stiff. We don't want to rush him." Which was true.

"Gotta go, Mom. You guys be careful, and try to have a good time the rest of your trip."

"Will do. And you all take good care of yourselves. When I get home with Tori and Billy's gifts, I want them both well enough to crawl on the floor with me and make a mess."

"I'm sure they'll be more than happy to comply. Love you, Mom."

"Love you, too, hon."

I snapped the cell-phone lid shut. And maybe I'd just take a little something special home for my two grown-up girls. To make up for all those traumatizing times I'd taken their temperatures or poured medicine down their throats to cure whatever illnesses had struck. Such a shameful parent, I'd actually expected them to get well.

I looked around. Most of the mourners had returned to their cars and were lining up for the drive back to the farm. Jack escorted me to Sadie, knowing that walking on uneven areas like grass was still a challenge for me.

"So," Jack said into the rearview mirror, "is the crisis with Tori really over?"

"Yes, she's feeling much better this morning. They've put her in a room. They just want to observe her for a couple of days."

"Now all we have to do is prove I didn't kill anyone, right?"

"Right. Or make a break for it," Leo suggested. "Few people know where Metropolis, Illinois, is located. I doubt if even Chief Wilburn could find us there."

"I wouldn't bet on it," Deb said. "He seemed pretty sharp to me. Probably even knows how to read a road map, unlike some people I could name."

"Low blow, Deb. Below the belt, even," I said, nudging her with my elbow.

"But accurate."

"Jack, before we leave for home, I'll have to make an emergency trip to that little antique store near our cabin," I said.

"Let me guess, something else for Tori, right?"

"And I suppose you think I'm spoiling her?" Which, of course, I was.

"Nope. Just wondering if I should pick up something for her, too. She loves Jolly Ranchers. Maybe I'll get her a bag of her very own at the grocery store, so she doesn't have to con me out of mine."

"I'm sure she'd love that. Let's take care of the necessary gifts tomorrow morning, then check in with Chief Wilburn to see when we can go home. With any luck, the autopsy will show that Jerry Beadle died accidentally, and Wilburn won't need to keep us here any longer."

TWENTY-NINE

By THE TIME we arrived at the farm for the gathering after the funeral, I was more than ready to sample the offerings the Beadles' friends and family had brought along to comfort the mourners. The meat and vegetables were great, and the amount of food could have fed half of the county. True to her word, Copper Penny sent over a basket the size of a small Volkswagen, stuffed with good things to eat. And for all I knew, half the county was present at the farm, with the kitchen and parlor full of female mourners eating and chatting, and most of the males spilling out into the yard to sit in the ancient metal lawn chairs. Jack and Leo joined the men outside, neither of them ever at a loss for words, even in a yard full of strangers. I just hoped they'd remember to ask a few discreet questions between bites of the delicious food.

Deb and I, not quite as at home yet in a kitchen full of women we'd never met, chose to sit in a corner with Sassy Bentley, paper plates carefully balanced on our laps. Sassy was quiet through much of the meal, mostly nodding at whatever Deb or I could think of to say. When Sassy wasn't looking, I gave Deb a wink to signal her to work the room. We'd decided she should begin by asking various ladies for recipes to the dishes they'd brought, which would give them a reason to trust her judgment and give both of us some terrific new recipes, and then she could segue into asking about Charlie Beadle and his charming cousin, Jerry.

My job was to gently question Sassy Bentley. At least find out what it was she wanted from me. Blood out of a turnip would have been far easier, and I gained nothing beyond her promise to send me her prize-winning canning secrets after we returned home. She said we'd discuss "my kindness" when the kitchen emptied out a bit.

"I'll have Medina write my canning recipes down for you, and she'll mail 'em, if you'll leave her your address," Sassy Bentley said. "Holding a pencil is difficult with these old fingers."

I hadn't asked her for the recipes, and I was touched that she was willing to share them with me. I suspected she wouldn't have if I'd lived anywhere nearby. A lot of women guarded their much-coveted cooking secrets as closely as anything Washington, D.C., ever stored in secured files. But since I lived several hours away, Sassy Bentley could rest easy that I wouldn't publish her secrets all over the county. And I'd keep that trust. I just wished she'd confide in me about who she thought might have killed her grandson. Maybe she didn't know, or maybe she thought it was someone too close to her to reveal.

Deb returned to her seat, her hands clutching various wads of scrap paper and at least one bank-deposit slip, all with hastily scribbled recipes. She smoothed the papers out on the table and sorted through them. Most likely the instructions to some of the best dishes in the area.

"Eat your heart out, Martha Stewart," Deb said. "Wait until you see these recipes. Sweet-potato pie, Kentucky Derby pie, scalloped pineapple, bread-and-butter pickles, stuffed pork chops, Chinese slaw, and that's only the beginning."

"I'm surprised one of the ladies didn't try to sell you the latest cookbook Medina's homemaker's club published this year," Sassy Bentley said. "Her group is pretty aggressive about sales. They're raising money to feed hungry folks in our area."

"Then we each need to buy a copy," I said.

"Gotcha covered," Deb said, pulling two of the coveted copies out of her over-sized purse. "Early birthday present. The line to the food seems to be slowing down. How about I get us each a smidgen of some of those delicious-looking desserts?"

Sassy Bentley declined. Deb motioned me to stay seated, saying she'd get us each a good sampling.

By the time Deb had made her way down the dessert table and returned with our over-loaded plates, Chief Wilburn stepped into the kitchen and arrested Mose Beadle for the murder of Charlie Beadle and his cousin, Jerry.

I was frozen to my seat.

Medina Beadle dropped into a nearby chair, covered her face with her apron, and bawled.

Deb went to her. I stayed beside Sassy Bentley, placing my arm around her shoulder for support. This couldn't be happening.

"We'll drive you to the police station," Deb offered.

Medina swallowed hard and pulled herself together. "Thank you, I'd appreciate that," she said.

"I'm going along, as well," Sassy Bentley said.

Medina stopped wrestling with her apron ties. "Mother, that really isn't necessary. You'll be fine here for a few—"

"I'm going with you, Medina!" Sassy Bentley reached for my hand.

Medina sighed her resignation and grabbed for her purse.

"I'd be happy to come along," I said, "unless you'd prefer someone to stay here and help finish cleaning up the mess."

There weren't many dishes to wash up as some thoughtful person had brought a carload of paper plates, cups, napkins, and plastic utensils, but there was a ton of food left over and a couple of neighboring farmwives had just begun putting it away.

"Leave it," Medina said. "I'll throw away anything that's likely to spoil when I get back. Right now I need to be with Mose, but I'm not at all sure I can drive."

"You go ahead, Medina," the lady with the hand-embroidered apron said. I wished I'd paid closer attention when she'd told me her name. She'd been extremely helpful all afternoon, and her lemon meringue pie was to die for, if the other mourners' assessments of it were on target.

Medina nodded at her, and off we went to the pokey to face Chief Wilburn and see what we could do to get Mose Beadle out of jail.

Jack drove Mose Beadle's ancient farm truck with Leo, as usual, riding shotgun. The Beadles didn't seem to have any other means of transportation, and they'd need that truck at the station if we got Mose out of jail. The wheel-chair quickly stored in Sadie's trunk, I drove Sadie with Sassy Bentley sitting up front and Deb and Medina Beadle in the back seat.

There was total silence during the long ride to the police department, but I had an eerie feeling there was a battle of wills somehow going on between mother and daughter. But would Medina Beadle defend her husband if he'd actually killed their son? And would Sassy Bentley, given her apparent lack of respect for her son-in-law, give him up to the cops, assuming he was guilty?

Something strange had gone on in that old farm house, beginning long before Charlie Beadle's death. But I couldn't tell what it was beyond the boy's apparent take-over of the sale of the car. Kids in general didn't seem to have the amount of respect for their elders they'd had when

I was a girl, way back in the dark ages. And there were always reports in the news of children taking advantage of older parents or grandparents for financial gain. Could that be what was behind the deaths of the two boys? And could mild-mannered Mose Beadle be a killer, particularly of his own son and nephew? Somehow I couldn't bend even my suspicious mind around that one.

We arrived at Wilburn's office, and, to my surprise, Sassy insisted we accompany her and her daughter in there. To my shock, Wilburn agreed. He ordered extra chairs brought in, and we all lined up against the cold cinder-block wall, except for Medina, who took the visitor's chair in front of Wilburn's desk.

"Mrs. Beadle, I've advised your husband of his rights, and he's waived them. He's confessed to the murder of your son. He'll be arraigned first thing tomorrow morning. If—and I doubt he will—the judge allows bail, you can take him home then."

Medina fished in her purse for a handkerchief, but Deb snagged a tissue from a nearby table.

"He didn't kill our son. He's covering up for me," Medina said.

"Medina!" Sassy exclaimed.

"No, Momma, not another word. I'll handle this." Medina turned back to Wilburn. "I assure you it was accidental. Charlie wanted some of my home-canned pickled peaches, and he went down to the basement and got a jar of them. I was in a hurry because I knew these folks were coming out to see our car again. I'd stored the pickled peaches down there without checking the seals properly. Charlie grabbed a jar that had evidently unsealed, and he ate from it. The next day he became very ill. We tried to get him to see the doctor, but he wouldn't. I've canned long enough to know the danger signals. It was botulism."

Medina stopped talking and sobbed into her tissue for several minutes. Sassy Bentley reached for my hand. Hers was cold and limp, just like my brain. Wouldn't a farm boy know better than to eat from an unsealed jar? Something else struck me as odd, but I couldn't think what.

Deb moved her chair up and put her arm around Medina's shoulder. What a mess. Her son was dead because she'd been in a hurry to greet us. Could this disaster possibly get any worse?

Chief Wilburn sighed and shuffled the papers on his desk. "Why didn't you call for an ambulance and let the authorities handle the body, Mrs. Beadle? Even if what you say is true, that doesn't explain how your son wound up in that ditch, beaten to a pulp."

Medina wiped her nose and sat up straighter. "Mose was trying to protect me. I suppose everything will have to come out now. I just pray that you'll understand."

Wilburn didn't look as if he was prepared to be particularly understanding. Sassy Bentley's hand tightened on mine. Her lips were a straight line, as if she was forcing herself not to speak. I wondered what was coming next.

"Mose was afraid I'd be arrested if the truth came out, so he—" Medina paused. "He tried to make it look as if our son had been attacked by a bear. We often see them at the edge of the bean field. Then he took Charlie's body away, to the other side of the county, so you'd think it happened there."

Wilburn thumbed through the shuffled papers, as if looking for important information he needed. Something strange was going on here. I still couldn't grasp what it was, but I wasn't buying Medina's story. Apparently, Wilburn wasn't, either.

A door slammed somewhere down the hallway. Sassy

Bentley cringed. Wilburn said, "What do you mean, 'Charlie's body'? The body we found in that ditch wasn't your son, Charlie Beadle, and you know it as well as I do."

THIRTY

THE VICTIM WASN'T Charlie Beadle? Then who was he? And where was the real Charlie Beadle?

Wilburn leaned forward and placed his elbows on his desk, steepling his fingers. "Now then, why don't you tell me the real story, Mrs. Beadle? And start from the beginning."

Medina leaned back, as if to escape from the chief's glare pinning her to her chair. Jack had stopped chewing his gum, and he and Leo stared at her as if she'd just threatened to torch one of their prize-winning vehicles.

By this time, I seriously needed a bathroom break, but I didn't think Sassy Bentley would let go of my hand, and I certainly didn't want to miss anything happening in here. Deb glanced over her shoulder at me. Her eyes were as wide as the Depression glass plates she used to serve cake to our car club. I didn't figure my eyes were much smaller.

"The young man you found in the ditch was someone who'd been in jail with our son, Charlie," Medina answered at last. "He took the trouble to befriend our boy, get to know all about him, and more important, all about us. When he was released from jail a couple of months ago, he came to the farm, asking for our help. We took him in because he knew our son, and because we wanted to help him. It was the biggest mistake of our lives." She blew noisily into her tissue.

"He took over our home, threatening to have Charlie

killed by some of his friends still inside the prison if we didn't do whatever he wanted."

So, Charlie Beadle truly wasn't Charlie Beadle after all. And who in the world was Jerry Beadle?

Deb coughed to cover her shock. Sassy Bentley gripped me even tighter. At this rate, I wouldn't have any fingers left by bedtime. Still, she remained silent. Then it dawned on me. She'd been a prisoner in her own home. They all had been. For months. I think my blood pressure jumped several points.

"So you're saying the young man basically held you hostage?"

Wilburn checked the file again.

"Yes, that's exactly what I'm saying."

"A.F.I.S. fingerprint identification is sometimes a bit slow, particularly if we don't put a rush on it, and I didn't in this case because one of the officers on the scene checked the driver's license on the body—which I presumed belonged to your son—and your husband confirmed the identification. But I got the report today. The dead boy's name was Lanny Ottwell."

Wilburn looked from the file back to Medina. "Why in the world did you identify his body as that of your son? Why didn't you tell me at the time that he wasn't your boy?"

"Because," Medina said, "the other one was still there in our home, the one who called himself Jerry, and he insisted we tell people he was Mose's nephew. The two boys were in on it together. When Lanny Ottwell died from eating the tainted food, the other one took over, saying he could still contact someone inside the prison and have Charlie killed if we didn't continue to do what he said." Medina leaned forward and placed her outstretched arm on Wilburn's desk, as if begging him to understand.

"He damaged the body and made Mose dump it so you would think our Charlie had been mugged or something and not check into the situation at our farm too closely. There was still a chance to save our son, so we did what he said. What other choice did we have?"

"Which gives your husband a perfect reason to kill 'Jerry,' or whatever his name was. I'll put a rush on that identification. Maybe your husband killed the second kid so you would be out of danger and could rescue your son."

"His name was Alvin Ottwell, and they really were cousins," Medina said. "And Mose didn't kill Alvin. I swear to you he didn't. Mose said he wasn't anywhere near the boy when the hook flew out of his hand and his arm was cut. Mr. Bloodworth can probably back him up on that. Maybe the shock of the accident killed him, or loss of blood."

"The injury to his arm didn't kill the boy," Wilburn said. He straightened the papers again and set them down. I was tempted to rip them out of his hands and file them away so he couldn't keep tapping them on his desk, but I didn't think Sassy Bentley would let go of me long enough for that. In the silence a siren blared as some unseen officer roared out of the police-station parking lot and off into the evening.

"Alvin Ottwell died from blunt-force trauma to the head," Wilburn said.

"Then he must have hit his head when he fell off the trailer," Medina said. "It was an accident."

"But there was no evidence of a head injury at the hospital, only the injury to his arm. The doctor checked him over carefully," Wilburn said.

"If he landed on his head rather than being hit by something, isn't it possible the injury might not have been diagnosed right away?" Deb asked. "The boy was carrying on so much that the doctor struggled just to get the stitches in his arm."

"The medical examiner can't say for sure at this point what caused the head injury. He's still waiting for some of the tests to come back. I can't charge your husband for that crime yet, if it was a crime. But I'm still investigating, and there's still the problem of the body of the other boy, Lanny Ottwell."

"I told you, he got sick after eating the fruit I'd canned. Like I said, I didn't think to check the cans down in the cellar after they'd cooled, and it never occurred to me that he'd go down there and get one for himself. He never waited on himself. He always made me fix his food, and he made me taste it first, to be sure it was okay. He must have assumed that something sealed in a jar would be safe to eat without having me taste it first."

Which made sense. And yet, somehow it didn't. My stomach turned to cold concrete, thinking of what this family had been through, thanks to those boys.

"Alvin planned to carry on with their original idea of living with us while stealing from the tourists. They hadn't managed to squirrel away much before Lanny died," Medina said. "He threatened to hurt my mother if we didn't continue to do whatever he wanted."

"And what exactly was it that he wanted?" Wilburn asked.

Medina Beadle wiped her eyes, looked at Deb, then turned back to look at her mother and me. Sassy Bentley nodded as if giving her daughter permission to speak. Medina turned back to Wilburn and took a deep breath.

"Alvin said if these folks—" she gestured toward Jack "—had enough money to buy our old car, they had enough money to pay him off. Mose insisted he couldn't ask them for more money, and Alvin said he wouldn't have to. He'd fake some kind of accident, pretend to be injured, and their insurance company would take care of it. I couldn't imagine what he meant, and I didn't dare warn you—" she turned around to face me again "—for fear he'd hurt Mother or have Charlie killed, as he'd threatened."

So our suspicions had been right, the accident hadn't been an accident after all. And Leo had nearly been killed in the process. If I could have gotten my hands on Alvin Ottwell right then, he'd certainly have begged for a quick death.

"Mose promised me he'd keep an eye out and not let anything happen to anyone else. And we never dreamed he'd cause one of you folks to get hurt, only himself and only a fake injury. I couldn't believe it when I heard the ruckus out in the barn."

Wilburn said, "So Mr. Evans's injury in the barn, caused when Jerry—I mean Alvin—let go of the cable, was done on purpose? And injuring his own arm was planned?"

Medina nodded and wiped her nose again. I thought about Mose Beadle standing like a statue after the accident, not moving to help his "nephew." No wonder he'd been frozen to the spot, reluctant to help the boy. And Jerry/Alvin had planned to get money from us? Until he died from the head injury! Was that a miscalculation on his part, or had Mose Beadle somehow put a permanent stop to the boy's plan? He could very easily have hit Alvin Ottwell again with the winch hook while the rest of us were tending to Leo and Medina was busy flagging down the ambulance. Except that would have meant bleeding or bruising and neither the doctor nor the medical examiner had spotted that kind of trauma.

"I swear it happened that way. We were too afraid of him to try to harm him. Too afraid of what he'd do to Charlie and Mother if we failed."

Jack said, "I was pretty busy working on Leo, but I was the closest person to the injured boy. I glanced over there several times, and Mr. Beadle appeared to be trying to stop the bleeding. I think I'd have heard something if he'd hit the boy. And the winch hook would've landed somewhere near us, after it struck Leo in the chest, wouldn't it?"

"I suppose it would have," Wilburn agreed. "You'd probably have seen anyone picking it up. Were there any other possible weapons nearby?"

"Not that I saw. That side of the barn was pretty empty, except for the old car. Like most farmers, Mr. Beadle stores his necessary tools near the door."

At least that much made sense to me. I glanced at Sassy Bentley. She still had a vise-like grip on my hand and was staring at Wilburn. Her lips moved but no words came out.

Wilburn picked up the case file and shuffled it around for the umpteenth time. Then he blew out a big puff of air. "At the moment I can't prove whether or not the head injury was deliberate or an accident. Nor can I prove that the fake Charlie Beadle was poisoned by accident. What I can do is check with the prison to see if any of your story pans out." Wilburn stood. "If you ladies and gentlemen wouldn't mind stepping outside for a few minutes, I'll make some phone calls."

We all filed out of his office into a waiting area. For the next half hour or so we sat in the hard chairs that lined the wall, carefully not looking at each other and not daring to speak. Various employees and officers whizzed by, but no one paid us any attention. At long last, one of Chief Wilburn's officers ushered us back into his office. Wilburn leaned back in his chair, arms behind his head as if he didn't have a care in the world. I hoped that meant good news.

"According to the warden at the prison, Charlie Beadle

is indeed still an inmate there. He has six months to go on his sentence."

Medina Beadle reached for a fresh tissue. At least she knew for sure her boy was alive and well. For the moment.

"The warden also confirmed that Lanny and Alvin Ottwell were released a couple of months ago, and having served their time, weren't on probation. Nor had anyone kept track of their whereabouts. The warden did say he wasn't surprised to hear of their activities and had expected to see them back in prison before too long." Wilburn took a sip of coffee from a cup nearly as large as his desk top. "Their deaths came as a bit of a surprise. The warden said he'd always considered the Ottwells too tough to be taken down by anyone or anything, considering they'd been forces to be reckoned with while guests of his facility. He had no trouble believing you all were too afraid of the boys to take any action against them. He'd received a tip or two about the boys forming a gang while they were still inside the prison, but nothing could ever be proved against them in order to lengthen their stays."

Wilburn paused to let that information sink in. "I also spoke to our local prosecutor. Since we don't have enough evidence to charge any of you in the death of Lanny Ottwell, and the only crime we can prove is tampering with evidence and moving his body, and since you appear to have been victims of a hostage situation, we're going to let all of you return to your homes, including your husband, Mrs. Beadle. We will want to take a close look at the canned goods stored down in your cellar."

Medina nodded and wiped her nose again.

"In light of the eyewitness account given to me by Mr. Bloodworth, that your husband couldn't have caused Alvin Ottwell's head injury, the prosecutor is willing to drop that case as well, unless something comes up in the toxicology reports."

"They were both inside the house that day, until Lanny came outside to take charge of the sale of our car with these folks," Medina said. "It's entirely possible that Alvin ate some of the peaches as well but never showed any symptoms of being sick like Lanny did. And I'm afraid I threw all the jars into our incinerator after Lanny died. I didn't want anyone else getting botulism."

Score another one for Medina Beadle. The incinerator would take care of any evidence of botulism poisoning. Regardless of what the toxicology reports showed, it would be difficult to prove how Lanny Ottwell was poisoned.

"What about my grandson?" Sassy Bentley asked, speaking for the first time since we'd arrived at Wilburn's office. Her voice was even more quivery than the first time I'd heard it, and her hands shook.

"I spoke to the warden about that. Since there is a possibility of his being in danger, assuming Lanny and Alvin Ottwell still have friends on the inside willing to do their dirty work even though they're both dead, your grandson will be moved to a secure area right away, with round-the-clock protection, until his time is up. If our investigation confirms everything you've said, I'll put in a word with the governor and see if we can get him released a bit early."

Wilburn came out of his chair, around the desk, and perched on the edge in front of Medina Beadle. By far, the most sympathetic thing I'd seen him do. "I think your boy got a bit of a stiff sentence for his crime, ma'am. He wasn't driving the stolen car that night, just along for the ride. Not smart, but not as criminal as the actual driver's actions were. And he's been a model prisoner. Hopefully, the warden and I can do something about the length of his incarceration. Meanwhile, he should be safe enough where he is. But I suggest you don't contact him until we know it's okay so you don't alert anyone on the inside that things might've changed out here. The warden isn't going to mention the deaths of the Ottwells to anyone, and I'll see if I can keep their real names out of the news."

"Thank you, Chief Wilburn. You don't know how much this means to us. Can I see Mose now?"

"His papers are being processed, so if you'll all wait outside again, he should able to go home very soon."

We filed back into the waiting area. Medina Beadle turned to Jack and me. "Why don't you folks go on back to your cabin? You all must be exhausted. I can never repay your kindness to us or apologize enough for what's happened to you because of us. I'm so very ashamed." She began to sob again. Jack and I both put our arms around her.

"I'm sure we'd have done much the same thing in your situation," Jack assured her.

I nodded. "Any parent would do whatever was necessary to protect their child. Not to mention protecting your mother. We're just thankful those two boys were the only ones hurt in all of this."

Still crying, Medina plopped into a chair. By morning her eyes would be swelled shut at this rate. Sassy Bentley wheeled over to her daughter's side and comforted her, insisting Medina and Mose had done the best they could under the circumstances.

I heard Sassy murmur, "I didn't know you were trying to protect me from those boys. I appreciate you and Mose for that. And if it hadn't been for our Charlie, I'd've run those worthless good-for-nothings off my place a long time ago."

I didn't doubt that for a minute.

Deb squeezed Medina's shoulder. "We'll leave you alone

now, but we'll certainly call and check on you before we leave for home tomorrow."

Medina nodded, and we headed for the door. I turned to look back as I exited and caught Sassy Bentley's eye. I was expecting to see relief, and maybe even a bit of joy, given that the family's ordeal was over at last and her grandson was safe, but instead I saw something akin to what? Exhaustion? Resignation?

I went back and bent over her chair to give her a gentle hug. Her eyes now held that same hard-as-coal look I'd seen there before.

She put her hand on my arm and whispered into my ear, "Thank you ever so much for your friendship to an old woman, Kitty. And could you possibly come out to the farm tomorrow morning before you leave for home, instead of calling? It's very important or I wouldn't impose on you so."

"It's no imposition," I said, "and it's not that far out of our way. We'll see you tomorrow morning."

Her face was as grey as the surrounding walls, and her hands shook. Suddenly, I was very cold in the warm waiting area.

Jack took my arm. "Let's go, Kitty. The family needs time alone to deal with all that's happened. We'll drop by and check on them in the morning, on our way home."

THIRTY-ONE

I PULLED MY robe tighter around my shoulders as a defense against the early-morning breeze and took a sip of hazelnut coffee. Deb's favorite. I preferred cinnamon flavored, but it was her turn to make our morning coffee. Thankfully, the bear had somehow missed our coffee stash in the pantry.

I was now convinced that the "bear" was really Lanny Ottwell, aided and abetted by his cousin Alvin. And I thought I'd figured out why they'd targeted us. I was willing to bet it had something to do with my camera and the picture I'd inadvertently snapped of Alvin Ottwell on our first visit to the farm. It hadn't surprised me to learn that they'd been involved in the rash of hotel burglaries in the area. Singing at the restaurant put Lanny Ottwell close to the multitude of customers wandering by, and it would be easy pickings to nab a purse now and then. Or a key, if they hoped to steal even more.

The sky was somewhat overcast and the radio announcer was predicting rain, which I didn't mind. Rain always made the late-autumn foliage stand out more. But it would also make pulling a trailer toward home that much more difficult, at least until we drove out of this area.

The cabin patio door slid open, and Deb stuck a bare arm out, her way of checking the weather on the terrace.

"C'mon out, Deb, it isn't nearly as cold as it looks or I wouldn't be out here, either."

She took my word for it and joined me on the terrace. "Are the chairs wet?"

"Nope, it hasn't started raining yet, and the overhang protected them from the dew. But it probably will start raining any minute."

"The guys are hogging the bathrooms again, so we might as well enjoy our coffee before they start yelling for breakfast. What time are we heading out?"

I shrugged. "Whenever the guys give us some time in the bathroom, I suppose. All our stuff is packed. Jack just has to load it into Sadie. What about you and Leo?"

"We're packed, but I'll have to be the one to load up the truck. Jack said he'd help me. Leo says he's still too sore to lift anything much heavier than his eyelids, and you can't lift much while navigating with your cane. Is there anything else we need to take care of before we leave? The cabin is all nice and neat. What time does the antique store open?"

"The sign says nine o'clock. We can grab a quick bite first. It won't take me long to get Tori's gift and a little something for the girls, if I'm lucky. Then we'll head out to the farm. We should be well on our way before lunch and home for supper, if we don't run into any trouble."

"Did Sassy Bentley say why she wanted to see you again? Does she still need a favor?"

"No, she just said it was important. And I think Jack wants to talk to Mose Beadle about the car one more time. Get some details on her history and what she needs. He said he forgot to do that with all that's happened. But he's ready to see home again, and as quickly as possible. I suspect we'll be buzzing up the road toward Illinois just as soon as that's taken care of. We'll be lucky to grab a sandwich on the way."

"I confess, I'm ready to see home, as well. I'll definitely need to rest up from this vacation."

"Me, too. I'm excited about my new car and about the trophies we've won, but I feel like I've been carrying Betty Blue around on my shoulders for the last couple of days instead of her being loaded on the trailer." I stretched to ease the kinks.

"I wonder," Deb began but stopped as Jack slid the door open and stepped out onto the porch. From the look on his face, something new had cropped up, and it wasn't good.

"What's wrong? Is it Tori?" I knew I shouldn't have left my cell phone inside.

"No, Kitty, it isn't Tori. I just spoke to Mose Beadle. Sassy Bentley passed away in her sleep during the night. Mose said his wife would still like for us to come out there whenever we can. No rush, but she'd like to speak to you women."

I nodded. Jack stood there for a few seconds, but when I didn't respond to the news, he went back inside the cabin. I warmed my stiff hands on my coffee cup and blinked back the tears threatening to slide down my cheeks.

"You do realize Sassy Bentley killed that boy, don't you?" I said to Deb when Jack was safely out of earshot.

She frowned at me. "You mean Lanny Ottwell, the fake Charlie Beadle?"

"Yes."

Deb thought that over. "The pickled peaches?"

"Yes, indeed. The famous pickled peaches. I knew something was wrong last night when Medina said her son died from eating them, but when Wilburn announced that Charlie wasn't really Charlie, everything flipped upside down in my brain. This morning I remembered what she'd said and figured that was probably what Sassy Bentley wanted to see me about today."

Deb sipped her coffee. "So why didn't you say something about it when I first came out here?"

"Because I thought I should talk to her first. Now I'll never have the chance."

"But you are convinced it wasn't an accident, like Medina Beadle claimed? You really think her mother killed that boy on purpose?"

"Sassy Bentley won all those prizes at the county fair for her pickled peaches, remember? No other woman's peaches in the entire county could match hers. She'd canned for most of her adult life, so she was an expert on botulism, as is any woman who cans her own fruits and vegetables. We have to be, if we don't want to kill off our entire family. Pickled peaches were Sassy Bentley's particular specialty."

Deb nodded. "I seem to remember her saying pickled peaches were the one thing Medina wouldn't try to can because she didn't think she could match her mother's prize winners. Or did Medina tell us that?"

"I think it was Sassy Bentley who said it. But last night Medina told Chief Wilburn that the boy ate some of her pickled peaches before he died. Peaches that hadn't sealed properly? She said she was sure he'd contracted botulism as a result, but he wouldn't go to the hospital for treatment. Medina didn't can pickled peaches, and Sassy Bentley hadn't canned them for several years. And Sassy certainly wouldn't have kept those old prize winners around until now. It would have been far too dangerous. Home-canned goods usually don't survive that long. Besides, you read my canning books when we canned together."

"Right." Deb sat up and snapped her fingers. "Botulism usually happens in low-acid foods like green beans or corn. High-acid foods like fruits aren't as easily tainted. But Medina said Ottwell got the peaches from the cellar. That could've pointed suspicion at her own mother, so why would she even suggest such a thing?"

"Wilburn would know her mother couldn't make it to the cellar in a wheelchair. He'd probably assume she couldn't even do the canning chores anymore, given her age. Medina knew it was safe to say it because she'd told the chief she'd tossed the jars into the incinerator. Which, of course, she did, sometime after Lanny Ottwell died and Alvin was off somewhere persecuting us."

"I'm betting Alvin Ottwell was poisoned, as well," Deb said. "Medina practically said so. And if so, how did Sassy manage it without him suspecting a thing? Medina claimed she always tasted the food. And why are you so sure it was Sassy Bentley and not her daughter who did the poisoning?"

Before I could say anything, Deb smacked her own forehead. "Duh, never mind. Medina was too afraid to try anything on those boys for fear of her son being hurt or killed. But Sassy Bentley had the nerve and the knowledge to pull it off, right?"

"Right. And she had the means. Medina Beadle was canning green beans the second time we went out there to see the car. I remember hearing the pings as the jars sealed in the kitchen. If one from an earlier batch unsealed while all of us were outside in the barn, Sassy Bentley could have hidden that jar in her wheelchair, under her lap quilt, waiting until she knew it was ripe enough to poison those boys."

"Medina took the blame last night for the poisoning, and made it seem like a terrible accident. That took the heat off her mother," Deb said. "She was willing to risk jail for her because if you are right, she knew who was really responsible. No way either of those boys fixed their own food. Too dog lazy."

"I will be surprised if the medical examiner's report doesn't turn up botulism in Alvin Ottwell's tests. We learned at the Citizen's Police Academy that the medical examiner's reports often take several weeks to complete, so a body might be buried before all the information comes in."

I took another sip of coffee to warm up. It wasn't working very well, but I didn't want to move the conversation inside, where the guys might overhear us.

"But why would Sassy Bentley risk killing Lanny and Alvin Ottwell now?" Deb asked. "They'd been living there for months, holding the family hostage. Mose and Medina endured it out of fear for Sassy and their real son."

"Because Sassy Bentley met us and liked us and knew those boys were after us. I'm pretty sure Lanny and his cousin broke into our first cabin and trashed it. I believe they were looking for my camera, but neither minded causing us other problems while they were about it."

Deb started to sip from her cup and stopped. "Alvin was just about the size of the kid who knocked you down and stole your camera. It's a shame we never had a chance to quiz him."

"The guy who stole your purse was much fatter, but Alvin could have layered his clothing that night. And the purse thief was pretty much a blur. I'm betting Plan B was to make sure we didn't have any pictures of Alvin to show to Chief Wilburn or anyone else."

"No telling how much money they could have gotten for that injury, fake or real," Deb said. "Are we going to tell the guys about this? And what about Chief Wilburn?"

I put my empty cup on the table and snuggled down

into my robe. "Not just yet. Let's see what Medina Beadle has to say for herself. Then we'll know what to do. I'm only guessing at a lot of this. We don't have any real proof."

THIRTY-TWO

After a jump-in-jump-out shower we began loading up our vehicles. Leo and I did most of the directing and Jack and Deb did most of the huffing and puffing.

Shopping for the girls and our grandkids hastily taken care of, along with a fast drive-through for breakfast sandwiches, we made the winding drive to the Beadle farm in record time, now knowing the way almost as well as we knew the way to our own homes.

I missed riding in Sadie's back seat with Deb, talking things over while Jack ferried us all, but she was busy driving their truck so Leo wouldn't have to strain with the twists and turns. Sometimes owning a prize-winning antique vehicle restored to its original condition, sans power steering, wasn't all it was cracked up to be. Sadie didn't have power steering, either, not to mention air conditioning, so I was glad Jack would be driving her for the long haul home. Since I didn't plan to enter Betty Blue in any contests, I aimed for her to have every modern-day bell and whistle known to woman.

Medina Beadle met us on her front porch. "My man's inside." She nodded toward the front door.

Jack and Leo headed through the open doorway, with Leo still moving well below snail speed, keeping one hand over his chest so the muscles stretched as little as possible. Deb said he had a bruise the size of Paducah on his chest and his backside looked as if he'd been run over by a semi. Far more information than I'd needed.

Deb and I moved up the steps, but Medina Beadle stopped us in the doorway with a gentle pressure on my arm.

"Indian summer day," she said, "so let's sit on the porch for a bit."

We nodded and took seats, with Medina shoving the old hound off his favorite rocker. "Git, Buddy. We women have things to talk about that you don't need to hear."

Buddy slunk off the porch and headed toward the nearest shade tree. Medina took his seat, fanning herself with her gingham apron despite the fact that the temperature was in the low seventies.

"When Chief Wilburn called this morning, I told him Mother passed away in her sleep last night. Given her age and the fearful time she'd just been through, he said he wasn't surprised. He promised again that he'd talk to the governor to see if he could get Charlie out early. Until then, Charlie is in a protected area of the prison. So all we can do for the time being is pray for him."

"We'll pray, too," Deb assured her. "You deserve to have him back home with you after what those boys did to your family."

Medina Beadle began to cry softly. "We didn't know what to do to get rid of them without Charlie or Mother getting hurt, or worse. Mother thought Mose was weak because he wouldn't do anything to stop them from taking advantage of us, but she didn't know they'd threatened her or that I wouldn't let Mose stand up to them."

"I'd have done the same thing if Jack had been in any danger," I said.

She gulped. "Mose is one of the most courageous men I've ever known. I've had to hold him back every single day to keep him from trying to take those boys on. They would have killed him and kept Mother and me prisoners.

And when Charlie finally got out of prison, they'd have been waiting for him, as well."

I couldn't even imagine what this poor family had gone through the past few months. Nor did I want to. At least they were free now. And as far as I was concerned, Sassy Bentley had killed in self-defense.

"Chief Wilburn said the medical examiner looked at the autopsy report again this morning, and he says he still can't tell for sure what caused Alvin's head injury, so he's going to assume the boy fell on his head and the bleeding was internal. He's willing to accept your husband's word that it was an accident, and ours that it was caused by the boy's own stupidity and greed."

I nodded, not knowing what to say.

"I assured the chief that the rest of us didn't eat any of the pickled peaches. Only the two boys ate any. He's reporting the case to the CDC, but he isn't charging me with anything as of yet. Not until he hears back from them."

"There have been several reported cases of botulism poisonings from canned carrot juice lately," I said. "I heard about it on the news. They might want Chief Wilburn or one of his men to check out your canned goods. Maybe send them some samples to test."

"Likely they will want somebody to check out my kitchen and my cellar." She rocked and thought a while.

"But they won't find anything containing even a whisper of botulism in either place, will they, Medina?" I asked, hating to question her at a time like this, but needing the truth if I was ever to come to terms with what I suspected.

"Your mother was very careful," I continued, "and sharp though he is, Chief Wilburn doesn't strike me as someone who ever canned his own food."

She nodded. "You've figured it out about Mother, haven't you? I saw the look in your eyes when she said goodbye to you last night. I expect she saw it, too. But that's not why she died. Don't you ever even think to worry about that!"

When she didn't explain further, I said, "Your mother somehow managed to pour the juice from an unsealed can of green beans over one of the bowls of food you put on the table, didn't she? Something she was absolutely certain neither you nor Mose would ever eat, so she wouldn't poison the two of you, as well. I'd guess she did it sometime when the boys were busy washing their hands at the kitchen sink. And she made herself eat some of the tainted food right along with them. But I don't understand why she did that, unless it was guilt."

Deb sat quietly, watching both of us. A stray chicken hopped onto the porch, and Medina shooed it off with a wave of her apron.

"Near as I can figure, that's just exactly what she did. She'd been going downhill, starting about the time Lanny first took sick and getting worse all the time. I thought it was the stress from having them in the house, threatening us. She hid it from everyone, even me. Alvin started feeling ill on the way home from the hospital, but he wouldn't let us take him back there. I suspect he was afraid another trip might interfere with any false claims he had against you."

A hawk whistled above us, and we all looked up to see him swoop overhead. Buddy raised up and barked until the hawk flew off, keeping the stray chicken safe until Medina might need it for the dinner table. Hawks were predators. Like the two young men had been, hunting for easy prey. Except they'd seriously underestimated Sassy Bentley!

"I suppose she figured that was the only way to keep them from harming us or you folks, by pouring tainted juice into their food. And like you said, it would have been something she knew we wouldn't eat." Medina fanned herself with her apron again. "They wouldn't have suspected it from her. And I certainly didn't dare risk putting anything into the food I cooked for them. You see, I lied to the chief about more than just the peaches. Those evil boys made Mother take a taste from each bowl or platter first, every single meal I cooked. Not me, like I said. So there was nothing I dared do to the food. And they were big and strong and quick, so Mother assumed Mose couldn't overpower either of them at his age. Certainly not both at once."

"But how could she outlast two healthy young boys if she'd eaten the poisoned food when they did?" Deb asked.

I saw Medina's jaws working, as if she were grinding her teeth. "Those two boys shoveled in everything they could get their hands on, after Mother tasted it first. It never occurred to them that she'd be the one to doctor it since she was eating a few bites, as well. Then they'd let us eat whatever they left behind. Mother was a light eater, so she wouldn't have gotten as much of the tainted food as they did. And different people react in different ways to poison."

"That's why her hands were so cold last night when she held mine, isn't it? And why she didn't say much. She was afraid someone would notice if she slurred her speech." I wiped a tear away.

Medina reached for my hand. "You folks aren't to blame for any of this, and in a way, you saved us and our son. You brought things to a head. Like I told the chief, if they could have gotten more money out of you, they were going to take off out of here. What I didn't tell him was that they didn't plan on leaving anyone behind to tell tales."

"Oh, my word!" Deb placed her hand on Medina's arm.

I felt like throwing up. Sassy Bentley sacrificed herself

to save her family, and in a way, to save us. "How did she manage it?" I asked, thinking of how crippled she'd been and how carefully they would have watched her.

"After you left that day, Mose and I were outside feeding the animals. Lanny demanded she heat up his supper right then. She could still work around in the kitchen a bit, from her chair, and he had no reason to think she'd do anything to his food since she'd be eating it, as well. She must have heard one of the jars unseal at some point and hidden it, in case she needed it. How did you figure out what Mother did?" Medina choked out the question. "What gave her away?"

Deb and I exchanged guilty glances. Best to make a clean breast of it, especially since Medina was being so honest with us.

"When Chief Wilburn first hauled Jack into his office for questioning about what he suspected was your son's murder, we got worried. Somebody in our car club suggested we find out what we could about your family." I felt myself blushing. "We went to the library and checked all the newspaper articles about you. We read about your mother winning every county fair for years, particularly with her pickled peaches. This morning I remembered you said Lanny Ottwell died from botulism poisoning after eating your pickled peaches, and I knew. There was no way you would've kept her prize-winning peaches around for this many years. And she would have known how to avoid botulism and how to use it. I believed you when you said you and Mose wouldn't have done anything to those boys while your son was in danger. That meant it had to be your mother."

Medina nodded. "There is a jar of green beans missing. I counted them last night after Mother went to bed. There's nearly always one that doesn't seal properly, so all she had to do was wait. She'd pretended to be hard of hearing when they were around, so they assumed she wasn't listening when they made their plans. Last night she told me what they'd planned to do to us."

"And that's when she decided to take matters into her own hands and protect you, and even us. If she hadn't, once they had our money, they'd have been gone, and—" I couldn't say the words.

And what would I have done in her place, if someone was threatening my daughters or my grandchildren? I honestly didn't know, and I prayed I'd never have a reason to find out.

"I suppose what she did wasn't a whole lot different than if she'd taken a gun and shot them when they first invaded your home," I said. "I guess what I'm saying is that she killed them in self-defense, and herself along with them. Not many other choices left in order to keep them from killing her grandson or you and Mose."

In the silence, I watched as Buddy flopped over into a more comfortable position underneath the tree. The hound was the only one unaffected by the family's disaster.

"As to the real source of Alvin's injury, I'm guessing again," Medina said. "But Mother still had some strength left in her hands. And I keep my iron skillet hanging near the stove."

"But she was crippled," Deb objected. "She lived in a wheelchair. She couldn't possibly have hit anyone with that heavy frying pan, even if she'd wanted to."

"She might've been crippled, Deb," I said, "but remember how strong her handshake was?"

The look on Deb's face told me she did, indeed, remember.

"I'll certainly never be able to fry anything in that old pan again," Medina said, "because I do believe she used it to whack Alvin upside his head while Mose and I were outside feeding the animals. When we came back inside, Mother was in her room and we found Alvin lying in the middle of the kitchen floor. Not that he didn't deserve it. He was the most disrespectful of the two cousins. And I found some bruises on Mother's upper arms this morning when I got her ready for the funeral home. I'd bet he caused 'em."

You bet he'd caused them! Just the thought of what the old lady and her family had endured made me itch to get my hands on those two boys. If they'd been alive, I would have!

"Won't there have to be an autopsy on her body?" Deb asked. "Since she died at home, with no physician in attendance? Isn't Chief Wilburn bound to investigate?"

"No, there won't be any autopsy. I called our family doctor as soon as I found her this morning, and he rushed right over. I'd have called him last night, if I'd only realized she was so ill, but she swore she was just tired and needed her rest. She was trying to keep me from figuring out what she'd done to herself. She promised me she'd somehow managed to put the tainted juice from the green beans onto Lanny and Alvin's food without having to taste it first, and like a fool I believed her. I should have known better. Anyhow, the doctor's farm is just down the road, so he's known Mother most all of his life. He didn't hesitate to sign the death certificate for her. Didn't even examine her closely, and I'm grateful for that."

So there would be no questions from Wilburn on that score. A break the Beadles probably deserved.

"I'm certainly not condoning what Mother did, mind you, but I do understand it," Medina continued. "Once Lanny and Alvin had your money and they were done with us, we'd have been buried somewhere on this big old farm where nobody would've ever found us, and those boys would've disappeared from sight with whatever they could've carried off."

I shivered at the thought. Medina reached over and squeezed my hand again. "I know you cared for my mother. And she'd grown very fond of you ladies. I lied to Chief Wilburn last night in order to protect her. I knew she'd poisoned the boys, but I didn't dare say it. I'm too ashamed to care what happens to me now. Is there any way we could keep this a secret, between us?"

I looked at Deb, and she nodded.

"I see no reason to tell Chief Wilburn what we suspect your mother did to their food or hers," I said, "unless he decides at some point to arrest you. I couldn't allow that to happen to you, knowing you're innocent. But he seems satisfied the case is closed, and I'm satisfied to leave it that way. There won't be any real proof left, just our suspicions, and even if we had any proof, there's nothing he could do to your mother now."

"Thank you, for her and for me."

"I will have to tell Jack at some point because we don't keep secrets from each other, but I'll wait until we get home. He'll be less likely to want to dash out and tell Chief Wilburn about it by then."

"I think Leo deserves to know, too," Deb said. "Having been injured by that young jerk, he won't want to tell Chief Wilburn, either. There's too much chance Wilburn might want us to come back down here and make a statement. And like Kitty said, what good would it do now, with all three of them dead?"

No good that I could think of. And besides, while Chief Wilburn was excellent at his job, I'd seen enough of the inside of his office to last me a couple of lifetimes.

"I appreciate it. My mother was well respected in this

area. Most of her friends are gone now, but I'd still hate for folks to know what she did in order to save us. She had more courage than Mose and I, but then we didn't know what they were about to do to us."

I couldn't think of anything to say to that, so we three sat in silence for a few minutes until Medina Beadle reached into the pocket of her dress and pulled out the tiny little case that protected my beloved camera whenever it lived in my tote bag.

As she handed it to me, I said, "Where did you find it, Medina? Or would you rather I didn't ask?"

"I searched Alvin's room this morning. Your camera was underneath the mattress. He saw the pictures you printed out for Mother. Apparently he knew you'd taken one of him near the outbuilding and didn't believe you'd deleted it, like you promised. He swore he'd get the camera and all of your pictures away from you. When you told us your camera had been stolen, I knew he was the guilty one. I didn't dare look for it before he died, and I forgot about it afterward, until this morning."

"He swiped the camera after knocking Kitty down at a restaurant," Deb said. "If I could have caught him, your troubles would have been over right then, because I'd have strangled him on the spot."

I grinned at Deb. Alvin Ottwell was double her size, if not more, but he would have had his hands full if she'd caught up with him that day. Or if I had. My lovely cane had more than one use.

"Thank you, Medina, for finding and returning my camera to me. It was a gift, and I hated losing it."

I quickly checked the memory-stick compartment and was relieved to see the stick still in place. It hadn't occurred to young Alvin that I might have e-mailed those pictures to my daughter.

Or that anyone might be strong enough or brave enough to take care of him. Certainly not an elderly woman in a wheelchair. Never underestimate the power of a senior citizen.

"Stealing your camera wasn't all Alvin did. After Lanny died, he started following you folks around. Watching where you went and what you did. He was probably after the camera, but he might have been up to more mischief, as well. I don't know any of this for sure, but he took to being gone from time to time. We could have called for help right then, except for putting Charlie's life in danger. And Mother's."

I thought back to the noises in the woods outside our cabin, the trash strewn everywhere, and the glimpse Jack caught of someone hanging around Sadie when we left Copper Penny's show. "There were some incidents," I said, "but we didn't put it all together back then. We were a bit suspicious of him, particularly after the accident when Leo was injured, but Alvin died that same night and that pretty much held our attention from then on."

"I'm just thankful your friend wasn't killed. I don't know how I would have lived with that."

"Us, too," Deb said. "But it certainly wouldn't have been your fault. Let's not take any of the blame onto ourselves that rightfully belongs to those two would-be killers. And I agree with Kitty, your mother did what she had to do to save you and your son. Not to mention us."

"That reminds me, as I tucked her in last night, Mother insisted I ask you folks to come out here again today so she could give you something she wanted you both to have. She must have wanted me to give them to you. I believe she somehow knew she wouldn't wake up this morning."

Medina opened the front door and stepped inside. Seconds later she returned carrying two antique quilts folded across her arms.

"Mother wanted each of you to have one of the friendship quilts she'd made many years ago."

"Oh, I couldn't possibly accept," I said, as my eager arms shot forward of their own free will. I adored the older, hand-pieced quilts, and these were absolutely beautiful. I could smell cedar from the chest they'd been stored in for who knew how long. I didn't have to look at Deb to know she was drooling. Medina placed one across my arms and handed the other to Deb.

"But you should keep them," Deb said, clutching the quilt firmly to her chest. "These old quilts are worth a fortune. They're a family heirloom!" She sounded sincere, but I doubted Medina Beadle could drag that quilt out of Deb's steely fingers, even if she hooked it up to Mose's old tractor with a strong chain.

"Yes, they are heirlooms, but Mother belonged to a quilting circle for several decades and she made dozens of quilts over her lifetime. I have them in every room of the house, so I have plenty to remember her by. And I want you to have them. Mother created these two quilts for her best friend, Nelda Booker, during her long battle with cancer. When Nelda passed away, there were no family members left, so the quilts came back to Mother and she stored them in her cedar chest. Most of her other friends were gone, until you two ladies came along. Last night Mother decided to see that you each got one. I think it's a wonderful idea."

I fingered the delicate stitching on mine. I'd quilted some over the years, even won a ribbon or two, but my stitches looked as if they'd been made by a bear with swollen paws compared to Sassy Bentley's. And the colors mingled so beautifully. I'd never seen a quilt with such lovely pastels.

"She embroidered her name and the date on the corners," Medina said. Which, of course, made them all the more valuable. I truly was dumbstruck, embarrassed to take such a valuable gift, but not knowing how to say no. And certainly not wanting to.

"Please," Medina said, sensing my inner struggle, "Mother really wanted you both to have a quilt she'd made. To keep you warm and to thank you warmly for befriending her. Those are her words, and mine."

"Thank you."

I struggled to come up with something else appropriate to say without crying when the men joined us on the porch, having discussed all they needed to in regard to my car. Jack carried what looked like the original car owner's manual. That alone was worth a small fortune, and now we wouldn't have to hunt for one on the Internet. It would help him make the appropriate repairs and find any original parts he needed that might be missing, just by using the part numbers.

"I really appreciate you finding this," Jack said, shaking Mose Beadle's hand. Jack waved the book at me. "You gals ready to hit the road yet?"

I turned to Medina. "When is your mother's funeral scheduled?"

"She requested a graveside service only, and it will be held tomorrow morning at ten o'clock. She had all her arrangements made, and she didn't want to be embalmed, so we have to bury her quickly. There'll be a gathering again here, after the service, if you folks would like to come."

"We checked out of our cabin, so we'll spend the night at a nearby motel and meet you at the cemetery tomorrow.

I doubt we'll be able to stay afterward. We really do need to get home and check on our granddaughter."

"I thank you kindly, and Mother would, too, if she were here. Is your granddaughter still in the hospital?"

"Yes, but the doctor promised to release her tomorrow if her fever stays down today and nothing else changes. My daughter says Tori has recovered enough to start driving everyone crazy. I'm taking that as a positive sign."

"Indeed it is."

We said our goodbyes and climbed back into Sadie. I didn't think Jack or Leo would thank me kindly, or any other way, for agreeing to attend Sassy Bentley's graveside service, particularly since we were packed up and ready to go home. But stay we would. I'd see Sassy Bentley settled into her final resting place and wish her well. Then we could go home and try to forget, assuming we ever could.

THIRTY-THREE

ATTENDING SASSY BENTLEY'S graveside service was one of the toughest things I'd had to do in a long time. Thankfully a graveside service meant no visitation and a closed casket. I didn't want to see those bright, intelligent eyes closed forever—eyes that had watched so many amazing changes take place in the world during eighty-plus years and survived a life full of hard work and hard times.

I was surprised to note that the Bentley family plot was several spaces away from where the Ottwell boys were now buried. I suspected Sassy had bought extra plots at the graveyard situated beside the church she'd attended, probably when her daughter had been young and still unmarried. Country families often did that, as a hedge against future family growth through marriages and births. At least Sassy wouldn't have to lie near those awful boys.

I wondered if Chief Wilburn would be able to find anyone willing to claim the Ottwell bodies once the real Charlie Beadle was safely home and Wilburn's office could release their true identities to the media. Awful as they were, I'd hate to think there was a family somewhere wondering where those boys were.

The fall air was crisp and cold. The breeze slid over the hilltop, ruffling my hair and making me shiver. Jack put an arm around my shoulder. Deb scooted close to me on the other side since Leo's arms still wouldn't reach as high as her shoulders.

"I'll be glad when this is all over. I've had enough funerals to last me a decade or two," she whispered.

"So have I, but I couldn't miss this one. Sassy Bentley deserved to have a couple of friends here to say goodbye."

Deb nodded. The mourners consisted primarily of Mose and Medina Beadle and all of their church friends. They'd attended the same congregation as Medina's mother for most of her life, but Sassy Bentley's friends had pretty much all gone on to their eternal reward.

We declined to join the Beadle family at the farm for the gathering after the service. Mose and Medina had plenty of support in their grief without us, and it was high time we headed back to Southern Illinois and the comforts of home.

Deb, Leo, Jack, and I were exhausted from our so-called vacation, and I was eager to get Betty Blue safely tucked into her new home—Jack's huge, climate-controlled pole barn behind our house where he stored his trophies and his enormous collection of Fifties memorabilia. That was where Sadie napped when she wasn't in a competition or attending a car-club meeting. And hopefully, Jack would be able to whip Betty Blue into driving shape in a few months. I was more than ready to take her for a spin with Deb, maybe to a workout with our aerobics class or lunch with our fellow Red Hat members. Wherever we went, Betty Blue was certain to make a good impression, and I'd be riding in a car similar to the one my daddy owned when I was a little girl.

As we were preparing to leave the cemetery, Medina gave Deb and me a final hug while Jack and Leo shook hands with Mose. I ripped a deposit slip out of my checkbook, tore off the part with our name and address, and passed it to Medina. She whispered her thanks to us again for not going to Chief Wilburn with what we knew about her mother, and from the look on her face, Deb was as un-settled about the whole situation as I was.

But I still didn't see any purpose in ratting out the elderly woman when nothing legally could be done about her actions now and it would only serve to blacken her name. Who knew if a court hearing would result in label-ing her actions as self-defense or outright murder?

"I'll write and let you know when our Charlie is home again," Medina said. "And I'll send you Mother's recipes, like she promised."

"I appreciate it, and I hope Charlie is released very soon." I also hoped the boy had learned his lesson and didn't cause his parents any further problems but didn't say it out loud. They'd had enough trouble to last them a life-time. Would Charlie Beadle ever realize what his grand-mother had sacrificed to keep him and his parents alive? Who knew?

Driving out of Sevier County, Jack very nearly rear-ended another car by frequently checking his rear- and side-view mirrors. A tad too frequently, if you asked me.

"She's not going to be out here today, Jack Bloodworth," I said. "You might as well give up."

"Who?" he asked, the absolute picture of innocence.

"Copper Penny. Most likely she's at a rehearsal. And she's not likely to hang around on a major highway in the hopes of waving goodbye to you and Leo. If she's as smart as I think she is, she's avoiding this busy area today like the plague."

Jack sighed. "You're probably right. But I'll see her again when she does her show over in Paducah. Remem-ber? I promised to take her for a drive in Sadie, touring the sights of Metropolis. Besides, a man can dream, can't he?"

Jack's question earned him a punch on the arm. "We

will take her for a ride," I said, "assuming she hasn't come to her senses and cancelled her Paducah appearance in order to avoid you and Leo."

Jack bit his lower lip, whether to keep from yelping in pain or snickering back at me was anybody's guess.

The cell phone chirruped a Merry Christmas again, and I dug into my tote bag, around the snack bars and under the camera case, wondering if I could stand to listen to that tune clear through Christmas. Maybe Sunny could fix it for me since she'd helped us get our cell phones in the first place.

"Mother, I'm at the house. Where are you and Daddy?" Sunny said. "I thought you were coming home yesterday."

I swear, if I'd demanded to know her whereabouts in that same tone of voice, she'd have had a conniption fit. Given her jangled bride's nerves, I decided not to mention that fact, discretion being the better part of valor, or so I've heard tell.

"Something came up, and we had to spend an extra day, Sunny. We're on our way home right now. We should be there by suppertime."

"Great. I'll rustle up something in your kitchen. Maggie can help me. She's on her way home, too. Is anything wrong? Is Leo okay? Why did you stay an extra day?"

I didn't like lying, so I skirted the truth as closely as possible without telling her every single thing that had happened. Time enough for that later. "The elderly woman we bought the car from died in her sleep, and we thought it only polite to attend her graveside service, which was held this morning. Leo's fine, but he's still a bit sore, so that was also a good reason to stay over another night and leave today. How's Tori?"

"How's Tori?" Jack parroted before Sunny even had a chance to answer me. I waved him off.

"She's fine, Mom."

I motioned the answer to Jack. If I hadn't, he'd keep asking until I bopped him with the cell phone.

"She has to be careful, like you did when your lung collapsed, and she'll be about as easy to keep still as you were," Sunny said. "I'm wondering if I should go out and buy some soft rope."

I didn't dignify that with an answer. I figured Sunny had other, somewhat nefarious reasons for calling me, not to mention offering to cook supper for her father and me.

"Okay, Sunshine, what's up? Why the family meeting tonight over supper?"

"Mother, what makes you think—"

"Sunny!"

"Okay, okay, you do know me too well."

As if I hadn't been with her practically twenty-four/ seven from the day she was born until she left to go back to college at SIU!

"What's up with Sunny?" Jack asked. I waved him off again.

"The wedding is off, Mom. It was a mutual decision."

"But, Sunny, if you two love each other—"

"You're not listening, as usual. I said the wedding was off. I didn't say the whole marriage was off."

"They're not getting married?" Jack said. I held up my hand. If I hadn't needed the phone to talk to my daughter, I most certainly would have bopped him with it, although it was probably too lightweight to do much damage.

"So, where are you getting married?" It would be a long drive back down here in a couple of months for the wedding, if she'd decided she liked the pictures of the chapel I'd e-mailed to Maggie, and the weather would definitely be more challenging by then, but at the moment I was willing to take a rocket ship to the moon if necessary.

"On the cruise ship. Craig and I were going to the Bahamas anyhow, for our honeymoon, so we'll do it on board the ship."

"Do they still do that? I mean, is the captain allowed to marry passengers?" I asked, wanting this marriage to be legal as well as lovely.

"Yes, Mother, the captain is licensed to marry couples. They do it while the ship is still docked, or berthed, or whatever. Craig checked that out for me this morning. Apparently, it's done all the time."

"Are we coming back here for the wedding?" Jack demanded. "It's likely to be snowing in the Smoky Mountains by then. Not to mention cold. You know how you freeze in August."

I punched his arm again. Perhaps a bit of pain would get him to stop interrupting until I could hear Sunny out.

"But, Sunny, what about all the millions of people you've invited to the wedding? They might not be able to afford a trip to the Bahamas. You can't afford to pay their way, and your dad and I certainly can't."

She was silent for so long, I wondered if my phone had dropped the call. I was about to try re-dialing when she said, "You want the truth, Mom? I'm not sure I ever wanted a big wedding in the first place. Somehow I thought you and Daddy did."

No matter that I'd hinted for months about how saving for a down payment on a home made more sense than spending a wad on a one-day affair. She and Craig had insisted on paying for most of their own wedding since Jack and I were helping her through school, so I hadn't been able to outright insist on telling her how much she should spend of her own money.

"Your father and I will be happy with whatever you and Craig decide. But what changed your mind?"

She sighed. "I thought about Maggie's wedding, how beautiful it was at the gazebo in the park and how little it cost. And she enjoyed it as much or more than any of my friends whose weddings cost the earth. You and Daddy eloped, and you've never minded not having a huge wedding."

And she was right, I hadn't. "But are you sure this is what you really want to do?"

"Yes, I'm very sure. Okay, it took me a while to figure it out, but this is what I want. I'm ashamed to admit this, Mom, but I was so busy keeping up with school, I hired a wedding planner. He was the one who insisted on the chartreuse because it's back in style. He kept telling me what I had to do or had to have and finally I got a belly full. I fired him over the phone this morning, on the drive home from the hospital. Then I called Craig and asked how he'd like to get married on the ship. He was thrilled."

I coughed to cover a snicker. "But you haven't said what you're going to do about the guests."

"I've been so busy fighting with the wedding planner, I hadn't gotten around to telling anyone else the details of the wedding. I didn't even send out invitations. So, we're keeping it small, family only, meaning Craig's sister, you and Dad, Maggie and Joe and the kids, assuming Maggie wants to bring them along. If not, I'm sure Joe's mom will keep them. She's always a willing baby-sitter. Um, Mom?"

"Yes, dear?" I figured I was about to get a difficult request, since she was being so ultra-polite. Far be it from me to decline.

"I thought maybe we could throw a big reception after we get back from our honeymoon. You know, rent the union hall or something, and have a real blow-out for our friends and family. What do you think?"

"I think it's a terrific idea, and I'll take care of it my-self, assuming you want me to."

"I was hoping you'd suggest it. We can have the small, private wedding Craig pleaded for, and you guys can go on the cruise with us. I know you've always wanted to take one. And a big party later on will make everyone else we know happy. We can even keep it casual so they don't have to buy something fancy to wear."

"I think that's the perfect solution to your problems with the wedding. Particularly since it will make both of you happy."

"You have no idea, Mom. Craig's been trying to sub-tly talk me out of a huge wedding for months because he found out someone he knows is building a new set of con-dos right on the river front. The cost of the huge wedding that the planner was working on for us would just about cover the down payment on a condo, and Craig knows I've always wanted to live near the river. He was going to try to swing it anyhow, on his own, as a wedding gift for me, but with helping pay for his part of the large wedding, he was going to have to take a second job, plus finish school. Would you believe he was willing to do that for me? And all the while I was busy letting someone else plan our spe-cial day!"

Knowing Craig, I did believe it. "Sunny, all brides go a bit insane trying to plan their weddings. I figured you'd come around. The important thing is, you're back in charge, and a wedding aboard a cruise ship will be lovely."

"Cruise ship? What if I get seasick?" Jack whispered. I poked him again. Had the man never heard of Drama-mine?

"I think so, too," Sunny said. "Just our families. Daddy giving me away. Maggie for my matron-of-honor. You bawling your eyes out, drowning out the captain. Even the kids, if Maggie wants them there. And guess who Craig picked to be his best man? His sister, Patricia."

Patricia Tanner was the queen of histrionics and very nearly as irritating as her poor dead mother had been, but she and Sunny were close friends. I couldn't wait to see her performance as the "best man." I wasn't convinced that a large ship was a good place for Billy and Tori. They were likely to sink it. But I'd let Maggie make that decision on her own.

"We'll be home in about five hours. How about something simple for supper, like chili and crackers and cheese? I could use some comfort food."

"Great idea. I'm sure Maggie will bring dessert. And Billy and Tori are dying to see you. I hope whatever you brought them doesn't get you into trouble with Maggie again."

"Don't count on it. This illness will require some serious spoiling on my part. Maggie will just have to deal with it."

"I forgot to ask, did you buy a dress for the wedding yet? And if you did, I sincerely hope it isn't chartreuse."

I'd totally forgotten to look for a dress to wear to the wedding in all the stress and confusion, but I wasn't about to admit that to my daughter.

"Haven't found anything I like, but you and I can go shopping when I get home and have a chance to rest up from my vacation. Have you found one?"

"Yes, I did. Maggie likes it, but I asked the store to hold off on ordering my size. I want you to see it before I make my final decision."

That nearly made me cry. My independent daughter wanted my opinion on her wedding dress.

"I'd love to." And maybe I could get Sunny to drop me some hints for a wedding gift while we shopped. Now that they were buying a condo, something for their new home might be appropriate, even though it would be a while before construction was finished. "And we could have a mother-to-daughter chat about the birds and the bees," I said, hoping to get a snicker out of my sometimes uptight daughter.

Sunny rewarded me with a loud guffaw. "See you tonight, Mom."

She hung up. I snapped the phone shut and turned to fill Jack in.

"A ship-board wedding does sound more, um, intimate," Jack said.

"Meaning you don't have to walk your daughter down the aisle in front of a large crowd, right? And I'm really going to have to turn the sound down on my cell phone so you can't hear every single word!"

"Hey, I missed a word or two here and there. But I know how to fill in the gaps. And yes, Craig and I will both be much happier with a small wedding. Not to mention the money the kids will save. Did she say exactly where those condos would be built? That's something you and I might need to consider, one of these days."

"One of these days, yes, but not today. I'm nowhere near ready to give up my sun porch or my large kitchen. And where would you keep Sadie and Betty Blue and all of your garage stuff?"

The resulting silence let me know he hadn't carefully considered any of that. We would have to downsize one of these days. But hopefully we still had several good years ahead of us on the farm.

THIRTY-FOUR

BY THE TIME we helped Leo and Deb unload their stuff at their house and headed back down the highway for our farm, I was beyond exhausted. Even a short nap on the trip home hadn't helped. Hot chili and a dessert would be just the thing to perk me up. And some hugs from my grandkids.

"Grandma, I was sick just like you," Tori announced when we walked in the door, throwing her arms around my good leg. She didn't even give me time to put my stuff down. "My lung lapsed."

"Collapsed," I corrected, "but I heard you were really brave about the whole thing."

"I was, almost as brave as you were. I only cried once when the nurse stuck a needle in my arm. She left it there, with a yucky tube. I couldn't even move my arm. They tied it to a board."

I figured she meant taped. "I cried about the very same thing," I confessed. "You were mighty brave. Grandma is proud of you."

She grinned up at me. I knew she was waiting to see what I'd brought her. "Grandpa is unloading the car. Once he has everything inside, I'll see if I can find a little something for you." Actually, it was a big something, but I'd been in a generous mood, particularly since I hadn't been with Tori when she'd been hospitalized and I still felt a bit guilty about that.

"What is it? What is it?" she demanded.

"Tori, you can't bounce around like that. Your lung is still healing," Maggie warned.

Time for us to sit down. Tori and I both needed the rest.

"It's a set of golf clubs. Grandpa and I figured you could learn how to play, then teach us. Maybe you could even become a pro some day. Then you could support us."

"Grandma!"

"Patience. Grandpa has orders to unload your stuff first before he brings in our suitcases. And he's bringing in something for Billy."

I couldn't help but notice that Billy was being extremely polite, not shoving his older sister out of the way or demanding to know what his gift was. Had he matured that much in a few days, or had his mother threatened him within an inch of his life?

Jack elbowed the front screen door open and entered the living room, carefully lugging the large antique wooden doll house I'd found at the shop near our cabin. The small dolls and their furniture were carefully wrapped inside. Joe and Craig followed him in, carrying the rest of our luggage.

"Oh, Grandma." Tori's tone was as reverent as mine had been when I'd first set eyes on Betty Blue.

In seconds she was on the floor, carefully unwrapping the items inside the doll house and exclaiming over each one. I eased down onto the floor beside her, remembering my own doll house from the Fifties. I wondered what had become of it when I'd outgrown it. My mother hadn't been one to save things for me. No telling where my wonderful old dolls had wound up. Not to mention my favorite teddy bear. He'd always been a welcome guest at my tea parties.

"Is it really mine? Do I get to take the doll house home with me, Grandma?" she asked, looking at me hopefully. Billy and Tori often begged to take home the toys I stored on the sun porch to keep them busy. And I always had to refuse, or I'd quickly run out of things to occupy them while we visited with their parents. The doll house out on the porch dated back to when my girls were small, and it was plastic. Fun to play with, but certainly not nearly as detailed or wonderful as this one. Nor as expensive.

"It's all yours, Tori, to take home and keep."

She stopped placing the tiny furniture in the upstairs bedroom long enough to give me a big hug, then went back to business.

I'd brought each of my daughters a collectable lighted Christmas house, which went over extremely well. Billy, with Grandpa's help, was busy running his new remote-control fire truck into or under the living room furniture. Apparently, neither of them could get the hang of steering the thing, and the roar of the motor hadn't endeared me to Billy's mother. Thankfully, before Maggie could chastise, Sunny called us in to dinner.

I was more than ready to sit down and eat. But somehow, in spite of my relief at being home, I couldn't get the Beadles out of my mind. Or Sassy Bentley. At least she didn't have to live in fear any longer. Or ever face gossip and speculation over what she'd done to save her family. I honestly didn't know if I could have survived the ordeal as well as that family had.

SLEEPING IN MY OWN BED that night would have been wonderful if only I could have gotten to sleep in the first place. Sunny's wedding plans appeared to be well in hand, so I could put that worry aside for the moment. But the sights and sounds from the last few days in the Smoky Mountains kept playing through my head like a piece of movie film that had somehow looped over into a continuous reel.

Had we really unknowingly set into motion the events

that led to the deaths of three people? And supposing we'd never even made the trip to the Smoky Mountains? Or if we'd eaten at a different restaurant and not met the Beadles and Sassy Bentley in the first place? What would've happened to the family then? Was Medina's prediction that the boys would have buried the family on the farm and headed for greener pastures really true? I very much feared it was.

Would Chief Wilburn eventually come up with any information that would make it necessary for him to get in touch with us again? And if he did, would I have to tell all I knew about Sassy Bentley? Would he file charges against me for not telling him at the time? My head was absolutely spinning from the possibilities.

As I rolled over on my side for probably the twentieth time, Jack put his arm over my shoulder and pulled me into a snuggle, spoon-to-spoon style.

"Stop fretting, Kitty. We're home, and the Great Smoky Mountains murder mystery is well behind us. Chief Wilburn solved this one all by himself, and without much help from us, I might add. We're finished with solving murders. And no way are we getting involved in another one. Not in this lifetime. No, siree."

I hadn't told him what I knew about Sassy Bentley yet. Maybe I'd do it tomorrow morning over breakfast. Jack was usually at his best with a plate full of bacon and eggs in front of him. I might even throw in some fried potatoes to sweeten the deal. I wondered if I had any canned biscuits in the fridge.

As for us not getting involved in another murder? Of course we wouldn't. Well, not unless we absolutely had to.

* * * * *

REQUEST YOUR FREE BOOKS!

2 FREE NOVELS
PLUS 2 FREE GIFTS!

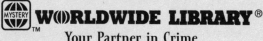

Your Partner in Crime